LIGHTNING IN JULY

Lightning in July

a novel by

ANN L. McLAUGHLIN

JOHN DANIEL, PUBLISHER · SANTA BARBARA, CALIFORNIA · 1989

Cover design by John C. McLaughlin
Design and typography by
Jim Cook/Book Design & Typography
Santa Barbara, California

LIBRARY OF CONGRESS CATALOGING-IN-PUBLICATION DATA
McLaughlin, Ann L., 1928-
    Lightning in July: a novel / by Ann L. McLaughlin.
        p.   cm.
    ISBN 0-936784-72-5: $9.95
    I. Title.
PS3563.C3836L54   1989
813'.54—DC 19   88-37410 CIP

Published by
JOHN DANIEL, PUBLISHER
Post Office Box 21922
Santa Barbara, California 93121

Distributed by Texas Monthly Press
Post Office Box 1569, Austin, Texas 78767

For Charlie

1

*I*n the hot darkness of that July night in 1955, the outdoor theatre on the Boston Esplanade was a glowing island of sound. The audience lay on blankets, listening or dozing, as the rich music spread over them. Programs waved here and there like white fans, stirring the humid air. A baby whimpered somewhere and was hushed.

Dan had arrived late and stood, leaning against a metal fence at the side. The tall light above him turned the dry grass a queer blue and he was conscious of an ache between his eyebrows. A drone enveloped the music; Dan looked up to see a plane, its tail lights blinking, as it made its way toward Logan Airport. In Colorado the stars were much brighter, he thought. Here the glow of the city drained the blackness from the sky. If he could only finish his library research this month, he could get back there in August to do the field work for his thesis. He would be busy mapping, making notes, but he would be in that country again. The metallic glitter from a French horn made him squint. He closed his eyes and saw his bed in the Harvard Graduate School dorm with its wrinkled madras spread and yearned for the moment when he could crawl in and turn out the light. Why was he so tired, he wondered, and gave his head a shake, as he focused on the stage again.

A thin girl with long dark hair, parted severely in the middle, was standing in front of the conductor, her flute raised in position. Dan stared. He had forgotten it was a flute concerto. The high solitary notes sounded strangely naked after the rich orchestration that had gone before. The tone was clear and light; it conveyed a mixture of courage and vulnerability,

[7]

Dan thought—a quiet passion. He peered at his program. "Harriet Elizabeth Blessing." The typed words on the substitution notice were faint. He gazed at her straight figure, taking in the shape of her small breasts in the white, high-necked blouse, and the way the wide waist band of her long black skirt emphasized her delicacy. He saw her gaze travel out into the audience beyond the conductor's moving arms and all at once he had the hot conviction that her eyes had settled on him. Dan held still. When the orchestra began again, he watched her raise her hand to flick her hair back from her shoulder, then massage her throat with a quick movement of her fingers. Was she worried about her breathing, he wondered. He felt her eyes again and watched as she played a lively passage, then a slow one, then another lively one. My God, she was good.

The concerto ended; the conductor smiled, as the applause rolled toward him. He turned, signaled the orchestra to rise, and pointed his baton at the young woman, who bowed briefly, while Dan clapped. The lights went on at the back of the amphitheatre. People rose and stood blinking, folded blankets between them, gathered up picnic baskets, and sleeping children, and began moving toward the parking lot. Dan hesitated. He would make his way back to the stage, he thought. But what would he say? "I enjoyed it. You were really fine." She would be surrounded with friends and family probably. No. This was not the time.

The night narrowed into a bright tunnel of concentration for Hally. There were the pages of notes on her music stand, the conductor with his lock of white hair bouncing on his forehead, his raised arms, and his baton pointing, and the audience out there in the dark. Just hours earlier, the first flutist's appendectomy had become Hally's important chance. She had played Mozart's Flute Concerto No. 2 in D Major in other concerts, but never with the Boston Pops. What if she forgot? What if her fingers slipped, or her breath gave out on that final cadenza? And yet, even as she fitted her flute together onstage, while the concert master sounded the A for the strings to tune, Hally knew she would be good. Pick out someone in the audience and play to him, her old music teacher used to tell her. Mom was out there somewhere in the dimness and a group of friends she had alerted that morning. But Hally fastened on a tall young man by the fence. She played the *Allegro aperto* to him, then the *Andante ma non troppo* and finally the concluding *Allegro*; he would know they were gifts for him.

2

Hally's practice time the next morning was broken by phone calls from friends, eager to congratulate. When Esther answered, she laughed happily and told callers that, as Hally's mother, she took full credit for her achievements. All at once their focus shifted; a phone call came from Washington announcing that Hally's sister was in labor. Esther made train reservations, while Hally pulled a plaid suitcase from the closet and put it on the bed. "You won't have to market for a day or two," Esther said, as she stood with her back to her daughter, so that Hally could button up her navy blue dress. "There's that chicken and. . . ." Esther turned and stared at Hally a moment. "You look flushed, dearie." She put a hand on Hally's forehead. "You feel hot."

"I'm just tired," Hally protested. "Last night was a big deal after all."

"But there're summer viruses going around," Esther started. She studied Hally as she twisted the top of a cologne bottle. "You just don't look. . . ." The taxi honked below. "Listen. Promise me, if you don't feel better by afternoon, you'll call Dr. Lester. All right?" Hally nodded, zipped up the suitcase, and carried it down the apartment stairs. She signaled the cab driver that her mother was coming and handed him the bag. "Good-bye," her mother said and kissed Hally. "I'll call just as soon as I can. Don't forget about Dr. Lester. Please."

When Dr. Lester arrived after supper, Hally felt annoyed that she had called him. He had always been fussy and over-cautious, she thought, and yet he had been their family doctor all her life. He examined her throat, confirmed the fact that her temperature was 103, and then, as she lay stretched out on her bed, he made her say "prunes and prisms" twice. "Lift your head from the pillow," he ordered. Hally let out a sigh of irritation, but felt confused when she discovered that she couldn't bring up her head.

"I'm just tired," she told him. "The concert last night, the...." She looked up at him and waited.

"I'm going to take you over to a hospital in Telford for some tests," he announced. "It may be nothing. But I want to be sure."

"Wait," Hally objected. "I can't do that. I haven't got time. I'm not sick really. I just have a little sore throat—a summer cold. I...." Her voice was hoarse; all at once talking was difficult. But she couldn't possibly spend the whole evening at some hospital, she told herself; she had to practice for the chamber music group on Wednesday and besides she wanted to be near the phone for news of the baby. Yet, even as she struggled to explain, Hally half hoped Dr. Lester would take over. The room had blurred, her music stand was merged with the chair, and her throat ached with a queer dryness. She felt a guilty yearning to curl up in some warm bed somewhere, far away from the press of the concert excitement, her jobs ahead, even from the impending news of her sister's child. When Dr. Lester told her to put a nightgown and a toothbrush in a bag, Hally obeyed, then followed him down the stairs and out to his car.

Dr. Lester was doing an extraordinary thing, Hally realized, driving her to the hospital himself. He kept consulting some scribbled directions he'd put on the dashboard and once he held his wrist to his ear, as if to judge whether the watch he wore was really ticking. But for Hally time had grown loose and soft, as they drove through the evening streets. She felt warm and quiet in her cocoon of fever, watching as they passed porches with gliders, where people sat chatting, and narrow front yards, where sprinklers turned. From time to time a rational voice within urged her to ask questions—why did her throat ache so? what were these tests? and what would they show? But Hally ignored the voice; it was uncomfortable to speak now. Besides she just wanted to keep on driving through the quiet streets and never find that hospital—at least not soon.

They turned into a street, ribbed with trolley tracks. "There it is," Dr. Lester said and pointed to a brick building on a hill, its dry, sloping lawn surrounded by an iron fence. Two gateposts, with lamps, stood on either side of the driveway entrance and, as they passed between them, Hally saw a large HOSPITAL ZONE QUIET sign on one. The other had a dark metal plate, whose raised letters were hard to read. "Wahl Doctors' Hospital," she thought it said. But maybe it was "Wall." The windows of the brick building made harsh yellow rectangles in the soft evening light. Several were open and Hally could see a nurse standing at one, her elbow resting on a bedpost, as she stared down. Hally peered up at her, wondering if the nurse was watching them, but the young woman turned and disappeared. Dr. Lester parked at the side of the emergency entrance. The car doors slammed, then the evening quiet enveloped them again. As they walked across the tarred surface to a ramp, Hally heard a cricket singing somewhere in the dry grass. Dr. Lester pushed the door open; it crashed shut behind them, cutting off the sound.

Hally stood squinting a moment in the lighted hall, surrounded by a strong chemical smell. "Name?" the nurse at the desk asked. Hally stared down at the manila folders and overlapping charts. She was dizzy, she realized, and put one hand on the wooden desk to steady herself.

"Harriet Elizabeth Blessing," she started. The sound was thick, almost unintelligible. Hally turned back to Dr. Lester, but remembered that he was conferring with the head doctor. "Hally Blessing," she said and stopped. The words were painful to enunciate. What was happening? How could she loose her voice like this? The nurse behind the desk looked tired. Some strands of blonde hair straggled down from one side of her stiff cap and she was massaging the small of her back with one hand, as she sat looking up at Hally.

"Don't worry," she said when Hally paused. "We'll get this information later. I'll find a wheelchair and take you up to your room." She rose and hurried down the hall, as Hally stared around her. There was a long jagged crack in the pale green wall behind the desk and the black and white tiles on the floor seemed to overlap and swirl. The disinfectant reek was loosing its sharpness, she realized, as she watched the nurse push a rattling wheelchair toward her.

Hally stared at its caned back, then settled herself in it with a sigh. "Watch it there. Watch it," said a male voice in a thick East Boston accent. The swinging doors at the end of the hall opened and two men in green orderly uniforms pulled a large cylindrical tank on long metal legs with wheels into the hall. Hally stared. An iron lung, she thought. She'd seen pictures of them in the newspaper. The men looked tired; their uniforms stuck to their backs in dark patches and their faces were sweaty. "Call Critical, will you, Marge?" the older man at the front of the lung said to the nurse. The skin under his eyes sagged and the hair above his ears was gray. "Tell 'em we're going to need some help with that door up there. Okay?" The men pushed the clumsy-looking machine on down the hall and through another set of swinging doors, while the nurse dialed a number on the black phone.

"Lou and Georgie are bringing up the new tank," she said into the receiver. "Right. That's what he said to tell you." Hally closed her eyes. Some saliva was leaking from the side of her mouth, but she couldn't remember where she'd put her kleenex. Never mind, she thought. Never mind.

Dan stood by his bed watching as his roommate studied a white prescription slip Dan had just handed him. He had told Mort the story of his visit to the infirmary in the late afternoon and now he felt a strange sense of objectivity as Mort read the directions on the square slip of paper.

"Where is this hospital anyway?" Mort asked and swung his bare feet from the cracked leather footstool to the rug. "Telford? Jesus! They want you to get tests out there tonight?" Dan nodded. A guy in his historiography seminar—someone he barely knew—had been diagnosed with a light case of polio and Dan had gone to the infirmary for an examination and gamma globulin shots, as the whole class had been asked to do. But unlike the others, Dan had been asked to wait.

"The doctor said I might well not have it or it could be mild." Dan stopped, aware that he was mouthing the intern's words. He had thought of FDR, as he left the infirmary, and now he saw that face from his childhood clearly, the head tipped back, the chin jutting up, the smile.

Mort fumbled for his loafers on the rug. "I think I can find it," he said rising, and turned over the slip. "These directions are pretty clear. I've got a map in the car anyway."

"I better take a cab," Dan began and glanced at the open window, where the rattle of a distant trolley car rose through the dusty leaves. "It's contagious, see. I mean I asked the doctor about you and he said you should definitely get the shots. If I have it, that is." Dan looked down at a folded newspaper on the bed. "President Eisenhower and Secretary of State John. . . ." The fold broke the headline. "Foster Dulles," Dan thought, finishing the name. That meeting in Geneva wouldn't amount to much. He stared at Mort again, confused by the irrelevant movements of his mind. Mort could contract this thing too after all. "I'll get a cab," he repeated.

"Look, if you've got it," Mort said, "I'm thoroughly exposed anyway and if you haven't. . . . " He paused and looked at Dan. "Come on. I'm taking you." Dan stared at him, then nodded gratefully. A crowd of little decisions seemed to hover just beyond him. Perhaps he should take pajamas, a toothbrush even, since he might have to spend the night, and he ought to give Mort his parents' number, in case Mort had to call. Dan stared at the sloping line of books at the back of his desk.

"I'll probably be sitting around there waiting, you know," he told Mort. "I oughta take something to read." He stooped and peered at the titles, unaware of Mort across the room, stuffing a pair of pajamas into a duffel bag. "I think I'll take Gabriel," Dan said and pulled a blue text, entitled *The Course of American Democratic Thought* from the row so that the line of books sagged slowly. "I oughta go through this again for background stuff anyway." Mort looked over at his friend and left the room. When he came back from the bathroom with shaving things and a red toothbrush, Dan was still gazing down at the unopened book in his hand.

"Come on," Mort said and zipped up the duffel. "Let's get started." Dan glanced around the room, taking in the curling Winslow Homer poster on the wall, the two desks back to back, and his dusty cowboy hat hanging above the door. He followed Mort into the hall and heard the ring of their footsteps on the metal stairs as they went down to the entryway and out to the car.

The windowless cafeteria in the hospital basement was dingy and dimly lit. Chairs had been turned upside down on all the masonite-topped tables but one, where two interns sat beside empty paper coffee cups. One was dozing, his head sunk heavily onto his white-coated arms, which were resting on the table. The loop of a black stethoscope dangled from his jacket pocket. The other intern folded a newspaper back to the sports page and sighed. He read a moment, then glanced up at the round clock above the door. "We oughta get back," he said. "Two more admissions already and I think they've brought that Connely case down." The resting intern raised his head and stared.

"I'll be there in a minute," he said and let his head sink to his arms again. His companion slapped the paper together and rose. He pushed his way through the doors, which swung back, their scratched aluminum covering glowing dully in the dim light. The hall was empty and a penciled out-of-order sign, taped to the Coke machine against the wall, fluttered as he passed. He turned the corner and stopped at the second door, where he pulled a ring of keys from his pants pocket, unlocked the door, then closed it behind him. The sign on the wooden surface read, NO ADMITTANCE. MORGUE.

_H_ally moved her bare legs under the starched sheet and eyed the unfamiliar room around her. She felt she had been waiting in this dim space for hours, isolated on this high hospital bed. The brown bureau against the opposite wall was bare, except for a thermometer, held upright in a glass holder. The bedtray, on casters beside the bed, held a metal-backed chart and, next to the bedtray, was an intravenous stand, supporting a glass bottle hanging upside down. Hally gazed up, as a bubble rose slowly in the transparent liquid and broke on the surface. She was connected to that bottle, she remembered, and glanced down at her arm; the black tube at the bottom of the bottle ran downward to a needle that had been pushed into a blue vein on her upturned wrist. Her extended arm felt stiff, strapped to a narrow wooden board with white bands of adhesive tape. Hally stared up at the bottle again. Why did she need that stuff trickling into her anyway?

The window beyond the bed was open and Hally could see that the evening had turned to night. The vague loveliness of her drive with Dr. Lester was over. He had left and now she must wait for another visit from the doctor who had come earlier. Maybe he would give her medication and tell her about the test. Clearly she was going to have to spend the night. But Dr. Lester had said he would call Washington and would bring her news of Ellie in the morning. He would take her home tomorrow, she planned, and then she would call the chamber music group about the rehearsal Wednesday night.

It was an old hospital, Hally observed, this Wall or Wahl, or whatever it was. The room smelt of disinfectant, like the corridor outside, and the walls were painted the same pale green. A long wavering crack led from the top corner of the door frame to the ceiling. Hally sighed and gazed up at the round gray light overhead which that head doctor had snapped off when he left the room. Dr. Mostello? That was his name. Dr. Lester had spoken of him in the car. But the darn test had hurt—that needle going into the bottom of her spine. She pushed her free hand down under the sheet, past the end of the johnny they had made her put on. Tunneling her fingers under her hot buttock, she touched the sore knot at the end of her backbone.

"Careful, dear. That's where they did the spinal tap." Hally jerked her head up. A nurse was sitting in the armchair beyond the bed in the orange glow of a lamp. When had she come? Had she been here all this time? Hally stared. A handkerchief with a pink embroidered border sprayed from the breast pocket of her white uniform and Hally could see a gray bobby pin at one side of her head, anchoring her stiff nurse's cap to her blue-white hair. A magazine lay open on her lap, its glossy pages reflecting the light.

"How are you feeling now?" the nurse asked. Hally swallowed; her unawareness of the nurse's presence must seem rude. She swallowed again and tried to raise her head. There were questions she must ask.

"Spinal tap?" Hally repeated and paused at the gargly sound of her words. "What do you mean 'spinal'?" Her voice was thick and Hally realized as she tried to repeat herself that she could not make it clearer. "What are they going to do?" she began, rushing to the most urgent question. She was just tired, she told herself. Her natural voice would return in an hour or so. Two soft hairs, protruding from the nurse's chin, glowed in the light. She pulled a kleenex from the box on the bedtray and mopped a thin ooze of saliva, that had started to dribble down Hally's chin. Hally murmured apologetically, but the nurse didn't seem to mind. Her hand was warm and clean-smelling. Perhaps she hadn't understood the question, Hally thought; perhaps she didn't know.

"Can I have some ginger...?" Hally began. She stopped halfway through the word and moved her mouth, working to swallow some of the saliva. She would get that word out, she resolved; it was important. "Ginger ale," she enunciated with an effort and searched the middle-aged face beside her to gauge the nurse's comprehension.

"Ginger ale?" The nurse shook her head. "No. I'm afraid not. You see they don't want you to have anything by mouth right now." She glanced toward the half-open door, as though *they* might be listening out there in the hall.

"But if I ... if I could just. ... " Hally's throat was tight; each hoarse word demanded effort. She stopped and sighed. Obviously the nurse was following orders. Hally would have to wait and ask the doctor. Ginger ale would help though, she thought. Those hard little bubbles in the cold liquid would force themselves down her aching throat, making a passage through the slimey soreness, eliminating the sour taste. Ginger ale was what Mom had always brought, when they had colds, when she and Ellie were little.

Hally moved her tongue over her lips, surprised at their prickly feel. Some more saliva was dribbling down from one side of her mouth; she should try to swallow it back. But the movement was too hard. She would just leave her mouth open, and let it ooze onto the pillowcase a little while. She could sit up and try to swallow it back later, when she felt more herself again. The nurse leaned over, holding a fresh kleenex. "There," she said, as she mopped Hally's chin once more. "That's better." It was odd to have a nurse all to herself; Hally tightened. Oh God, what would this cost? She stared at the pink veins around the nurse's nostrils and breathed out slowly. Never mind that now, she told herself. Just get through the night; I can ask the doctor in the morning. Behind her rimless glasses, the nurse's eyes looked kind. Hally let her lids drop. Thank you, she thought, as the nurse mopped her mouth again. Thank you.

Mom was holding out a glass of ginger ale. Hally could see her long freckled hand, with the silver wedding band at the base of the ring finger, holding a familiar blue glass. Its sides were dewy with wetness and the ice cubes knocked together softly, as the liquid fizzed. Hally smiled. "Mom," she whispered. "Mom." She turned her head to see her mother, expecting the wisps of white hair over her ears, the little brown mark at the side of her chin, her smile. She would have her glasses on, because she was about to read Hally, *The Wind in The Willows* maybe or *The Blue Fairy Book.* But when Hally opened her eyes, the woman in the armchair was the nurse.

Dan pulled himself up in bed and reached out for the book he had left on the armchair. The plastic seat cover was torn so that a string of gray stuffing hung down. Beyond the brown bureau, a mound of dirty sheets floated like a ragged cloud on the tiled floor. Dan turned. The window was open to the hot night; he listened and heard a cricket singing somewhere in the grass.

Dan sighed and pulled the pillow up behind him so that the metal bars at the top of the bedframe would not press against his back. They ought to give you an extra pillow, he thought, and glanced at the door, which stood half-open to the lighted hall. That intern, that Dr. Rickley, had promised to come back soon with the results of the spinal test. They must have finished it by now, he thought, and sighed. Did he really want to know? Maybe it would be better to save the news for the morning. But suppose he felt worse? Suppose he really had the disease? Oh God. What would happen then? He heard a phone ringing somewhere in the hall, then footsteps. He waited, but no one appeared at his door.

Dan lay back against the pillow. What was really going on? What if he was paralyzed, unable to walk, or to walk only with crutches, maybe a cane? He had planned to map the Oregon Trail this summer for his thesis. The disease might well be over soon, but if he couldn't get that stuff done in August, how the hell could he fit it in before his teaching assistantship began in September? Dan stared up at the shadows on the ceiling. What about Valley, his father's ranch? Suppose he couldn't ride? Suppose he could never mount Star, his graceful palomino with the white mark on her long forehead? Suppose . . . Oh, for God's sake, shut up, he told himself, and pushed his bare feet out straight.

He stared down at his naked legs, protruding from the stupid white johnny they'd made him put on. That old pink scar, where he'd fallen off his first pony the summer he was nine, still marked his left knee cap and his big toe had a red place on the top, he noticed—probably those damn shoes he'd bought last month at the Harvard Coop. He sighed and flapped the johnny, creating a little movement in the still air. They ought to have air-conditioning at least, Dan thought, and pulled up the sagging pillow again.

He opened the book he'd brought to the page marked with the torn jacket flap. "The harmony between science and Protestant orthodoxy in the Middle Period," he read, "arose chiefly from the fact that the mechanistic concept of the universe derived from Newton's. . . . " The words blurred; Dan let the cover close. What would happen? What had they found?

The overhead light went on and Dan jerked himself to a sitting position, blinking in the brightness. Had he been asleep? The room seemed crowded by the presence of a heavy-set doctor, who was standing beside the bed in a white medical coat. Dan glanced down at his johnny and jerked up the sheet.

"Dr. Mostello," the doctor said, introducing himself. The man exuded authority as he stood griping the bedframe with one large hand. Strands of crinkly black hair were combed across his balding head and his eyes were dark and serious, as they traveled over Dan's half-covered body. He must be one of the big guns, Dan thought, noticing the curling gray hairs at the doctor's temples. "I've just seen your spinal tap," Dr. Mostello said.

"Oh," Dan said. "What's the news? Have I got it?" He waited, held by the direct gaze of the doctor's intense black eyes. Dr. Mostello stood a moment, assessing his new patient.

"Yes, you've got it," he announced. "But it's a mild case." Dan stared at the doctor, then down at the white ridges of his legs under the sheet.

"I thought so," he said slowly. "I've been feeling weird for the last day or so. I mean I sort of thought I . . . so what happens now?" Dan looked back at the doctor. "What are you going to do? Medicine or what?"

"Well, as I told you," Dr. Mostello repeated. "It's a mild case. Right now the best thing is to keep you here under observation a while."

"So I've got polio," Dan said and gazed around the room. "I read something recently about the rise in cases this summer, but I. . . ." He leaned forward and the pillow dropped to the bed with a thump. "What do you mean 'mild'?"

Dr. Mostello pushed his fists down into the pockets of his medical coat and studied Dan again.

"The fact is there's really no valid way to predict right now what the virus is going to do—not at this stage. Your case is mild tonight, but it could get worse by morning or your fever might lift and you could go home in a day or two." He rocked forward on the balls of his feet. "This disease runs the whole gamut from symptoms that are no more than a bad cold to acute paralysis, requiring respirator care and. . . . " He let his breath out slowly, studying Dan. "Your case is 'mild' now, but I can't tell you whether it's going to stay that way." He held Dan in his strong dark gaze a moment longer, as if to indicate that his speech was a compliment to the patient's intelligence. "Diagnosis in the early stages is vital, prognosis is difficult though—foolish in fact."

"But what about treatment?" Dan asked. "Don't I get some kind of medication, some shots or something?"

"No. The fact is there is no treatment at this stage of the game," the doctor said. "We just have to wait and watch—see what the virus is going to do." Dan stared at the doctor.

"There's nothing you can do now?" he asked. The doctor shook his head.

"Just watch you carefully," he said. "Believe me that can make a vital difference."

Dan nodded and looked down at his legs again. All at once he wanted to show the doctor that he had some awareness of the overall situation and the problems the doctor was facing. "There's been a lot of disappointment about polio recently, hasn't there?" he began. "That Cutter Lab business last month. That sounded like a real mess."

"Terrible," Dr. Mostello said and clasped the bedframe again. "Terrible. Cure seemed close, then it slipped. Now we're facing another summer of epidemics."

"Epidemics?" Dan repeated. "But it's not that bad here, is it? In Boston, I mean."

"Not yet. Not yet. But. . . ." He paused and glanced toward the hall. "You can never tell."

"What I don't understand," Dan went on, eager to keep the conversation going, "is why it's called 'infantile paralysis'? I mean, I always thought it was a children's disease." He saw the picture of FDR again. Funny that he had almost never been photographed in a wheelchair.

"You're right," Dr. Mostello told him. "It used to be largely children. But this summer it's almost all adults. Young. In their late twenties mostly. Thirties. Practically no children this time." He jerked up one arm and peered at his wristwatch. "Look," he said, and patted one of Dan's sheet-covered legs. "You take it easy now. All right? I'll be back in an hour or so to see how you're doing. Meantime, the staff'll stop in." He glanced toward the lighted hall. Dan nodded. The man was okay and he seemed bright—or at least, I hope to God he is, Dan thought.

"I think Rickley's on down here tonight. He should be in soon," Mostello added.

Dan started to explain that Dr. Rickley had already been in, but the doctor turned. "You try not to worry now. We'll keep our eyes on you." He snapped off the overhead light and Dan lay in the dimness once more, listening to the doctor's hard-soled shoes retreating down the hall. Maybe he should have told the guy to call his parents in Colorado. Or would Mort do that? But did he really want them to hear this news now? They would begin packing, making plane reservations—at least Mother would. But that wasn't necessary yet, not if his case continued "mild."

Dan turned on his side and listened to the insect sounds outside in the grass. Dry stirrings like that used to rise from the shadowy weeds beside the north trail at home, he thought, and closed his eyes. He and Dad would emerge from the lower pasture, riding toward the lighted barn together, side by side. He would be on Star, of course, and Dad on Graylie or the other mare. He thought of his father pointing to the mountain range, rationalizing some decision not to sell this pasture or that. "About the most beautiful view in the world—at least it is to me," Dan could hear him saying and opened his eyes. The lights on the brick posts at the entrance to the driveway made orange globes in the dark. Dan closed his eyes again. It was easier to see Dad coming home through the meadow on Graylie or hear the horses munching their evening feed, moving in their stalls, as night closed in around the barn.

When Hally opened her eyes before dawn, she saw a dark-haired young woman in a white skirt and jacket, sitting in the armchair where the nurse had been. The young woman held her chin cupped in one hand, as she watched Hally and, when Hally stared at her, the young woman smiled. The queer sequence of last night's events came back to Hally: her arrival at the hospital, the tests, the nurse, the waiting. She raised her eyes; the bottle was still there above her, its side gleaming in the orange glow from the lamp, and her arm was still taped to the board. She sighed and looked back at the young woman in her medical jacket.

"You're not a nurse, are you?" Her voice sounded thick and strange in the still room. Hally waited, wondering if the girl would understand.

"No." The young woman smiled; her face had a vivid look that made Hally turn her head on the pillow to get a fuller view. "I'm a third year medical student. We do our training in contagious diseases here. My name is Artemis," she added. "Artemis Thermodopolis. I come from Greece." She smiled again. Hally could feel a drool of saliva spilling over her bottom lip and she raised her free hand to her mouth, embarrassed in front of this interesting stranger. "I'll get it," Artemis said and plucked a kleenex from the box on the bedtray. She bent over, wiped Hally's chin, then dropped the kleenex into the wastebasket beside the bed. Hally stared. Had she been wiping away her saliva while she slept, Hally wondered.

"My name's Hally Blessing," she began. "I'm a . . . a . . . I play the. . . . " Talk was painful, not simply uncomfortable now; it hurt her tight throat to make sounds. And yet Hally felt an urgent need to present this young woman with her professional identity. If Artemis was a doctor, Hally wanted her to know that *she* was a flutist, not simply a frightened patient, lying here. Hally lifted her free hand above the sheet and held it at the side of her mouth, as though supporting one end of her flute. Then she raised and lowered her fingers, manipulating imaginary keys. Artemis studied her and nodded.

"You're a flutist?" she asked. Hally nodded with relief and dropped her half curled hand. "That's wonderful," Artemis went on. "I've always loved the flute. I wanted to play it myself once, but I went into medicine instead." She laughed, then studied Hally again. "You're pretty uncomfortable now, aren't you?" Hally nodded. Her sore mouth hung open, for it was too painful to try to swallow the oozing drool. The dim shapes in the room—the bureau, the lamp, and the shadowy mirror—wavered and ran together; she closed her eyes. "They want you to stay awake as much as you can," Artemis told her. "It's hard right now, when you're so feverish. But I'll talk. Okay? That might help." Hally opened her eyes and stared.

"I bet you've played Purcell's *Dido and Aeneas*?" Hally nodded. "It's beautiful, isn't it?" Artemis went on. "When I was little, I used to think it was written for me. You see, Dido's the Phoenician name for Artemis."

Hally sighed. Questions hovered beyond like the blurred shapes around her. What was the matter with her? What were the doctors going to do? How long would she be here? Why couldn't she have any ginger ale? She moved her aching mouth and tried to swallow. But she would ask the questions later, when she felt stronger. Right now she would just lie here quietly and listen to Artemis talk.

"Artemis is a wonderful goddess really," the intern was saying. "She wasn't just a huntress. She was a birth goddess too, you know. Women prayed to her in childbirth. Which is curious, isn't it?" Artemis paused and wiped Hally's chin again. "You must visit Ephesus someday." Her words fell softly, enclosing Hally. "You would like it—the temple, the trees, the birds singing nearby. It's very quiet there. Sometimes in the evening you can sit on the temple steps and it almost seems as if deer are in the woods nearby." She paused a moment and studied Hally again. "Can you see it?" she asked.

Hally's wet cheek shone in the light, as she moved her mouth to answer. "I'm trying," she said and closed her eyes.

*T*he round clock above the door into the first floor hall said 9:07, but the sun, streaming across the damp tiled floor, was already hot. Roy, a graying janitor, stood stuffing a pile of dirty sheets into a laundry bag, as if he were filling a large, white sausage case. His body bulged in loose folds above his gray uniform pants and dark half moons of perspiration were already visible in his armpits. A nurse with a blonde ponytail approached, pushing a rattling intravenous stand. Roy straightened and bowed. "Good morning, m'darling," he said, sweeping the floor with his freckled hand. "You're looking very lovely today." The nurse smiled, rolled her eyes upward with a weary expression, and continued down the hall. A buzzer sounded from a patient's room and a red light went on above the abandoned nurses' desk.

"Where's Lou?" Marge Flaherty, the head nurse, demanded as she hurried around the corner, clutching an armload of metal-backed charts. She put the charts down on the desk and reached up to flick off the buzzer light. "It's after nine," she muttered, as she glanced down at a list on the crowded desk. "Four more admissions last night."

There was a sound of male voices in the outer hall. The swinging doors opened and all at once the space beyond the nurses' desk was crowded with white-coated men. Dr. Mostello led the way, followed by the head resident in horn-rimmed glasses, carrying a clipboard. A group of students in white duck pants and crumpled jackets, trailed behind. Several carried spiral pads; one had a pencil tucked behind his ear and the black loops of a stethoscope protruded from the pocket of another student's white jacket.

Dr. Mostello strode into Hally's room; the others crowded in behind him, leaving Roy alone with his laundry bag in the empty hall.

The heavy-set doctor stationed himself next to the intravenous stand and peered down at Hally, while the students grouped themselves in a semi-circle around the foot of her bed. Hally lifted her head with an effort and stared down at the group below. Artemis was not among them, she noted, and let her head drop back, so that she was staring up at Dr. Mostello.

"How are you feeling this morning?" he demanded.

"Fine. I mean I . . . I. . . . " Hally's words were thick. "What are you going to . . . ?" She swallowed and started again, aware that she was barely understandable. "When can I go home?" she asked. Dr. Mostello turned to the student group.

"This is your typical bulbar involvement," he explained. "Thick nasal voice, swallowing difficulty, high fever." Hally waited for a moment when she could interrupt—could force some answers to the questions crowded inside her.

"When can I go home?" she asked again. Dr. Mostello glanced down at her and then back at the group.

"The breathing capacity is reduced, you see. That salivation, the lip paralysis—that's seventh nerve involvement." He looked back at Hally, who lay with her mouth half open, exhausted by her effort to speak.

"What are you going to do?" Her thick, throaty sounds enveloped her and she raised her hand to her mouth, as if to pull out the words that were stuck inside. "What's the matter with me?"

Dr. Mostello looked down, taking her in all at once. "What you've got is bulbar polio," he said slowly. "You see, Hally, the virus has settled at the top of your spine." He raised his white-coated arm and gripped the back of his neck to illustrate the area. "See? People often think of polio as paralysis in the legs or back. But it can paralyze the throat too." Hally stared up at him and nodded. His explanation seemed less important than the fact that he had called her "Hally"; this head doctor actually knew her name. "The paralysis has affected your swallowing and your breathing," he continued. "That's why your throat's so sore."

Paralysis, Hally thought. Paralysis in her throat? But how could you have polio in your throat? Children got polio in their legs and had to wear braces, but she only had a bad summer cold. That was all, wasn't it?

When could she go home? The doctor's deep black eyes seemed to sweep across her body like a searchlight, assessing her with their intelligence and authority. They were like her father's eyes, she thought, her young and brilliant father years ago before he died—her father, who had given her her first flute. She heard the Mozart Flute Concerto in D Major—the difficult run in the *Allegro* which she had done well. She was playing for the doctors, she realized—giving them a gift of music in return for their willingness to help her, because they were right; it was more than a summer cold. She was sick; she needed them.

Hally could see notes in front of her and realized she was climbing up a music staff, ascending the black bars diagonally. She climbed onto a cluster of joined eighth notes and ran up its back, then leapt to the next cluster, and the next, jumping lightly, moving higher and higher, until she was at the top. Panting a moment, she stared down. She was above them all now—high up, here at the top of the room, as the concerto continued. Below her, she could see the heads of the students—one with greased dark hair, another with a furry blond crewcut, and one with a cowlick nodding in back. Beyond them was the doctor's head with its crinkly dark strands combed across the balding area in front. She saw the bed, where she had been lying, the sheet pushed back, the dented pillow, and the black intravenous tube, hanging limp. She had escaped, she realized, and was above them all; she was alone with her music and free.

"Are you with me, Hally?" Dr. Mostello asked. His voice had a parental sharpness. "Do you understand what I'm saying?"

She should go back, Hally thought. He was kind; he was like Daddy. He was taking time to explain the situation to her; she must return to that bed, nod, and show her appreciation. "Yes," she said and stared up at the doctor again. Now the green and blue stripes in his tie were just above her once more.

"The reason your speech is so thick," the doctor said, "is that the polio virus has settled in your throat. See?"

Hally nodded. She would concentrate later, she told herself. Right now she felt hot and dizzy; she would pretend to understand. The saliva was building up in the corner of her mouth and soon it would begin to ooze down her chin. Hally sighed. She was sick. That was clear. The green walls were swaying gently in and out. But it was all right; this was a good man. He knew what to do to make her well. "Thank you," she mouthed, as Dr. Mostello turned to go.

"I'll be back in a while," he told her. There was a shuffling sound of feet and all at once the room was empty again. Hally tried to lift her head. If only Artemis were here or better yet—Mom. But the Mozart was around her still—the *Andante,* the beautiful *Andante ma non troppo* that she had done so well; Hally closed her eyes and smiled.

Dr. Mostello turned to Dr. Baldwin outside in the hall. "I want her monitored around the clock," he said.

Roy stood beside the elevator. "Slam that door, will ya?" he yelled down the shaft and gave the elevator button an angry punch. "I'm stuck up here." There was a crashing sound as someone downstairs jerked the collapsible metal gate inside closed. The elevator began to rise with a clanging noise and shuddered to a stop. Roy pulled the outside door open, held it back with his hip, pushed in two laundry bags, and stepped inside. The crashing noise of the collapsible gate was followed by more clanging, as the elevator began its descent.

"Her breathing's getting tricky." Dr. Mostello raised his voice over the sound. "The virus's close to the brain."

"I'll get in there right after rounds," Dr. Baldwin said. "I'll put Schmidt on her now." He tucked his clipboard under his arm, and spoke to a dark-haired intern, then followed the head doctor into Dan's room.

Dr. Mostello strode to the head of the bed, while the students grouped themselves around the bottom. Dan had heard them in the hall and was sitting up in anticipation, his back pressed to the pillow, which was mashed against the metal bars of the bedframe once more. He had shaved earlier and now he felt hot with questions he wanted to ask.

"How are you feeling this morning?" Dr. Mostello demanded. "Any pain?"

"A little," Dan admitted. "Down there in my legs, sort of." He looked up at the doctor. "I don't think it's very serious though. What I want to know is what if . . . ?"

"Lie out straight," Dr. Mostello interrupted. Dan stared at him a moment then pushed himself down in bed. The guy was so damn abrupt. Such a power figure. He settled his head on the pillow and pushed his legs out straight. After all he had a right to know if. . . . The doctor pulled back the sheet and moved to the bottom of the bed. He lifted Dan's left leg slowly, supporting the heel in one hand, the calf in the other.

"That hurt?" he asked.

"Feels a little stiff," Dan answered and bit down on his lip. It felt a hell of a lot more than "stiff," he thought to himself; the leg was hot and ached all the way down the calf. But if he didn't acknowledge the pain, if he acted stoical and removed, maybe it would disappear. Dan winced as Dr. Mostello lifted the leg higher. He watched the doctor put it down on the sheet again and take a small test tube from his breast pocket. What now, Dan thought, and opened his mouth to ask, but the intent look on the doctor's face silenced him. He saw him remove the stopper and extract a straight pin. Dr. Mostello bent and pressed the point of the pin into the top of Dan's foot with a quick jab.

"Feel that?" He glanced back at Dan, who nodded.

"Sure," he said and started to add, "of course." But he waited and watched the doctor push back his loose pajama pant and prick his naked calf, about an inch further up. "What about that? Can you feel that too?"

"Sort of," Dan said. "It's not quite as sharp." He peered at the doctor's face, but the intent dark eyes divulged nothing. The next prick felt distinctly muted, almost remote, as though someone else's leg was being pricked nearby. This is it, Dan thought with a rush of panic. This is paralysis. It's in my legs. My legs. He looked at the doctor and then down at the students. *Do something, can't you, he started to shout. Do something. Don't just stare. There must be something you can give me, something to stop this or. . . .* Dan swallowed. Dr. Mostello jabbed the pin again. Was it really not as sharp as the one on the foot or was he just scared? Dan stared down at his naked leg in confusion. It was hard to tell. He felt a tension had spread out in the room, as the students watched Dr. Mostello continue up Dan's leg, pricking the skin at intervals, then turning his head for Dan's response. Dan scanned the group for Jim Rickley, the tall, friendly intern who had come into his room last night to talk. There he was, standing on the side, watching Mostello. He turned his head, met Dan's eyes and nodded; the look filled Dan with relief. He gazed down at his leg again. He would talk with Jim later. Jim would be sure to stop in; he would explain this procedure and . . . . Mostello had said there were many gradations after all. Dan watched the doctor straighten and replace the pin in its tube. "I can feel them all more or less," Dan told him. "It's just that they're not as sharp up toward the top of the calf, I think."

"Right. Right." Dr. Mostello nodded, his face was stern. "This gives us a better idea of what's going on."

"What?" Dan demanded in a rush. "What is going on?"

"Well, there's some paralysis. Some involvement. But this is often the pattern while the temperature's high. This isn't much and it may well recede."

"But what if . . . ?" Dan started.

"I can't tell you much more than that right now," Dr. Mostello said. "You get some rest. I'll look in later." He moved to the door, followed by the students. "By the way," he said, turning back. "I talked to your parents last night. They'll be here tomorrow."

"Tomorrow?" Dan repeated. "They will?" He watched the backs of the two doctors as they filed through the door, then the students' backs; the room was empty again. Dan fixed the pillow under his head and stared up at a network of cracks in the corner, that looked like the mouth of the Nile. Mother would be trembly, but busy, packing the suitcases in the master bedroom, telephoning. But Dad . . . ? Dan gazed down at his legs again. If they were paralyzed or partly so, if he couldn't ride, couldn't help manage the ranch, if had to walk with a cane, a limp . . . ? Oh God, Dad would be sick with worry, trying to get information on what Boston doctors were best, what hospitals, plus all the details of leaving. He imagined his father, standing outside the barn with Harley, the ranch manager. He thought of them going over the list of chores together: the plowing in the north field, the rye harvest, training the new hands. Damn, Dan thought. July was a lousy time for Dad to leave. If he was really flying here with Mother, he must think this polio thing was more than "mild."

I might still be out of here in a week or ten days, Dan told himself. I might still finish the research and leave for the Oregon Trail by mid-August. And yet if I lose ten days of library work. . . . It isn't just the research itself, he thought, I've got to finish the maps. Suppose I'm still here in August? Suppose. . . . Stop it, he told himself, and reached for his book again.

Suppose he was left with a limp? He opened the book, then let it close. Suppose he had to use a cane? He imagined a brown stick, its curved top rubbed with use. He could work, Dan told himself, teach, do research. He could climb the library steps slowly. Hell, Dad had hired a hand four years ago with a wooden leg. Red, they called him, and he had been a good herder, a good worker too.

Dan slid down in bed and thought of Jill, her blonde hair covered with that orange scarf. When would she hear that he was in a hospital, he wondered. Not for weeks maybe, since she was in France for the summer. She'd be sorry then; she'd think back on that fight in May. Oh, honest to God, he told himself. Shut up, can't you? He rolled cautiously on his side and thought of Valley again. It was dawn there now, the fields growing light. Star would be shifting on her long slender legs out in her stall. He thought of her deep brown gaze, the white mark on her forehead and her velvet mouth, nuzzling his hand. All that could not just stop, he told himself. It was his life, the life he knew.

"How are you doing now?" Jim Rickley asked. Dan looked over at the tall medical student standing in the doorway in his wrinkled white jacket and smiled. "That pin prick test is kind of hairy," Jim said. "But it's not that big a deal really. I mean as Mostello said, waiting's all we can do right now."

"But what about medicine?" Dan asked. "I can't believe there isn't something they can give me to arrest this thing? Stop it spreading or something. I mean. . . . "

"There isn't anything," Jim said and sat down in the armchair. "There literally isn't. There might have been if we'd had that Cutter vaccine. But that's out for now."

"No penicillin, no. . . . "

"Nothing. Intelligent, conscientious observation is it and you're lucky. Mostello is tops, not just here, you know. All over the country. He's a polio expert—a brilliant diagnostician."

"Well, that's one good thing," Dan said and sighed. "It's so weird. I mean I don't really feel terrible—just sort of hot and aching. But . . . Jeez."

"It's a strange disease," Jim said. He stretched out his long legs in his white duck pants and sighed. "God, I'm bushed. I've been on since nine last night."

"Nine last night?" Dan said. "That's terrible. Why such long shifts? If there's such an emergency, why don't they get some extra help?"

"They'd love to, but it's tricky. Polio admissions have been rising steadily for the past two weeks—here and in other hospitals in the city too. We had four more last night and ten the night before that. It looks damn close to an epidemic. But the city won't admit it. Bad for tourist trade. The fact is the hospitals can't get extra help until an epidemic is offically declared." Jim sighed. "In other words, it's a mess."

"God," Dan said and stared.

"It's a mess, but it's temporary. They'll have to do something soon. Tomorrow or Monday maybe. They'll have to."

"Well, at least then you can get some sleep." Dan pushed back the sheet and swung his legs over the side of the bed.

"What're you doing?" Jim sat forward.

"Just going to grab that book on the bureau," Dan explained.

"Stay there. I'll get it. You're supposed to stay put."

"Could I walk now if I tried?" Dan demanded and stared at him.

"Probably not," Jim said. "But that's not the point. There's no way of knowing what's going to happen. That's why you've got to lie flat and wait."

"Okay. I don't really want the book anyway. I just wanted to see." Dan lay back again. "You know it isn't my legs. I just feel so achy, so. . . . My stomach hurts and. . . . " He paused. "I bet you envy me the bed rest anyway." Jim stretched his legs out again and gave a long sigh. He let his head sag forward on his chest and his eyes closed. The room was quiet; the only sounds were the ticking of Dan's bedside clock and the soft breathing of this exhausted young man, at ease in the armchair. Dan studied the figure beyond him a moment, smiled to himself, and closed his eyes.

5

*I*t was late afternoon; the glare had faded from the hospital steps outside and gray shadows lay across the lawn. Dr. Baldwin stood beside the intravenous stand, looking down at Hally. The frame of his horn-rimmed glasses was held together on one side by a piece of adhesive tape and a line of ball-point pens stuck up from the breast pocket of his medical coat. Hally opened her eyes and moved her tongue over her chapped lips, as Dr. Baldwin watched. These bulbar cases were the trickiest of all, he thought—two deaths last week. So much depended on the patient's ability to fight. Could this girl do it? She was a musician apparently; that took discipline and persistence. Still, you could never tell—not with fever like this. The only thing to do was try to help them keep fighting until the fever went down, if it did.

"Any history of diabetes in the family?" he asked, bending toward her slightly. "What about measles? Did you have measles when you were a child?"

"I've already told you that," Hally's thick voice held an edge of annoyance. "Aren't you writing anything down?"

"I don't need this information," Dr. Baldwin confided, as he watched her. "I'm only trying to keep you awake." She would work better with him if she sensed the seriousness of the situation, he thought—if she didn't panic, that is, and he would take that chance.

"Awake?" Hally stared up at him with a puzzled look. "But why? I'm so tired . . . so. . . . If I could sleep. That would . . . would help." She turned her head to gaze beyond him at the lamp by the armchair, part of an island of orange light in the dim room, then she closed her eyes again. "Say 'Kellogg's Corn Krispies' for me," Dr. Baldwin ordered. Hally gave him a tired smile. "Again?" "All right then, how about 'prunes and prisms'?" He paused. Actually those diagnostic phrases were pointless now; they had long since established the problem. "Would you rather talk about music?" Dr. Baldwin glanced at the hall. It was quiet for the moment; the interns on duty were in the respirator ward. "Artemis tells me you're a flutist. I'm a Mozart lover myself." Hally stared, then brought out two words slowly. "Me too." If he loved Mozart . . . . His hand rested on the bedtray; she studied his clean blunt fingernails, with their grayish moons. If he loved Mozart, he must be a good doctor; he would help. In a minute she would lift her head and ask him if he liked the Flute Concerto No. 2 in D Major. But right now she would lie quiet a little longer, for the music had started again—her solo was ending, the strings were beginning, their bows pushing up, then withdrawing. The conductor raised his baton and nodded at her. Now she was playing. The notes were rising, light and sure, moving up and up.

A taxi stood in the driveway circle late in the afternoon. It was parked just beyond the front steps of the hospital, its back door hanging open. Tom Lewis, a tall, tanned man in a blue seersucker suit, was standing beside the driver, taking money from his billfold, when Marian Lewis sat forward on the back seat and called out to him. "Wait, Tom. Ask him if this is really it." She leaned to stare out at the brick building with its rows of windows, the venetian blinds pulled up crookedly at some, or lowered to cover others. "It looks so small," she said. She was partially visible within the cab—a gray-haired woman in a green linen dress with white beads at her neck, whose peering face looked tense, despite her careful make-up. "Tell him it's the Wahl Doctors' Hospital we want—part of the Fiske Medical system." Tom Lewis took the change the driver handed him, gave him back two dollars, and turned to his wife.

"This is it, Marian. The sign back there said so." He bent and offered her his hand. Marian's high-heeled shoes and stockinged legs emerged first. She stood, smoothed her skirt, and settled her pocketbook at her side, before she took her husband's arm. They glanced back a moment, as the cab started down the long driveway, then they turned to the building and mounted the front steps together.

They had waited so long to see the head doctor, that when he finally appeared, Tom felt secretly angry with him, as though it was somehow Dr. Mostello's fault that Dan was sick and they had had to leave the ranch before dawn. They had visited Dan in his hot room, talking to him of Valley, the family, his horse. When a nurse appeared with a small machine on casters and announced that she must test his breathing, they left and stood in the hall, leaning back against the tiled wall, for there was no waiting room apparently and the whole place seemed old and crowded. The doctor held his conference with them right there in the hall. The waiting method he described made Tom clench and unclench his fist in his jacket pocket. Still this Mostello fellow was supposed to be tops in his field; Tom had checked on that. But my God, to just wait—to leave Dan in increasing pain, to just sit in there and. . . . He tried to focus on a question Marian had asked. The doctor paused a moment. "That's right," he said. "At this point there is no medication, no real treatment. The only thing we can do right now is watch him carefully. Later, when we know what we're dealing with, when the fever has subsided, then there are a number of treatments, if he needs them. But for now the only thing to do is wait." Tom narrowed his eyes, assessing the man. He was clearly used to exercising authority. Yet he was not condescending, and, more importantly, those dark intense eyes conveyed intelligence, brilliance even. Dr. Mostello glanced up at the clock on the wall to indicate that the interview was ending; he looked from one face to the other with a professional nod.

"But doctor, when will we know just exactly what the . . . the . . . " Marian hesitated. This was so tough for her, Tom thought. But there was nothing more the guy could say; he was doing his best. The place was coping with a crisis; apparently Boston was close to epidemic status. Tom touched her arm and she let the question trail.

"I wish I could be more definite about it. But I can't. Nobody can be right now. We just have to be patient and see what happens." Dr. Mostello glanced up at the clock again. "I'll talk to you tomorrow. All right?" The Lewises nodded and watched the doctor walk down the dingy hall, past the rooms on either side to the swinging doors of what seemed to be a ward at the end. When the doors closed behind him, Marian looked up at her husband. Tom nodded and let out a long sigh.

It was four in the morning when Dr. Baldwin paused at the door of Dr. Mostello's office, then raised his hand and knocked. "Come in," said the brusque voice. Dr. Baldwin opened the door. The head doctor was sitting with his white elbows on the blotter, his head sunk in his hands. But he raised it, as the door opened, and gave the head resident a searching look. "What's the situation now?" he demanded. Dr. Baldwin paused. The weariness in that familiar, heavy face moved him and he felt a sudden urge to confess his own discouragement, his heavy fatigue. But he glanced down at the uneven stack of manila folders on the desk instead, the medical text lying open, its pages weighted down with an empty coffee mug. A solitary seersucker jacket hung on a coat rack in the corner. It must have been waiting there unused for more than thirty-six hours, Dr. Baldwin thought. He himself had not been home in all that time—so certainly the chief had not.

"How is he now? That Murphy fellow?" Dr. Mostello demanded.

"Gone," Dr. Baldwin answered and sighed. "Twenty minutes ago."

"Ah, Christ." Dr. Mostello pushed his desk chair back. He rose and turned abruptly to the small window behind him, where he stood staring out, his back to the head resident. "I ought to have put him in a tank this morning," Dr. Mostello said, without turning back. "This afternoon at the latest."

"We didn't have any extras." Dr. Baldwin said dully, aware that he was repeating an obvious fact. "We still don't."

"I know, Goddamnit," Dr. Mostello muttered and turned back to Dr. Baldwin. "I know." He let out a long sigh. "How about that Blessing girl? How's she doing now?"

"Tricky. Could go either way," Dr. Baldwin said. "Schmidt's with her this shift, but I'm going back. Pre-dawn," he said and glanced down at his watch. "Could be crucial."

"Yes. Sure." Dr. Mostello nodded. "I'll be up in a while. Going back to the ward first." The men nodded at each other and Dr. Baldwin left the office, closing the door behind him.

Dan's room was already hot, although it was not yet ten in the morning.

Dust motes twirled in a bright shaft of light, slanting through the crooked blinds. Dan lay flat on his bed, his face damp. His eyes were closed and his jaws were clenched. Marian Lewis, who was sitting in the armchair beside the bed, smoothed back a page in the heavy book that Dan had brought.

" 'Chapter 4'," she read. " 'Emerson and Thoreau.' " She paused and peered over at her son. "Shall I go on?" she asked. The material seemed so remote, she half hoped he would say no. Dan opened his eyes, gazed over at her, and shook his head. Marian studied him. "The pain's pretty awful right now, isn't it?"

Dan nodded and closed his eyes. Had that elegant woman in the armchair with her coiffed gray hair and beads really sat by his sandbox and decorated the cuts on his knees with mercurochrome flowers? Strange. He breathed out and felt himself swinging back and forth between a need to moan and be her hurt baby and a need to stay stiff and stern and be her stoical son. He sighed, too weary to choose. Mother meant well, but he would feel better when Dad came back, filling the room with his quiet sanity.

"What about *The New Yorker*?" Marian asked and reached for the magazine. "Would you like me to read you the 'Talk of the Town'?" No thanks, Dan indicated, rolling his head on the pillow again. He had leg paralysis all right and this was no mild case, Goddamnit. He could barely move his left leg at all now and the right one hurt like hell. Oh God. He'd be an old man at twenty-five. Why me, Dan thought, and clutched his side as another spasm began in his thigh. Why me? He heard his mother rise, heard the jangle of ice cubes in the plastic pitcher on the bedtray and opened his eyes. "How about some water?" Dan shook his head, as he felt another spasm spread down his leg; right now he must simply endure.

Marian gazed down at him. "Dr. Mostello says this might be over by tomorrow," she announced and paused, one finger pressed to her lips. She lifted it and added, "He says you'll feel much more comfortable soon." The spasm ended.

"I hope to God he's right," Dan whispered hoarsely and stared up at her. Was she just telling him a soothing lie? How the hell would Mostello know when this would end? Dan closed his eyes again. Jill once said his mother was duplicitous. But that was last spring when Jill was full of criticisms of his family and they both suspected that the thing that they had had was gone. Dan felt his mother's eyes move over him. Dishonest?

No. She was desperate; she was trying to comfort her son. Another shudder began in his back; Dan felt his fingernails dig into the skin on his side. How much longer? God in Heaven, how much longer would this go on?

Marian stood by the bedtray staring down. Dan's eyes were closed and his face was sweaty and unshaven. One of his hands was clutching his shoulder and the fingers of the other were kneading the bottom of his rib cage. Another spasm of pain. Poor child. Surely a fabricated hope was better than none.

She settled in the armchair again and picked up the book. Ralph Gabriel, *The Course of American Democratic Thought*—peculiar reading for a boy as sick as Dan, still he had listened with interest yesterday. His world was so different from theirs now. Long ago he had been a browned little boy in faded jeans, with a blond cowlick nodding at the back of his head like a flower. He had loved the ranch, but Harvard was in their plans from the first; both Tom and her brother were Harvard men after all. She had grown up in Boston and would be there or in Connecticut still, if it hadn't been for Tom's heart attack in '39 and their move West. Dan's acceptance to Harvard had important secondary benefits; it created an excellent new excuse for Marian to make more trips East, visits with her son, as well as her father, Friday afternoons at the symphony, shopping. Marian sighed. Without her trips East, her Denver life would have been insupportable.

Marian looked back at the bed. Why a doctorate in History, she wondered. Dan said he was going to write a thesis on the Oregon Trail. He meant to drive the length of it this August and write . . . what? Something about the accuracy of a book by a man named Parkman? She wasn't sure. But why not Harvard Law School? That's where her brother had gone and Dan would make such a fine lawyer. He could build up a good practice back in Denver and write history as a hobby maybe. He would inherit the ranch someday after all and . . . . Marian glanced back at the bed and sighed. Nothing mattered now, she thought, as she pressed the fingers of one hand to her lips, nothing—if Dan could just be well, could just be out of pain again.

It was noon and the weedy grass felt wiry with dryness, as Roy led a young repairman to the side of the building, where an air-conditioner protruded from a first-floor window. Roy was talking busily; the new listener was an opportunity and he himself was an authority on this polio crisis after all. The repairman glanced at the machine, put his tool box on the grass, and crawled under the heavy metal box. Roy watched the young man select some pliers from among his tools and rotate his shoulders a moment to unstick his uniform shirt from his back.

"It's like I said," Roy told the man. "Nothing gets fixed around here no more. There just ain't the time. Only one other fella besides me now and he's a three-day man. Sink stops up, wheels on the meal trolley don't roll right and like this here—the air-conditioner breaks down. The only thing them docs worry about in there," he jerked his head toward the building, "is them tanks—the respirators, you know. When they go, that's it." Roy sliced the humid air with a decisive gesture. But the man under the air-conditioner was oblivious; he twisted a rusty bolt, first with the pliers, then with his fingers.

"I've worked in better places than this, I can tell you," Roy went on. "Fiske Medical when she was new. Modern? I swear. All the equipment. And the floors. Beautiful! New, shiny. The halls must've been a good five feet across. Oh, that was a job, I tell you. Been here seven years this August." Roy paused. "But this summer. God. This polio business—it's getting real serious. Bad. Yes sir. Real bad. Fifty-four was no joke, you know. But this .... The pressure. It's gotten something terrible. Them admissions streaming in night after night. Been going on over two weeks now. Some of these doctors is working eighteen, nineteen hour shifts. And it's the city's to blame, you know. Politics. Pure politics. Weather too, if you ask me. This heat, it breeds them germs, brings them right up out of the dust." Roy put his hands on his heavy hips and shook his head ominously. "It's terrible, I tell you. There's people dying in there right now." He looked up at the building and shook his head. "Some of them won't last the night, God rest their souls. You mark my word."

Roy's grim prediction was lost on the repairman, however. He lifted off the rusty cover of the air-conditioner and laid it beside him on the grass, then stood, reached the controls in front, and turned a knob. The machine started up with a shaky roar. It drowned the sound of Roy's voice temporarily, but he simply spoke louder and kept on talking.

6

It was Hally's third night in the hospital and Hans Schmidt, the visiting intern from Vienna, who had a dark lock of hair that hung down on his forehead, stood beside Dr. Baldwin, watching the dial of a machine beside Hally's bed. An accordion-pleated tube, attached to the rubber mask that covered Hally's nose and mouth, gauged her "vital capacity." Her eyes were closed as she inhaled, exhaled, then inhaled again. Dr. Baldwin made a notation on the metal-backed chart that lay open on the bedtray, then lifted off the mask. He glanced at the window, half-open to the dark summer night, and back at Hally. Her chin was marked with a long pink scar of chapped skin, indicating the path of the oozing saliva, and her open mouth gave her a limp, unconscious look.

"She can't possibly make it now, can she?" Hans whispered. He peered at the chart and then at Hally. "It's a classic case of the double camel's hump. Right?" He looked at Dr. Baldwin, but the head resident did not reply. "I mean her temperature was 104 the first night and 104.5 the whole time I was with her last night. They say here it went down to 102 this morning." He pointed to the chart and his voice rose. "But look. It's up to 105 now. The body just doesn't have the strength. Does it? I mean if those extra tanks would come then . . . ."

"Careful. She's conscious." Dr. Baldwin's voice was sharp. He replaced the mask on a hook at the side of the machine and wiped the drool from Hally's chin. Dr. Schmidt gave him an uneasy look, then glanced out into the hall.

"I'm going down to the ward. Back in an hour. All right?" Dr. Baldwin

[39]

nodded, but did not turn to look at the man. He stood watching Hally intently as the sound of the medical student's retreating footsteps echoed in the empty hall.

Hally opened her eyes and stared at the side of the brown bureau beyond the bed. They think I'm going to die. Die? But death is for old people, other people. Not for me. She wet her lips with her tongue and moved her mouth to make a word. "I . . . I. . . . " She heard her frog-like croaking in the quiet room. Dr. Baldwin bent down so that his serious, bespectacled face was just above her. Hally studied a brown mole on his cheek and realized that the other doctor was gone. "He thinks I'm going to. . . ."

Dr. Baldwin put his hands on his knees. "Watch me, Hally," he broke in. "Do this." He inhaled deeply, then exhaled, letting his breath out with a light blowing sound. "See that? That's what you've got to do. In, out. See?" Hally breathed in, keeping her eyes on the doctor, then out. She paused and breathed in again. This wasn't hard, she thought. She had studied breath control after all. In, out. In, out. She could do it. She was strong. She had just begun. She had pushed wheelbarrows full of rocks, when they were making the wall at Grandpa's, and had bicycled twenty miles one day last summer in Vermont. After all, she often practiced five hours straight or more, she thought, and breathed out again.

"In, out," she continued, mouthing the words.

"That's the way," Dr. Baldwin encouraged. "Keep it nice and steady now." He straightened, keeping his eyes on her face. "That's it. Good girl."

"In, out," Hally continued and saw the doctor's face soften with relief. He loved Mozart; he wouldn't let her die. She let her eyes travel to the curved white bar at the bottom of the bed, which gleamed in the lamplight. A chipped place on the side was the shape of a sleeping cat. Hally saw Jeffy dozing beside the African violets in the kitchen window, the sun making a soft halo of the fur on his back. It's all right, she told herself. It's all right. I can go on.

A nurse passed in the hall, pushing a rattling medicine cart, then quiet flowed into the room again. Hally continued to mouth the words. "In, out. In, out." Dr. Baldwin massaged his neck with one hand. She was keeping the rhythm well. She hadn't panicked, despite Schmidt's unsubtle observations, despite the fact that she was still alone. They'd had trouble contacting her mother apparently. But she was on her way now, Mostello had reported. Five minutes passed, fifteen, then half an hour. Dr. Baldwin glanced down at his watch again and breathed out slowly. Five o'clock. One more crisis time had passed.

Dan looked out at the shadowy lawn and sighed; this would be the fourth night he'd spent in this damn place. Four nights and they felt like forty. He tried to think of his room in the graduate dorm, the line of books at the back of his desk, his shoe box card file with "O.T." printed in red ink letters on the label. Oregon Trail. Oh God.

Tom Lewis poked his head around the door and came into the room. His shirt sleeves were rolled up, exposing his tanned arms. "Look what I brought you," he said and nodded at a brown box-like object he was carrying. "A radio. I just bought it at the hotel. Ought to be fairly good reception here." He put the radio on the bedside table, stooped, and felt along the dusty baseboard for an outlet. He plugged the cord in and straightened. Dan twisted his head to look, but the movement made him wince. "Thanks, Dad," he said, covering his expression with a smile. "That's great."

"Thought it might break the monotony." Tom watched as Dan turned his head back again and let out a sigh. "Not feeling much better, are you?"

"Not a whole lot, but . . . ." Dan looked up at his father. "Listen, Dad. Baldwin was just in—that head resident, you know? He did a couple of tests—that pin prick thing again and . . . I can't feel anything now, Dad. Not the right or the left. I can't move either leg."

"I know," Tom said. "I just saw him. He told me."

"What did he say to you? He wouldn't tell me much of anything. I mean it's paralysis obviously. But how long will it last?"

"He doesn't know apparently," Tom said. "Nobody does." He took a handkerchief from his pants pocket and wiped some perspiration from his upper lip, then sighed. "We've just got to wait it out, Danny. Put the lights on in the barn, make some coffee, and wait." Dan opened his mouth to object. They weren't waiting for the arrival of some little filly after all. He closed his mouth and nodded; Dad was right. It was what they had all told him—Dr. Mostello, Baldwin, Jim Rickley, the whole crowd. He just had to wait—to keep on waiting and see. He closed his eyes and imagined the lighted barn at night, the coffee machine grumbling on the low desk in the harness room. With Dad here, it was easier anyway.

Tom Lewis lowered himself into the armchair, keeping his eyes on his son. He crossed his long legs in their blue cord trousers and wiped his palms with the handkerchief. "You've made it through the critical phase. Now there's this long waiting period, Baldwin says—seeing how the fever recedes, which nerves are damaged and which will recover. It could still be mild, Danny. We just won't know for a while." He gazed out the open window to the globe lights glowing at the end of the long driveway. "Several weeks maybe."

Tom let his eyes travel from his son's exhausted-looking face to his naked chest. An incongruous triangle of brown skin jutted down from his collar bone, indicating the open-necked shirts he'd worn in the summer days just past, when he had been a graduate student, crossing Harvard Yard with his green book bag on his shoulder. Tom himself had gone to Wall Street instead of graduate school and then to Colorado after his heart attack for a month or two of rest at a ranch. But he had stayed on; Colorado had been the best thing that had ever happened to him, outside of Marian, or his children, especially his son. He gazed at Dan's motionless legs stretched out in the faded pajama pants. The boy had been a natural rider from the beginning, an expert herder at twelve. Oh God. Tom clenched one fist in his trouser pocket. Why not me? He stared up at the crack in the corner, then looked back at the bed again. Put me there, God, will You, he pleaded silently. Me. Not my son.

The bed blurred. Tom turned to the radio beside him and switched it on. The tuning knob made a long bronze-colored needle rotate on the round dark face. "Remember Kent," an announcer urged. "Kent with the exclusive, scientific Micronite filter." Tom twisted the needle a few degrees further. "West German Chancellor, Konrad Adenauer, spoke today of the continuing desire of the German people for reunification and. . . . " Tom moved the needle on. A phrase of the Bach Chorale, *Sheep May Safely Graze,* spread out in the dim room. He turned up the volume slightly, and glanced over at Dan, who opened his eyes and nodded at his father, then closed them again. Tom settled back in the armchair as the rich, gentle music flowed around them. The room had grown dim, but Tom did not reach to turn on the light. He raised one foot, in its crepe-soled shoe, and rested it carefully on the edge of Dan's bed, so that his long leg in its blue trouser pant formed a bridge between them as they listened together. Tom let his breath out in a low sigh; there was always hope.

Dr. Baldwin stood beside Hally's bed in the room next door, watching his patient. Her eyes were half shut and her mouth hung open, as the saliva continued to ooze down her chin. But she was still at it, still breathing steadily, "In, out. In, out," though it had been close to fourteen hours now. With luck she would make it, he thought, as he crumpled and uncrumpled the wrapper of a Milky Way bar in the pocket of his medical coat.

The Bach Chorale drifted from Dan's half-open door out into the hall and on into Hally's room. She paused in her breathing and opened her eyes to listen. Dr. Baldwin saw her try to raise her head from the pillow, but she could not, and smiled up at him instead.

"Bach," he said. "That chorale. *Sheep May Safely Graze* isn't it?" Hally nodded and tried again to raise her head. "Don't get too interested," Dr. Baldwin warned. "You've got a job to do." He watched his patient resume her rhythmic breathing, but she did not close her eyes. Her face looked more alert, he thought, and her chest seemed to be rising and falling almost involuntarily. In, out. In, out. Yes, the movement was becoming unconscious again. Maybe that music was helping; it was certainly helping him. Dr. Baldwin crossed his white-coated arms over his chest and for a moment he closed his eyes.

*E*sther stood by the bed, gazing down at her sleeping daughter, as the chaotic hours churned behind her. Only last night she had been in another hospital, arranging flowers on Ellie's bureau while the baby nursed. The phone call had come after midnight; she had heard her son-in-law's voice in the hall. Dr. Lester had tried to reach her repeatedly before he left for a conference in London, but he had been calling Ellie's old number and, when he finally sent a telegram, it was a neighbor who retrieved the yellow envelope, that had been fluttering in the door of the empty apartment, and called the new house. By then Hally had been fighting for her life for more than forty-eight hours alone; that fact kept sweeping over Esther, making her shudder. But she had come as fast as she could, and, despite her unease about traveling through the air, the early morning flight was surprisingly beautiful. The cab driver had been kind and then there was the conference here with that head doctor, who was clearly a good man, although he looked exhausted, with deep rings below his eyes. Hally's polio involved something called the "bulbar" part of the spine, he had explained. The virus had almost reached her brain. But it had stopped; she had survived. Esther sighed. Whatever lay ahead—some form of paralysis, some change in Hally's career perhaps—they would deal with all of that in time. For now it was enough that her child had lived and that she was here beside her at last.

Esther was wearing a white surgical gown and her mouth was covered with a thin paper mask—precautions that had been added yesterday for visitors and staff, as the rush of admissions continued. The tapes of her gown were tied at the back of her neck and down below. But the ones in the middle hung loose, exposing her flowered dress behind and one of the elastic pulls on the mask, that slipped over her ears, was tangled in a strand of white hair.

Hally lay with her eyes closed, breathing steadily in and out, unaware of her mother watching over her. The liquid in the intravenous bottle gurgled softly, but it had just been refilled, Esther reminded herself. The doctor would be back soon. My child, she thought, my baby. Funny, intense little Hally, who had begun on music as soon as she could reach the piano. What would happen now? A dribble of saliva started to slide down Hally's chin and Esther pulled a kleenex from the box on the bedtray, blotted the wetness, then dropped the kleenex into the wastebasket, without looking down, for the task had become a familiar one.

Hally opened her eyes and stared down at the bedframe. Her gaze shifted and she took in her mother. "Mom," Hally croaked and stared in astonishment. She reached out to clutch her mother's wrist with her free hand. "When did you ... ?" Esther smiled and stooped to kiss her daughter's forehead, laughing a little at the awkwardness of kissing her through the mask. She straightened and smoothed back the tendrils of hair at Hally's temples. "How did you ... ?" Hally's thick voice stuck.

"Hush, dearie," Esther cautioned. "I'll do the talking."

"But Ellie ... " Hally objected, straining to bring out the words. "How did you ... ?"

"Ellie's fine. It's a girl, dearie, and guess what they've named her?" Hally shook her head. "Harriet Elizabeth. Hally for short," Esther announced. "What do you think of that? When Ellie came back from the delivery room, I asked if she'd decided on a name and she said, 'Why Hally, of course.'" Hally's eyes grew large with tears. She raised her free hand and pressed her fingers to her mouth, as if to hold in her feelings.

"So now you have a niece named after you," Esther said and wiped a trickle starting down from one of Hally's eyes. "That's another good reason to get well. They're proud of you here, Hal," she added and stroked her daughter's cheek. "That head resident, Dr. Baldwin ... told me you did a wonderful job." Hally shook her head.

"I just did what he told me," she whispered. "He's nice." She closed her eyes, then opened them again. "What about Ellie?" she demanded. "What about ... ?" Dr. Mostello had warned Esther that Hally would be hard to understand. Her voice was hoarse certainly, but Esther could make out the words perfectly well. After all Hally was her child.

"It's fine. Ellie understands." She paused. "You mustn't worry. This is where I want to be right now." Esther watched Hally's eyes close. Just last evening, her whole attention had been focused on her other child—Ellie with her baby and her new life of motherhood. Then the news of polio had come like a crash of thunder and it was Hally, her survival. How would this catastrophe affect her career? But no, Esther thought, even the questions were a long way off. Hally was alive. Esther gazed at her daughter's thin face on the wrinkled pillow, at the long pink scar, striping her chin, and the dots of perspiration above her loose lip. "I know what you need," she said and turned to her summer pocketbook in the armchair. She pulled out a small bottle of cologne and daubed some of the sharp fragrance on Hally's temples. "There," she said. "Now you'll feel fresher."

Hally smiled and raised her hand to push back her hair. But she paused with her elbow raised and her expression grew serious, as she stared up at her mother. "Mom, what if . . . ?" Hally curled her fingers to hold the imaginary flute. Esther nodded and breathed out slowly.

"I know," she said. "I told Dr. Mostello you were a flutist. But he says it's too early to know what the effects of this will be." She paused and studied Hally's face. "We just can't worry about that now, Hal. We really can't. You have more immediate things to do." Hally moved her eyes to the frame at the foot of her bed, to the mark of the sleeping cat. Esther watched her nod slowly. But it was an impossible caution, Esther thought. How could she not worry; the flute was Hally's life.

Dan woke from a doze and gazed around his room. It looked larger, brighter, more serene. The mouth of the Nile in the corner was like a tall-stemmed wine glass now, with elaborate swirls, and there was a vase of yellow roses on the bureau that he had not seen before. Out in the hall, nurses were passing, buzzers were ringing. An elevator clanged some-where nearby. The smell of detergent wafted toward him and Dan turned his head, hoping for a sight of the voluble old janitor, who might stand in his doorway and talk. But no one came. Dan turned his head to the other side and saw a group of sparrows collected in a sandy space beside the driveway, shaking their brown-gray wings as they gave themselves a dust bath. That twist of his head had not brought a shudder of pain, Dan realized; he rolled it back cautiously and stared up at the ceiling. No pain that time either. Marvelous. He reached under the sheet and moved his left hand down beside his hip, then his right. A little stiffness, but no spasm at all. Dan breathed out slowly. Even if the pain returned in an hour or two, this was an island of relief. Maybe the fever was receding; maybe he was getting better at last.

Down the hall he could hear a male voice talking on the radio, droning some message in a heavy Boston Irish accent. Dan listened. "Hail Mary, full of grace!" That was Archbishop Cushing, intoning the Rosary. Then this was Sunday morning, Dan thought. How queer. When had he come to this place? Tuesday night? Wednesday? He wasn't sure.

"Hail Mary, full of grace! Blessed art Thou among women and the fruit of thy womb, Jee-zus." The nasal voice seemed oddly reassuring, although it spoke to him from a world he barely knew—the Irish Catholic Boston that lay out there beyond the brick Georgian confines of Harvard. Yesterday, or had it been the day before, he wondered, he had lain here in the hot room with the blinds half-drawn and the pain wrapping him round and round, twisting him until he was dizzy and drenched with sweat and had only wanted to escape it all. To die? Yesterday that was almost what he had wished. Dan sighed and stared up at the wine glass again. Clearly he was better this morning. His legs were numb, his arms were. . . . But there was no point in assessing things now. It was all changing. He could see that vase of flowers on the bureau now and three yellow petals, lying on the brown surface beside it, and there were the sparrows outside, and he could think of . . . of . . . not the library perhaps and his shoe box file marked "O.T.," but of the Yard in the evening, of shadows, and the smell of mown grass, of supper with someone—not Jill maybe—but someone. . . . He heard footsteps in the hall, then a voice, a laugh, that sounded familiar. Jim Rickley, he thought, and turned his head. In a moment Jim would sit complaining, joking and. . . . Odd. This really wasn't such a bad place.

"The Lord is with thee," the Archbishop intoned. Who knows, Dan thought. It might be true. Right now at least, things would go on.

Dr. Baldwin pressed his ear to his stethoscope, which lay on Hally's naked abdomen, and listened, while Hally gazed up at the ceiling. She could feel the sweat trickling down between her breasts and her chest was still heaving. She had not meant to scream like that and kick his arm, but oh my God that tube poking its way up her nostril, then curving and snuffling down, down. Oh God. It had been awful. But the procedure was over apparently, over at last, and Dr. Baldwin's listening head lay just below her breasts—a position of peculiar intimacy, Hally thought, that she should enjoy perhaps, for despite this nasty tube insertion, Dr. Baldwin was definitely her favorite doctor.

"That's it," he said and lifted his head. "It's down." He straightened and stuffed his stethoscope back into the pocket of his medical coat as Miss Flaherty handed Hally a kleenex.

Hally wiped her mouth and stared at the red blood on the crumpled white surface. "You've got some on your nose too," Miss Flaherty said and leaned over to clean some bloody mucous from around her nostrils.

"Cut some adhesive, Marge," Dr. Baldwin directed. "We've got to tack it down now." Miss Flaherty snipped some strips from the wide roll and hung them on the end of the bedtray near Dr. Baldwin. "Okay. Here we go," he said and leaned over Hally again. Hally gazed down at the string of translucent tubing, that hung from one nostril, then peered at it cross-eyed, as Dr. Baldwin pulled it upward, stretching it along the bridge of her nose. She saw Miss Flaherty lean close, holding out a strip of tape, then felt Dr. Baldwin's thumb pressing it to her nose. She rolled her eyes upward, aware that he had pulled the tube up and was attaching it to her forehead with a second strip.

"There you go," he said and straightened. He cut the tube off near her shoulder and held it out to her. "That's the feeding end. I'll put a fastener on it in a minute. When you're not using it, you can push it back behind your ear. See?"

"My ear?" Hally stared.

Dr. Baldwin nodded and stepped back. "She looks like an Indian princess, doesn't she?" Miss Flaherty smiled. Hally raised her eyebrows cautiously and felt the stiffness of the adhesive tape as her forehead wrinkled. She lifted her hand to her nose and touched the thin tube protruding from her nostril, then reached up to feel the flat adhesive patch on her forehead. She didn't feel much like a princess right now. All at once she lowered her arm and stared at her hand. It was free; she could move it.

[48]

"You're all done with that intravenous now," Miss Flaherty told her. "I'll take it away." She pushed the metal stand with the bottle toward the door and out into the hall.

"That tube'll be a heck of a lot less trouble than the IV," Dr. Baldwin said, looking back at Hally.

"I'm sorry I screamed," Hally began, hurrying to take advantage of Miss Flaherty's absence. "I didn't . . . I didn't mean to hit you. I. . . . " She watched the doctor drop some wads of bloodied kleenex into the wastebasket and wondered if he had understood.

"Don't worry," he said. "I had to put one of those things down myself in medical school. It was awful. I remember."

"You did?" Hally saw him gather up the wet rubber tube that he had used to guide the thin one down. That thing had hurt, but she wished she hadn't yelled. "What will I be getting through this?" she asked and held out the loose end of the tube. "Milk or what?"

"Warm milk with some vitamins." Dr. Baldwin smiled. "You're going to get very used to that," he said. "It'll seem like part of you soon."

Hally looked cross-eyed at the ridge on her nose again, then back at the doctor. "It will?" she said and sighed.

Debbie Kent, a tanned nurse in a nylon uniform, entered Dan's room carrying an aluminum bowl of soapy water. Dan turned his head to peer at her. Her white uniform clung to her breasts and the small starched cap, pinned to her orangey blonde hair, looked unfamiliar. "You're new, aren't you?" he said.

"How can you tell?" Debbie gave him a teasing smile and dipped a washcloth into the bowl.

As she bent over him, Dan glimpsed the white mark of a bathing suit strap beyond the open neck of her uniform. "Because you're so tan and rested-looking."

"Oh, so that's it." Debbie covered his face with the warm cloth. Something in her manner reminded Dan of Jill—her figure maybe or her teasing.

She lifted the cloth and he added, "All the other nurses—Miss Flaherty, Arlene, and the rest—they all look so tired and gray."

Debbie laughed. "I was at the beach when my supervisor called and. . . . "

"You mean they've declared an epidemic?" Dan pulled himself up a little and peered at her seriously. "Are they going to get help?"

"Yup," Debbie told him brightly. "They've decided it's an epidemic all right." She wrung the washcloth out over the bowl, then turned back to him. "I had to drive all the way up here from Provincetown last night. Three hours in traffic." She lifted Dan's arm and swept the washcloth over his armpit. "My boyfriend couldn't bring me. He's a lifeguard, see, and he has a late shift." She put Dan's arm down and straightened. "I've been working on this tan of mine for almost a week and now I won't be able to finish it just because a lot of you guys have polio." She laughed and leaned over to start on Dan's legs.

The noisy, basement cafeteria, with its harsh ceiling lights and steamy smells, seemed pleasantly familiar to Esther on her third hospital day. Her milky tea felt warming and the toasted cheese sandwich was filling, for it had been six hours since her breakfast at home. She started to speak to the nurse across from her, but the girl looked tired, as though she would prefer to finish her pie in silence. A group of interns were talking at the next table, eating large plates of macaroni and tomato sauce. That might well be their first meal since last night, Esther thought. She looked up as a well-dressed, middle-aged woman emerged from the line by the cash register, holding her tray. She paused a moment, looking around her at the crowded tables for a place to sit down. She had a patient in the room next to Hally's, Esther realized. Esther had seen her last night, taking out a supper tray. She looked conspicuous in her shantung suit and beads, standing there amidst the doctors in their wrinkled white coats, and the other visitors, who looked as damp and rumpled as Esther felt. The nurse, who had been sitting across from Esther, rose suddenly and lifted her tray. Esther waved at the gray-haired woman and nodded at the empty place.

"Thank you," Marian said. "It's so crowded. Maybe I should have waited, but . . . ." She put down her tray, slipped off her jacket, and draped it carefully over the back of the chair before she sat down.

"Well, yesterday I waited until almost two," Esther said, "and it wasn't much better. Besides you get so hungry, you need lunch."

"Oh, but what a place to have it in." Marian glanced around her. "This noise." She rolled her eyes briefly, then looked back at her tray. Esther watched her lift a tea bag from a thick white mug, glance around her quickly, then drop it into the glass ashtray between them.

"I'm Esther Blessing," Esther began. "I think we must be neighbors. Don't you have a patient on the first floor, near the elevator?"

"Yes. My son, Dan. I'm Marian Lewis." She smiled and lifted her hand. Esther started to raise hers, but Marian pulled a paper napkin from the metal holder between them instead and spread it in her lap. "Do you have someone in that room next to his?"

Esther nodded. "My daughter," she said.

"Oh, I see." Marian lifted her sandwich, peered at the lining of ham inside, and paused. "What a time this is," she said, and took a delicate bite. "The suddenness of this whole thing. We got a call Saturday night and took a plane the next morning. We live in Colorado, you see. My husband runs a large ranch and it's difficult to leave, especially in the summer. I come East fairly often myself, but. . . . " Marian stopped herself and gave Esther a polite smile. "Do you live here in Boston?" she asked.

"Well, in Cambridge," Esther replied. "But I was in Washington when I got the news. There was some confusion about my daughter's new phone. She'd just moved, you see; she was having a baby. I didn't get the news about Hally for almost two days. I only got here Monday."

"Oh my. A delay. That must have been terrible."

The intercom blared suddenly, breaking in over the din of voices. "Dr. Baldwin," the machine voice demanded. "Dr. Baldwin. Respirator Ward. Respirator Ward immediately." The women twisted to look back as Dr. Baldwin turned from the line he had just entered, replaced his empty tray on the stack, and hurried out into the hall.

"They work so hard," Esther said. "Such long, long hours. I saw one intern napping here yesterday—sleeping away in the midst of all this noise."

"Oh, it's unbelievable," Marian agreed. "Even with this extra help they're supposed to be getting now. . . . It's all politics, you know. That's what my husband says." Esther nodded.

"There were six more admissions last night, Miss Flaherty told me."

"Six? Really?" Marian shook her head and took another bite of her sandwich. "You've already learned the nurses' names." She stared at Esther. "And you've only been here three days."

"Oh, names are easy for me," Esther said. "I like people. I'm a teacher, you see. But I can't say I understand much about this disease. It's so complicated."

"I don't either and . . . " Marian sighed and looked around her. "If only this was a decent, modern hospital. But it's such a depressing old place. So dirty and run-down." She raised her mug and took a sip of tea. "So you teach, do you?" She said, gazing across at Esther. "What level, may I ask?"

"Oh, elementary school. I help to train young teachers actually." Esther smiled.

"How interesting." Marian glanced away from her to the group of interns, who were rising. "I help support the Denver Symphony myself. I feel good music is an essential." Esther leaned forward.

"Hally, my daughter, is a professional flutist," she began. "She just played her first concert with the Boston Pops."

"How nice," Marian said. "I'm very fond of Cambridge. My son's a graduate student at Harvard, you see, and both my husband and my brother were Harvard men." Esther stared. Should she repeat the information about Hally? No. It was hard to listen here, hard to listen anywhere right now. "Dan's pretty much totally paralyzed," Marian announced. Esther heard the pain in the woman's voice and looked up, then down at Marian's red fingernails and the raised diamond on her ring, as she tried to think of something comforting to say. But Marian reached for another napkin and laid it over a sticky spot beside her mug. "Wouldn't you think they could keep the tables clean at least?"

"Well, it certainly isn't a slick, modern setting," Esther agreed. "But everyone says that Dr. Mostello is the best in the field."

Marian nodded. "That's what we've been told too." She dabbed at her mouth with her napkin, leaving a faint red arc on the white paper. "My husband's done quite a bit of research and the consensus is that Mostello's excellent. How is your daughter?" she asked.

"Well, she has bulbar," Esther began. "That's paralysis of the throat and voice, you know, and she has some involvement in one leg too, apparently."

"Oh, bulbar. That's the most dangerous form, I understand. How's she doing now?"

"Much better, thanks. They cranked her up for a little while this morning. So she's making progress."

"Good. Dan's progressing too. But, of course, it's very hard to tell right now what the situation really is."

"Yes, that's one of the hardest things of all, isn't it?" Esther said. "The uncertainty." She lifted her eyes, as an intern rose and carried his tray to the rack by the door. "But it helps to talk." Esther gazed at the woman across from her again. Was that true with this particular parent, she wondered, then squeezed her napkin together. Of course it was.

8

Visiting hours were over and a collection of parents, wives, and husbands had begun to descend the steps in front of the hospital and spread out in the shadowy parking lot. Behind them loomed the lighted building, dingy and familiar. Some of the men carried their suit jackets, slung over one shoulder. Some of the women's skirts were twisted, and their blouses hung out behind. One young woman held a dead plant, others carried thermoses or paper bags, containing the remains of sandwich suppers, eaten beside patients' beds. Some carried pajamas to be washed, get-well cards to be answered, or magazines to save. All looked hot and weary.

Mrs. Christy, a stocky woman in a flowered dress, clutched the iron railing as she started down the steps. Esther waited on the sidewalk, smiling back at her. "How's Kevin tonight?" she asked. Mrs. Christy descended the last step heavily, then planted herself beside Esther and lifted a crumpled handkerchief to mop her perspiring face.

"He's better, thanks. Got some bad bed sores though. Trouble is they can't move 'em enough in them tanks, you know. They do the best they can, but what I think is if they can just get him out of that thing in a week or so. That's what I'm hoping for."

"It all takes time, doesn't it?" Esther said, relying on the now-familiar adage. "At least that's what they keep telling us." She smiled and shifted a paper bag she was carrying to the other hand. It was so hard to extend sympathy when part of her kept thinking, thank God mine is not as sick as yours.

"Yes—time," Mrs. Christy agreed. "That's what they keep saying—

[54]

time and we just gotta trust to the good Lord that they're right." She smiled. "Hally's doing real good. Isn't she? I stopped at her door just now and she's coming right along with that new tube and all." Esther shifted; it had been a long day.

"Well, we all gotta get some rest," Mrs. Christy said. "You have a good night now. You hear?"

Hally lay on her side, watching as the last visitors passed through her view of the hall. Soon the ceiling lights would go out, the hall would be dim and the long, dull night would begin once more. Dr. Baldwin came into view and stood a moment with his back to her, conferring with Debbie. Hally pulled herself up in bed, and pushed back her tube. In a minute he would come to the doorway and talk. But Dr. Baldwin only raised his hand in a quick greeting and hurried off. Hally sighed and curled on her other side. The globe lights were lit at the end of the driveway and the long lawn had turned gray. Beyond the lights was the city of Telford, Hally thought, and beyond it was Boston. But the Symphony was playing in Tanglewood now or rehearsing or. . . . She turned and stared up at the ceiling. Oh God. How long would this go on? Another week? Two? If she could just get to Tanglewood before the season ended, if she could just play in one concert there. Mom kept telling her not to plan ahead; too much was unknown. But how could she help worrying, thinking of life out there, sliding on.

Debbie flicked on the overhead light, filling the room with brightness. Hally sat up, squinting, but alert. She smiled at Debbie and pulled her tube out from behind her ear. "Is it midnight yet?" she asked and watched Debbie dip the nose of a long syringe into a paper cup full of milk. "Is it midnight?" she asked again.

"About half an hour after," Debbie said. She pulled the plunger up and the syringe grew white, as it sucked up the milk. "You haven't slept any, have you?" Hally shook her head. "I tell you, that's one thing about this disease I really hate; no sleeping medication. 'Could inhibit the central nervous system,' they tell us, whatever that means. Meantime you people just wait through the whole darn night. I should think they could give you some chloral at least."

[55]

"I wish they could," Hally said, grateful for the sympathy, though uncertain what chloral was.

Debbie sighed. "Only two of us on this shift tonight." She attached the syringe to the metal fastener at the end of Hally's tube, then pushed the plunger. The milk began to climb, changing the tube from translucent gray to white as it traveled upward. Hally rolled her eyes to peer at it, as it approached her forehead, imagining its journey down the ridge of her nose, in through her left nostril to the dark passages inside—her nose, her throat and down into her stomach. "It's a zoo out there," Debbie announced. "I thought New York was bad, but . . . ."

Hally stared up at Debbie. "You're from New York?" She said, thinking of the Mozart Competition at Town Hall that she had won last April. That was the main reason she had been picked to substitute with the Boston Pops. Did this nurse ever go to concerts, she wondered? Could she have been at the Mozart?

"What?" Debbie had not understood. Hally reached up and held her sagging lip in place—a trick that Dr. Baldwin had taught her.

"New York City or New York state?" she asked slowly.

"Albany," Debbie said. "That's where I did my training, but I came here from the Cape. My boyfriend's working in Provincetown, see?" Hally smiled, trying to think of a friendly comment that she could enunciate clearly. She could ask about the beach, but "b's" were unpronounceable, coming out as "m's." She hesitated, imagining the nurse and her boyfriend in shorts and sandals, strolling through the tourist crowds on a weekend afternoon, or lying on the warm sand together, drinking Coke from cool green bottles.

"Your next feeding's at four. Right?" The nurse asked. Hally nodded and watched her toss the paper cup into a wastebasket, then flick off the light. She started to pull the door shut behind her, but Hally leaned out of bed and called out.

"Don't. I mean could you leave the door open?" Debbie turned, holding the used syringe upright in one hand, and stared at Hally. "It helps," Hally explained. "Having something to watch, you know. It makes the time go a little faster." Debbie nodded and pushed the door open again.

Dan lay flat, his head pushed upward, squashing the pillow against the white bars at the top of the bed. He gnawed his upper lip to repress a groan, then rolled his eyes upward to catch sight of the call light, gleaming red above his bed in the dimness. Debbie came into the room, dragging a hot pack machine, that looked like a small barbecue cooker on casters and made a rattling noise on the tile floor. "You want hot packs. Right?" She leaned over Dan's bed and flicked off the light.

"Yes. The pain's gotten sort of bad again." Dan sighed and watched Debbie plug the cord into the wall outlet, then stoop to take a pair of heavy rubber sheets from the bottom drawer of the bureau.

"Pain's always worse at night," she said and spread one sheet along the right side of the bed. "Now can you lift yourself onto this or do you need some help?"

"Some help, I'm afraid." Dan sucked in his breath as Debbie slid one of her arms under his shoulder, the other under his back. She lifted as Dan groaned and then half pulled, half tugged him onto the sheet. Dan sighed.

"Thanks," he said. "At this rate you'll be in better shape than your lifeguard friend by the end of the summer."

"Ha! With these shifts!" Debbie gave a dry laugh. "Twelve hours last night and who knows when I'll get off tonight." She turned on the machine, then lifted the cover, and peered inside. "These are almost cold. It'll take ten minutes to heat them up anyway. They don't do any good if they're not hot enough, you know." She moved to the bed again and handed Dan the bell cord. "Think you can hold out that long?"

"Sure. I'll ring when they're ready," Dan said. "They smell so awful, it's not hard to tell."

"Yeah. They really stink. My legs ache when I get home plus I feel almost nauseous from the smell of those things. Tonight I have to stay on until four."

"Lucky you," Dan told her and smiled. "I'm on all night."

Hally pulled herself up in bed and leaned out so that she could see the clock in the hall. It was only twenty after two; she had thought it was almost five. She sighed and lay back on her pillow again. Four and a half hours until morning. Six hours until Mom came, bringing clean pajamas, the mail, the *Boston Globe,* and a return of sanity. Hally's foot ached with its old night pain, intermittent, but uncomfortable now. She gazed out at the lights at the end of the driveway, then up at the shadowy ceiling. If only the dawn would begin, then the day at last. The pain in her leg increased, hot now, making her knee jerk upwards, as she lay on her side. Damn. She stared at the bell cord, pinned to her pillow, then pulled it. What the hell, she thought, and lay waiting in the dimness. It would fill the time at least.

"What do you want?" Debbie demanded and reached over Hally to flick off the light above her bed.

"Hot packs," Hally began. "I mean if you have time. My leg's hurting and. . . . "

"Okay," Debbie said. "But you'll have to wait. The patient in the next room is using the machine right now. I'll get the stuff out." Debbie took the rubber sheets from the bottom bureau drawer and spread one down the side of the bed. Hally lifted herself onto it and waited. "So you've got it in your legs too, have you?"

"Only one, apparently," Hally told her, "and it's not bad. Just hurts at night usually."

The outside door banged open; a middle-aged man was holding it back for a pregnant young woman in a blue sun dress. They stood together in the hall, talking in low voices. The man reached into the breast pocket of his sports shirt, drew out a pack of cigarettes, lit one, and handed it to the girl with an apprehensive look. She inhaled and turned to stare up the hall at the doors of the respirator ward.

"Her hubby's real bad tonight," Debbie said. "He came in late in the afternoon. Dr. Baldwin's down there with him now. Mostello too, I think." She spread the second rubber sheet over Hally and glanced back at the hall. "They oughta have some kind of waiting room here—a place where people could sit down at least." Hally nodded and looked back at the girl, who had turned away, as though aware she was being watched. She stood at the door looking through its small, square window, out into the dark; her shoulders were bare, and her light dress sloped outward over the bulge of her baby. She must be seven or eight months pregnant maybe and the man must be her father, Hally decided, and resolved not to keep staring at them. But when Debbie left to see about the hot pack machine next door, she curled on her side and continued to watch the strangers from her darkened room.

*　　*　　*

Hally stared out at the clock again; it was four in the morning. The hot packs had helped, but now they seemed a long way back. The outside door opened. The father and daughter, who had gone outside a while ago, came back into the hall. The girl was wearing a white sweater around her shoulders and a patent leather purse dangled from one arm. Hally could see her toes with their red nails protruding from her sandals.

The father pulled another cigarette from the pack in his shirt pocket, but pushed it back again when footsteps sounded in the hall. Dr. Baldwin came into view and stopped beside them. Hally watched him put one hand on the girl's elbow as he began to speak. The girl stared at him, then twisted back as if she were going to rush down the hall to the ward. A scream tore through the quiet. "Oh no. No. I can't stand it. No." Hally stared at her in horror. The sound seemed unconnected with the girl, but the man had put his arm around her, and was leading, almost pulling her toward the door, which Dr. Baldwin held open. "No," she screamed again. "No." The door crashed shut, obliterating the sound.

Hally leaned out of bed, trying to catch sight of someone in the hall. But it was empty. Everyone was in the ward, she thought, and the hall still echoed with that scream. Oh God, Oh God. Tears leaked down Hally's cheeks and the lights at the end of the driveway blurred. She watched a lone car depart, its headlights cutting a path along the dark drive. Was that the father taking the young wife home to her new widowed life? Hally glanced back at the hall, forcing herself to hear that naked scream again. "No. No. I can't. . . . "

Footsteps sounded in the corridor; Hally saw Dr. Baldwin pass. What discouragement, what fatigue he must be feeling. And she? She was only a selfish, spying patient, who had had the luck to survive. Her mouth was shaking. If only Mom were here, she told herself, and thought of Rosie, her aging golden retriever. "Oh Rosie," Hally cried. "Rosie." She sat up and pulled her knees to her chin, as the sound of her sobbing spread out around her in the dim room.

9

*R*oy parked his dolly outside Hally's open door in the morning. He pulled the handle of the wringer at the side of the bucket, squeezed out the gray strings on the mop, and carried it into Hally's room. "Good morning m'lady," he said and bowed. "How are you this fair morning?"

"Fine, Roy," Hally said, smiling with relief at seeing him. "Fine."

Roy pushed his mop around the bed, leaving a scalloped pattern on the tiled floor. "Well, we lost another one last night, God rest his soul," Roy said and leaned on the mop handle.

Hally straightened her sheet. Her curiosity rose, but she hesitated. "Is it going to be hot again?" she asked.

"Oh, it's gonna be another scorcher," he announced and gazed out of the half-open window. "Dry. I tell you. This summer beats all." He looked back at Hally, who smiled at her visitor. "You know who you remind me of?" He peered more closely, as Hally shook her head. "Katharine Hepburn," Roy announced. "That's who and you know what? There's a nice young fella in the room right next door, reminds me of Cary Grant." Roy nodded. "That's the truth. He does. One of these days I'm going to see to it that you young people meet." He lifted the mop and swished it over the floor again. "That's just what I'm going to do. Introduce the two of you."

"You just see to it that I get up," Hally said. "If I can just get out of this darn room, I don't care who I meet."

"Well, you've got to have a little patience, my beauty. Time. You know what they say. It all takes time."

A towel, sprinkled with hair snippings, was draped around Hally's shoulders; Esther held a pair of bandage scissors and stepped back to study her daughter.

"That's just about it," she said. "No wait. There's a little piece on this side." She bent and snipped a tail of hair, then straightened again. "It looks nice, dearie. Now it won't keep getting stuck in that adhesive tape or tangled in your tube." She pulled the bedtray closer. "Here. Look at yourself." She folded the top back and propped up the mirror inside. Hally glanced at her reflection a moment, then turned to the window, and sighed.

"Well, it's done," she said and peered at herself again. "Now I've lost my hair, my voice, my lip control, and any good looks I might once have had."

"Oh, dearie. Don't say that." Esther bent and fluffed out the sides of her hair. "Look. It's pretty and cool and...."

Hally raised her hands to cup the soft ends, then looked away. "It's fine," she said. "I didn't mean ... I'm sorry."

Dan lay flat on his rumpled bed in the room next door, naked except for a white towel covering his genitals. A thin orderly, with "Lou" embroidered in white on the breast pocket of his green uniform, leaned over Dan to wash his neck. "Not too hot for you?" he asked. Dan shook his head, as the orderly turned back to the aluminum bowl on the bedtray, squeezed out the cloth, and bent over Dan's legs. He washed the left one and placed it close to the edge of the bed.

"Did you hear that Sox game last night?"

"No. I missed it," Dan said.

"Oh, it was good. A cliff-hanger. Real exciting."

The sound of the intercom invaded the room—a woman's nasal voice, speaking in a heavy East Boston accent. "Atten-shun, all orderlies," the voice began. "A respirator truck has arrived at the ambulance entrance. Unloading help is needed immediately."

Lou straightened and looked back at the door. "Okay. Okay," he said, as though addressing the woman who had spoken. "I'll be right there."

"Atten-shun, all orderlies," the voice began again. "Help is needed...." Lou dried his hands hurriedly and wiped them on the sides of his tunic. His face looked animated, as he pushed back a strand of hair from his forehead.

"Back in a flash," he told Dan and turned to the door.

"Wait," Dan started. "Would you just. . . . " But Lou was gone. Dan lifted his head and peered down at his left leg. That foot's too close to the edge, damnit, he thought. If I could just grab the knee and. . . . His hand scrabbled on the sheet, but he could not reach the leg. Dan could see the foot tipping slowly, rolling toward the edge of the bed. He glanced out at the hall, reached for his bell cord, and pulled. Nothing happened; no one was passing. He stretched his arm again, but the leg was just beyond the grasp of his clawing fingers. He lay back, panting. Maybe it'll be okay, he told himself. It might not fall. There's an inch of bed at least and somebody'll come. Somebody'll come in time.

A cloud of hair clippings fluttered down into the wastebasket, as Esther shook the towel. She picked the longer ones from the terry cloth surface slowly, aware of Hally behind her, staring at herself in the mirror again. "You know even if I weren't a flutist, even if my life didn't revolve around a wind instrument," Hally began, "I would be horrified. Depressed. I'd be ashamed of the way I look now." She pressed her bottom lip into place with the fingers of one hand, then removed her fingers and watched the lip sag down again. "Look at that," she said. "I look like some kind of village idiot—someone whose mind is half gone."

"It isn't that bad," Esther told her. "And besides it's just temporary."

"Temporary!" Hally echoed in a thick shout. "How temporary? That's what I want to know. I can't play at all with paralysis like this." Her voice shook and she paused, then added, "You know that, Mom."

"But this is just a stage, Hal. You've been improving steadily. Dr. Mostello thinks. . . . "

"Dr. Mostello." Hally's voice trembled. "Oh God."

"You have to take things a day at a time," Esther said. "I know this is terrible for you. But at this point they simply can't tell which nerves will recover and which will not. Mostello really does think you might make an almost complete recovery."

" 'Almost complete.' What does that mean?" Hally flung herself back against her pillow and stared at her mother, but Esther did not reply. "I'm sorry," Hally said after a moment and sighed. "I know you can't answer.

Neither can he or anyone. But. . . . " She turned to the window with a groan. "Why couldn't it have been in my legs or my. . . . "

"Don't, Hally." Esther's voice was sharp. "Don't."

A buzzer rang outside in the hall, stopped, then rang again with a loud persistent noise. A shout came from close by. "Help. Goddamnit. Somebody help."

Esther turned toward the hall. Was anyone coming? There'd been that emergency earlier and the hall seemed deserted right now. The shout came again. It must be Marian Lewis's boy. Suppose he'd fallen out of bed? "Help," the voice cried. "Somebody, help." Esther hurried out into the hall and on to Dan's room. She stopped; the young man on the bed was naked. His frantic eyes caught hers and she saw at once that one long leg was hanging down over the side of the bed. The boy was clearly in pain. "Please," he said.

Esther bent and lifted the leg back onto the bed. "Thanks," Dan breathed. "Thanks a lot." Esther covered him with the sheet and folded it back over his chest.

"I'm sure that was a scare," she said. "But it's over now. Do you want some water?" Dan nodded. Esther fixed a bent straw in the paper cup on the bedtray and held it to his lips. He raised his head, sipped, then dropped his head to the pillow again, breathing heavily. "There's some emergency this morning," Esther said. "A respirator case arriving, I think. Everybody seems to be down there." Dan nodded wearily.

"I didn't know I couldn't even reach my leg," he began and paused. "I mean I knew it was paralyzed. But with my pajamas on, I can grab the material and pull it. See?" He stopped again. "I've never been so . . . I mean the orderly left and I thought I could pull it back, that I had some control, but. . . . " He sighed again.

"Well, it's over now," Esther said and smiled. "I'm Esther Blessing. Your mother and I had lunch together a few days ago."

"Oh sure," Dan said. "She mentioned that. Could you give me some more water? Fresh even?" He smiled wearily. "I asked for some fresh last night." He sighed. "But it doesn't do any good to complain."

"Oh, it may do some," Esther said and lifted the water pitcher. "Nobody can keep all this frustration in."

A large truck stood backed up to the short outside passageway, which connected the main hospital building with the patient wing. Its tailgate yawned open, revealing a mustard-colored respirator within. Lou and another orderly were straining to control the weight of the heavy machine as they started down a short wooden ramp. Dr. Baldwin stood at the bottom in his long white medical coat, calling directions. "More to the left." He leapt up the ramp and pressed his weight against the front of the machine near Lou. "Okay," he continued. "That's it. Easy. Easy. We're almost there."

Debbie stood at an upstairs window, watching with another nurse. "You can see the patient now," she said. "See. There's Marge Flaherty carrying the IV, talking to him or maybe it's a her. I can't tell." Debbie's voice was hard to distinguish over the roar of the generator in the back of the open truck. "This is the first time they've ever moved one of those things in here with someone in it—since I've been here anyway." She shook her head as she continued to stare. "Too darn dangerous, if you ask me."

The huge respirator bumped safely down onto the concrete passage-way, the patient's head, protruding from the end, revealed short blackish hair, visible against the white pillow on the head tray. The men regrouped, as Miss Flaherty hovered close, holding the intravenous bottle above her. Dr. Baldwin was at the head again, the others behind.

"I don't know," Debbie said, as the group moved beyond her view. "The whole thing makes you feel sort of weak."

Esther settled in the armchair beside Hally's bed several days later, after handing out the mail. "I just met a wonderful character," she reported. "Her name's Maureen Hogan and she has nine children. Imagine! She's so imperious and funny. I can just see her standing up to Mostello. I told her all about you, of course. She wants you to come visit her just as soon as they let you up. You'll love her, Hally. I know you will."

Footsteps pounded outside in the hall and Esther looked across at Hally in surprise. "Are they doing rounds in the morning today?" Hally shrugged and pulled herself up in bed. Esther rose quickly, straightened Hally's sheet, and stacked the magazines neatly on the bedtray. "God and his archangels," she whispered. "You never know when they're coming." Dr. Mostello pushed the door open and strode to the foot of the bed, where he stood a moment, looking large and authoritative, while Dr. Baldwin and the students crowded in behind.

"How are you this morning?" he demanded. "Any problems?" Hally hesitated, then shook her head.

"Not really. At least nothing new." Dr. Mostello studied her. "Your voice is better. Know that? I can understand almost everything you say now. No more need for a translator." He smiled at Esther as Hally looked down.

"Let's see that back." Dr. Mostello moved to the head of the bed. "Bend over," he ordered. Hally drew her knees up and bent her head. Dr. Mostello raised her pajama top behind and pounded her spine with his fist, moving it down one side of her backbone, then up the other in a series of steady thumps. Hally waited, her head on her knees. "There's nothing wrong with this back," he said to Dr. Baldwin and pulled Hally's pajama top back into place. "Dangle her tomorrow. All right? Wheelchair, Wednesday." He looked back at Hally and smiled. "We're going to get you out in the world at last. What'd you think of that?" He laughed, then turned and followed the group, which was already emptying the room.

"My heavens," Esther breathed in the sudden quiet. "A wheelchair! What did he mean by 'dangle' do you think?"

"I suppose they'll prop me up on the side of the bed, just to make sure I don't get faint or something," Hally said. "After all I've been in this bed a month now, haven't I?"

Hally sat in an old-fashioned wheelchair with a high, caned back, looking around her in astonishment. The walls of her room seemed to have grown taller, as though she had slipped downward suddenly within the green box. She stared at the dusty casters of her bed and the U-shaped curve of the pipe underneath her sink, surprised that they had been there all along. Lou, who had lifted her easily from the bed into the chair, stooped down to tuck a bath blanket around her legs.

"When can we go?" Hally said. "Aren't we ready yet?" Lou laughed and turned to Esther.

"Little impatient, isn't she? I thought you'd want to just sit right here." He laughed again and pulled the wheelchair back, then pushed it through the doorway into the hall. Hally leaned forward, staring to the right, then to the left. It was strange, she thought; it was all wrong. In those hours of lying on her side, peering out at her rectangular view of the hall, she had built the space out beyond it, she realized. There was a circular nurses' station with a panel of buzzers, she thought, not that scarred wooden desk with its jumble of charts. She had imagined a wide corridor with stainless steel sidings and rubberized tiles on the floor. But there were the same green walls out here, with cracks in the plaster, just like the ones in her own room, and the same uneven black and white tiles on the floor.

"It's so small," she said, glancing back at Esther.

"What did you think? That it was big and modern?"

Lou pushed the chair past the nurses' desk, where Miss Flaherty stood talking on the phone. When she caught sight of Hally, she raised her free hand in a cheering gesture. "You sure you want to take over?" Lou asked Esther. "You have to watch these old chairs, you know. They can tip forward suddenly, see? And the brakes aren't too wonderful either. You're sure you'll be all right?"

"Oh, I think so," Esther told him. "We won't go far anyway the first day." She took the handles and pushed the chair cautiously, as Lou stood watching. He nodded at her, then turned back down the hall. "That's a respirator," Esther told Hally and stopped the chair beside a long green tank on metal legs that was parked beside the wall. "Isn't it huge? That one must have arrived last night. They seem to leave them out here until they can check them over or whatever, then fit them into the ward." Hally eyed the heavy machine. Respirators were at the real heart of the hospital drama, she thought. She had felt inauthentic as an epidemic victim, who had never been in a respirator, but now her proximity to this empty one seemed to make her part of the crisis too.

"I think Maureen's expecting us," Esther said, "but I'll just knock." She tapped on a half-open door and waited.

"Come in," called a commanding voice. Hally peered around her, as her mother navigated the wheelchair past a large floral arrangement on the floor and pushed her to the bed. "So you're Hally," the voice exclaimed. Hally stared. The woman's face was almost skeletal with a brightly lipsticked mouth and dark inquisitive eyes set deep in her fragile skull. Hally moved her mouth into a polite smile. The patient was propped up among a collection of pillows that were clearly not from the hospital, some pink satin, others lavender, edged with lace. She wore a flowered bed jacket with a ruffle at the neck, that gave her a regal look,

Hally thought, despite the shocking thinness of her face. Her black hair shaded into wings of gray above her ears and her long fingernails were red.

Hally glanced around her. The room had the same shape and furniture as hers, but it felt busier and more crowded. The bureau was cluttered with pictures and get-well cards and, beside a statue of the Virgin Mary, was a framed photograph of Maureen and her husband with their nine children grouped around them, smiling and self-conscious in Sunday clothes. A bottle of perfume sat on the bedtray beside a pile of rosary beads. Hally felt the woman's gaze move from the strip of adhesive tape on her own forehead, to the tube in her nose, and down to the paper cup that Hally had brought for spitting into.

"Your mother tells me you're a flute player," Maureen began. "And you've just played your first concert with the Boston Symphony or was it the . . . ." Maureen twisted her head and inhaled with a hoarse, whistling sound, making the tendons in her thin neck protrude like tight cords. Hally glanced up at her mother in alarm, but Esther seemed to be waiting calmly. The sound subsided and Maureen smiled from one to the other. "That's just my regular deep breath," she explained. She laughed, then looked seriously at Hally. "You mustn't worry about your flute. You'll play again. Look at me. I'm a mother and I'm going to get back to that. I've got a big family." She nodded at the photograph on the bureau. "Connaught's the oldest. She's seventeen and the baby'll be a year next month. Nine in all. But I don't like odd numbers." Maureen laughed again. "I mean to have ten."

"That's wonderful." Hally raised her cup and spat discreetly.

Maureen watched. "You're not that hard to understand. Know that? I bet after a visit or two, I'd barely remember you had bulbar." Hally smiled and pushed back her tube more securely. "I wish I could serve you tea," Maureen went on. "But, of course, without a full staff. . . . " She laughed and glanced around the crowded space. "Wait," she said. "There's a bottle of Harvey's Bristol Cream on the bureau, Esther. And some cups." Esther lifted the bottle, then hesitated.

"I don't know, Maureen. I mean Hally can't have anything anyway and I. . . . "

"Well, we'll celebrate for her," Maureen said. "After all sherry's medicinal. Now hand me that Swiss army knife over there behind that missal. See?" Esther passed the knife to Maureen, who cut the tinfoil cover from the top of the bottle and drew out the cork. She nodded at the knife, as she folded the blade back into place. "When you have as many children as I do, these come in handy." Hally glanced at her mother and smiled.

There was a knock on the door. "Come in." Maureen called out and pulled her sheet up over the bottle. The door opened and a young, pink-cheeked priest in a high collar and black suit stood in the doorway. "Oh, Father Anthony," Maureen exclaimed. "How nice." She pushed the sheet back and lifted the sherry. "You're just in time to have a drink with my neighbors. It's Harvey's Bristol Cream," she added and poured a third cup. "You'll like Father Anthony," she told Hally. "He's one of the nicest young priests I know and I know dozens of priests, don't I, Father?"

Maureen laughed, then stopped to take another deep breath. Hally glanced down; the tiled floor was heaving. She hadn't tasted the sherry, of course, but these new faces, this sudden expansion of her world had filled her with a strange giddy feeling.

10

*H*ally leaned forward to pull the wheels on either side of her caned-back wheelchair, as she rolled herself slowly up the hall. She jerked one hand back to catch a box of kleenex, which had started to slide off her lap, then looked around, wanting someone to notice her. "Hi," Artemis called from the nurses' desk. "Are you all by yourself today?" Hally nodded. "Terrific." Artemis glanced at the clock on the wall. "I wish I could stay and talk, but I'm in a tear. I'll stop by this afternoon. Okay?" Hally nodded again and watched Artemis disappear.

A loud pounding noise rang out near the elevator. Hally looked back and saw Roy stooped over a metal bedframe, hammering in a bolt on the side. The noise stopped and, in the sudden quiet, Hally heard flute music rise. It was coming out of the room next to hers, she realized, and she pulled herself closer. The door was open. It was the last part of the Brahms's *Variations on a Theme of Haydn,* the Boston Symphony recording. They must be doing it on WGBH, Hally thought and pulled herself to the threshold to listen. The light, ascending notes seemed astonishingly lyric and familiar. She could see the open score before her, and felt her flute warm under her fingers, as the conductor pointed his white baton.

"Out of the way, m'lady. Out of the way." The music was drowned by a loud rattling noise. Hally turned to see Roy and Lou just behind her, dragging the bedframe down the hall. She pushed herself backward across the threshold into the open room, as the men pulled it past. Its shaking noise covered the music, then receded, so that Hally felt the flute melody enfold her once again. The violins were entering now, then the double basses; the movement was rising to its end. Somewhere beyond the music, she was aware of a room like her own—the same kind of blinds hanging half-pulled at the window, and the same view. The clarinet had joined in and now the horns. Everything was rising, rising toward the end. The last chords sounded. Hally saw the conductor raise his arms, hold the position a moment, lower them slightly, as the applause rushed toward him, then raise them triumphantly, saluting the players now, before he turned and bowed to the audience again.

"That was the Brahms's *Variations on a Theme of Haydn*," an announcer's voice intruded. "Opus 56." Hally stared at the radio, then at the man in the bed, startled to realize she had entered his room uninvited.

"I'm sorry. I . . . ." Hally glanced around her in embarrassment. A full urinal sat on the floor beside a jumble of dirty sheets. "They were pulling a bedframe and I . . . ."

"Don't worry," Dan said.

"This concludes our Saturday morning rebroadcast of Music from Tanglewood," the announcer continued. "We turn now to a Harvard Divinity School discussion entitled, 'Is there an Islamic Renaissance?' "

"I don't think we need that, do you?" Dan smiled and reached out to turn the radio off. "That Brahms was marvelous, wasn't it?" Hally gazed at the spread of soft hair on the young man's naked chest, then jerked her eyes to his face. He looked friendly; Mom had helped him one morning, she remembered. He was a graduate student or something and, according to Roy, he was Cary Grant. Not quite, Hally thought, but he was attractive. She glanced down at the urinal, then back at the man again.

"Sorry to barge in. They were moving a bed and. . . . "

"It's okay. I'm delighted to have company." His smile was surprisingly happy, Hally thought, as though he assumed the surrounding world was benign. He probably had a lot of girlfriends, she decided, and thought of her tube, the adhesive tape on her forehead, her chopped hair, and her lip hanging down. Then the memory of the music poured over her again.

"I bet that was Doriot Dwyer," Hally said. "Doriot Anthony Dwyer. She's the first woman the BSO hired."

"The Reesso hired?" Dan repeated, puzzled. "Oh, you mean the BSO, the Boston Symphony Orchestra?" Hally nodded. "Sure, of course."

"I have bulbar. I'm really hard to understand," Hally added. "But if people can take the time to listen, I can. . . . "

"Time's what I seem to have a lot of now," Dan said. Hally glanced down, confused by his smile. "You sound like you know the Boston Symphony well."

"Well, I . . . ." Hally paused. "I'm a musician, or I was." She glanced at the young man's legs in their wrinkled pajama pants. The drawstring from his fly hung down; Hally looked back at his face again. "I'm a flutist," she said. "That's why I know about Dwyer." Dan nodded as he watched her. "She's so . . . so. . . ." Hally lifted one hand. "She's just so good. Exactly the right tone, the. . . ." Her voice caught and a knot of saliva stuck in her throat. She raised her paper cup. "Sorry," she said and spat. Why had she gone on like that? Why should he care about the flute part? "What I mean is. . . ." Hally stopped. The humiliation of her ugly voice flooded over her again. Once she had prided herself on her clear, modulated tone. It was she who had been chosen to read the Bible verses in school assemblies. Other girls had pretty legs or glossy hair; Hally had a lovely voice. Would she ever have it again?

The young man was peering at her. "Wait. I know who you are," he said. "Mother told me you were a musician. No wonder you know about Doriot Dwyer. Didn't you substitute for her with the Boston Pops at an Esplanade concert back in July?" Hally nodded. "You were wonderful that night. You really were. That was the night before I came in here, the 13th of July. The Bastille fell the next day and so did I." He laughed.

Hally felt her face grow warm. He had been at that concert; he had heard her play the Mozart that long ago night in July? She thought of her own hot concentration, the stage lights, the lock of hair bouncing on the conductor's forehead, and then her notes rising up into the darkness. She put her hand to her chin to cover its sudden shaking.

"I didn't know it was Bastille Day," she said. There had been only one review, but it was positive, and the concert master had hugged her afterwards. Had this guy come with some pretty date? Probably. She stared, thinking again of the tension, the brightness onstage, and the audience spread on blankets out there in the dark.

"I was late," he said. "I had some stuff to finish at the library and . . . ." Hally shivered. There had been a young man by the fence, tall and. . . . She glanced down; she couldn't think about that time now. "I guess I was coming down with this thing at the time. I mean I definitely was, and you know . . . ." Dan paused. Should he tell her that he had watched her reach up and massage her throat? "You know I thought of going around back to congratulate you afterwards," he said instead. "But I lost my nerve." He smiled at her again and asked. "Are you a regular member of the Boston Symphony?"

"Oh no," Hally said. "I just get to substitute sometimes." She paused and glanced out at the lawn. "That was a big break for me—that solo. It was a big night. I just wish I could, you know, exploit that luck right now. But I got this instead." Hally watched a leaf drift down to the grass and clutched her arms around her. Without her flute, she was only a serious, awkward young woman, lacking any talk beyond her narrow music world.

Hally started to glance back at the young man's face, but her eyes stopped at his motionless legs. God, how self-centered she was. She'd sat here thinking about her bulbar troubles, but he might never walk again. She stared at him, uncertain what she should say. "I ought to go," she began. "This is my first time out alone and. . . . " She turned the wheel-chair and began to back out. One wheel caught the side of a straight chair behind her, where a long rubber sheet was hanging down. It swung, then dropped to the floor, blocking Hally's path. "Oh damn," she said and leaned over to catch the triangular fold of sheet, jutting up from the floor. But the wheelchair tipped forward alarmingly. Hally threw herself back-ward, as her paper cup and kleenex box slid off her lap with a clatter. "Good God," she exclaimed and let out a frightened laugh.

"That thing looks lethal," Dan said. "They ought to retire it. Stay here. Lou or one of the nurses'll be back in a minute." He smiled at her and rolled partway on his side. "When did you come in here anyway?" Hally glanced out at the hall, then back at Dan; they might as well talk.

"I came the night after the concert too. Our family doctor drove me. It was a good thing he did, as it turned out. I was pretty sick, but I didn't know it." Hally enunciated her words with care, trying to lift them out from under their blanket of nasality. She watched his face, pleased that he seemed to understand.

"It was a good thing for me too," Dan said. "I mean a friend of mine packed me up and drove me over. He's a wonderful guy." Hally watched the young man smile again. He thought a lot of people were wonderful,

ANN L. McLAUGHLIN

she decided, relieved to learn that the friend was male. But he did have
girlfriends, she told herself, and raised one hand unconsciously to cover
her sagging lip. Still they weren't around now and he did seem glad to
have her here.

"By the way," she said. "My name's. . . . "

"Wait," Dan broke in. "I remember from the program. It's Harriet
Elizabeth Um Um . . . ."

"Blessing," Hally supplied. "You've got a terrific memory. But most
people call me 'Hally.' I've heard your radio before," she added. "It's been
a real help."

"It has?" Dan said. "I didn't know you could hear it. Where's your
room anyway?"

"Right next door," Hally told him and pointed to the wall behind the
bureau.

"I'll be darned," Dan said and smiled again. "Right there? Mother
didn't tell me that." He lifted his right wrist with his left hand, supported
the elbow, and pushed the arm toward Hally. She stared. Was that whole
arm paralyzed? He had turned the radio off with the other, but this arm
must be badly affected and it was his right one, she realized, as she shook
the hand.

"My name's Dan Lewis," he said. "I've got general spinal involvement,
as you've probably surmised." He smiled, as though he enjoyed tucking in
the verb "surmise." "I've got it mostly in my legs and abdomen, but some
in one arm too." Hally nodded and busied herself with recovering the
kleenex box; she did not want to watch him resettle that motionless arm.

"Are you in graduate school at Harvard?" She glanced at the hall
surreptitiously, wanting someone to appear.

"Yes. I'm in an odd ball specialty called American Civilization."

"Oh?" Hally said politely. She wished Miss Flaherty would come. "Do
you have to write a thesis?"

"Yes. I've just gotten started really and I'm excited about it. You see I'm
planning to retrace the Oregon Trail—do a study of some of the writings
about it and. . . . " He paused. "I really enjoy the stuff. I want to teach and
I love this subject." Dan's face had changed somehow, Hally thought. He
looked eager, almost healthy, and his brown eyes were shining. He was
quite nice really, not one of those arrogant Harvard guys. "I'm kind of a
nut about the history of the West," he went on. "I come from Colorado.

[73]

So this Oregon Trail material is a natural for me." He was one of those out-going athletic Westerners, Hally thought, and looked down. Her only exercise was her bicycle and it had had a flat all summer. "I've done some of the preliminary research already," Dan continued. "But I've got more to do, more of the mapping and stuff. You see what I'm planning—what I was planning, I mean—is to follow the original trail, using a jeep and backpacking, and show the topography, the settlements, and . . . ."

"Sounds fascinating," Hally said and for a moment it really did. But how could he ever travel again, drive or hike? She felt her face flush and looked down at the tiled floor, lest he read her thoughts. "Would you mind pulling your buzzer?" she asked. "They don't know where I am out there and I don't want to worry anybody." Hally glanced out at the hall; her jaws were shaking with fatigue, she realized, and her mouth was painfully dry.

"Sure." Dan raised his good arm to pull the brown cord pinned to the side of his pillow case. The red light went on above his bed, as the harsh ringing noise sounded outside in the hall.

Dan and Hally looked out, expecting Debbie or Miss Flaherty, but instead they heard shouted directions close by. "Let the cord go. Easy. That's it." Two orderlies appeared in their view of the hall, pushing a green respirator. A woman's head projected from the end, supported on a narrow metal tray with a short pillow. Her eyes were staring up at the ceiling as she passed, her lips pressed together, and, below the tray, her loose hair made a soft brown triangle. A thick black cord was dragging along the floor beneath the machine. The men pushed the respirator past and she was gone.

"Lord," Hally breathed. "That's the first time I've seen that. I didn't think they could move them with patients inside."

"I guess it depends on the severity of the case," Dan said. "Maybe she's getting more independent of her tank and they're moving her from the critical ward down to the convalescent one." Hally stared at Dan. Were there two respirator wards? "Jim Rickley, that tall intern, fills me in," Dan explained. "He says respirator patients feel a terrific ambivalence about their tanks, anxious to get out, but terrified to leave." Dan paused. "Jim's a really nice guy. Do you know him?"

"No, not really." Hally looked back at the hall again. "All that machinery," she said slowly. "All that complicated stuff, just to keep one person breathing—doing what they naturally do."

"Yes," Dan said. "Strange, isn't it?"

"She looked about my age," Hally added.

"Makes you think about your own luck, doesn't it?" Dan said. Hally drew her breath in, wanting to add something, but Dan grimaced and eased himself onto his back again. "Sorry. My arm gives out after a while."

"Here you are, Hally." Miss Flaherty hurried into the room. "I was getting worried." She leaned over Dan and turned off the buzzer. "So you two have met, have you?" she said, smiling at them. "I don't need to do any introductions."

"Not necessary," Dan told her. "We were...." Hally tensed. She did not want him to reveal that he had listened to her play the Mozart Flute Concerto No. 2 in D Major when she had substituted for Dwyer with the Boston Pops in July. "We were at the same concert a month ago," Dan told her.

"Well, well," Miss Flaherty said. "But you mustn't overdo, Hally." She grabbed the handles of the wheelchair and kicked the rubber sheet aside. "Come on. I'll take you back to your room." Hally smiled at Dan as she clutched her cup and kleenex box.

"Thanks for having me," she said, and waved as Miss Flaherty pushed her toward the door.

"Come back soon," Dan called. "You know where I live now and chances are I'll be right here whenever you feel like dropping in." He wondered whether Hally had heard his invitation or his joke, as he watched Miss Flaherty's retreating back. He gazed across at the empty spot beside the bedtray where Hally's wheelchair had been. So Hally Blessing, the flutist, lived right next door.

*H*ally sat in her wheelchair beside Maureen's bed, feeding herself slowly from a large syringe. "You're getting pretty good at that," Maureen said, as she watched the milk climb. "I suppose it's easier to do it yourself, than keep waiting for somebody to come." Maureen pulled some sliding pillows up behind her and lay back. "You know about that plan to move some of the people in the private rooms upstairs? Well, this morning I told Mostello what I thought. I said, 'You just listen to me, Dr. Mostello. I'm staying right where I am. I need my privacy, and I want my things around me.' " Maureen swept her arm out in an expansive half circle. "Not that this is the Ritz exactly, but . . . ." Hally held her syringe upright and pointed to some knots of dust, lying beside a crumpled kleenex in the corner. "Local color, atmosphere—and it's mine." Maureen laughed. "Say. What do you think of your next door neighbor? Your mother said you stopped in to see him yesterday."

"I was forced in," Hally began and paused. "He's nice. Almost too nice," she added.

"What do you mean 'too nice'?" Maureen demanded.

"Well, he's in pretty bad shape—both legs and some arm paralysis too, you know. I mean he just seems so charming, so sort of optimistic, as though everything's going to be perfectly fine in a week or two."

"Could be one way of coping," Maureen suggested.

"It could." Maureen watched in silence a moment, as Hally continued to squeeze milk into her tube.

"Do you have a lot of boyfriends?" she asked.

"No." Hally paused. "I mean I used to go out with guys at the Conservatory some. But mostly I'm too busy for social stuff." Maureen studied her and nodded.

"Hmm," she said. "I see." Hally looked up, aware of Maureen's scrutiny.

"I like Dan," she admitted. "But right now Dr. Baldwin's my favorite." The syringe jerked out of the tube attachment, as she turned to smile at Maureen, spraying the front of her bathrobe with milk. "Oh, damn," Hally said. "I keep doing that." She put the syringe down and brushed at her lapels with a kleenex. "I think Baldwin's sexy," she confessed as she fitted the syringe back into the tube. "I just wish I. . . . " Maureen rolled her eyes.

"Dr. Baldwin? Sexy? Is that what you think?"

Hally smiled, then sighed. "What I really think," she began, and her voice had an irritated edge, "is that we must be awfully bored to sit around talking like this."

"Maybe," Maureen agreed and pulled a stuffed dog up from among her pillows. "Here's a really sexy fellow though. His name's Bertie." Hally put down the syringe and rubbed her forehead against the dog's fur one, as her long tube dangled down.

"Bertie, you're wonderful." Hally cuddled the dog against her damp bathrobe and rocked him, so that his brown face, with its static smile, peeped out from the crook of her arm. "He reminds me of Rosie, our golden retriever," she said, smiling down at the toy. "He makes even the Wahl seem cozy."

Mrs. Harding, an efficient-looking physiotherapist with a black ponytail, stood beside Dan's flattened bed. She held his left leg partly raised, his heel in one hand, his calf supported in the other. As she lifted the leg slowly, Dan grimaced and looked away from her, then let out a low groan. Marian Lewis, who stood at the foot of the bed, watching, glanced from the therapist to Dan, then back to the therapist again. "I'm afraid I don't see the point of this stretching every day," she said. "I mean it's extremely uncomfortable for Dan."

"I realize that, Mrs. Lewis," Mrs. Harding replied, turning her head to take in Marian's purple dress and paisley scarf. "But it prevents atrophy— tightening of the muscles, you see." Mrs. Harding looked down at Dan again. "If we just let him lie there, the muscles in his legs would tighten up and he could have some serious distortions later. He might even need an operation before he could walk."

"Yes, but. . . . " Marian put one hand to her throat. "Do you really have to. . . . " Dan looked up at his mother and sighed.

"Why don't you go down to the cafeteria and have some coffee, Mother? Take a break. Okay? I'll be done with this in fifteen minutes or so." Marian stared, then gathered her Italian leather pocketbook from the bureau and moved to the door.

"It won't be long." Mrs. Harding turned back to Dan, who clamped his jaws together, as she lifted his leg again.

As Marian started down the hall, she noticed a girl in a high-backed wheelchair rolling toward her. "Morning," the girl said. Marian stared, uncertain what that nasal sound meant or whether the girl had been addressing her. A tube was adhesive-taped to the young woman's forehead and her lip drooped down. How awful, Marian thought. Thank goodness, Dan didn't look like that.

As Hally sat by the window, leafing through a music score, she heard an unfamiliar cry in the hall. "Did you hear that?" Roy demanded, appearing in her doorway. "That crying?" He clutched the doorframe in excitement.

"What was it?" Hally asked and rolled herself toward him.

"A baby. A baby born in a respirator," Roy announced and raised his hands in a cheering gesture. "A little baby boy." Hally caught her breath and pushed the wheelchair closer, but Roy hailed someone up the hall, and disappeared. Hally pulled herself to the doorway and looked out. The doors to the respirator ward at the end were shut. The nurses' desk was deserted and Roy's bucket sat abandoned on its dolly, midway down the hall. Hally rolled herself toward Maureen's room, but the door was closed. She glanced at Dan's open door and pushed herself into his room.

"Hi," she said. "Guess what?" She paused a moment, confused. The room looked peculiarly crowded; a metal frame rose up around his bed, like a half-finished building. Two pillow ticking slings swung down at odd angles, as Dan lay stretched out on his back.

"It's an orthopedic frame," he said, following her stare. "They put it up yesterday." He nodded at the slings. "They crank me up and stick my arms in those things when I eat. Works pretty well." He smiled. "What's happened?" Hally pulled herself closer.

"A baby was just born in a respirator down in the ward," she said.

"In a respirator?" Dan pulled himself up on one elbow and stared at her. "Really? My God." He grabbed his pajama pants and tugged one knee up an inch. "When did it happen? Who told you?"

"Roy. You know, the janitor. I heard it cry. I didn't know what it was. I was studying a score and. . . . "

"I hope the mother's okay," Dan said.

"Oh, I do too." Hally paused and glanced toward the hall.

"Is Roy around? Somebody we could ask?" Hally turned her chair and pushed herself back to the doorway, but the hall was still empty. "You get so involved with people here, don't you?" Dan said, as she rolled back to the bed. "I mean complete strangers seem like family. You know? I keep thinking about them."

"I know," Hally said. "Did you hear . . . ?" She stopped. It would be better not to speak of that scream in the night.

The sound of footsteps came from the hall. An unfamiliar male voice was talking on the phone at the nurses' desk. "Mom? She's okay. Yeah. That's right." There was a pause. Hally and Dan stared at each other, as they eavesdropped. "No. The baby's good. Gonna take him over to the Children's Hospital." Another pause, then the voice added, "Sure. Mom. I'll tell her. I'm going back up there right now." Hally squeezed both hands together in a gesture of relief and realized as she smiled at Dan that she was wearing her faded bathrobe. "I've got to get back," she said.

"Don't hurry." Dan pulled himself up a little further on his elbow. "It's an historic afternoon." Hally stared. She felt herself swinging out into a wide, new space; her bathrobe didn't matter, even her sagging lip didn't matter right now. She had her voice and mouth problems and he had problems with his legs and arms, but there was a kind of democracy in this disease and he really wanted her here. "Have you ever thought of what it would be like to be a parent?" Dan asked. "Not you yourself necessarily," he added. "I mean parenthood as an objective thing." Hally laughed.

"My sister had a baby the same night I came into the hospital," she said. "And guess what? They named her after me. Harriet Elizabeth. Hally, for short. Isn't that something?"

"Wow. That's wonderful." Dan smiled. "How old is she now? Five weeks?"

"Five weeks and four days," Hally said. "I've got two pictures." She paused. "I'll bring them in and show you. I feel it's a kind of responsibility, you know. I mean I want to know her as she grows up—be part of her life."

"She's a lucky girl to have you for an aunt, especially if she turns out to look like you." Hally jerked one hand up to cover her mouth and glanced down at the floor. Stop it, she thought, and let the hand drop back into her lap. She looked at him again and smiled. He wasn't her type, but he was a good hospital neighbor.

"I've really got to go," she said and turned her wheelchair. "I'll see you tomorrow maybe."

12

*H*ally sat up in bed and glanced around her, confused by the gray look of her room. The morning sun was not streaming through the half-pulled blinds as usual and the space seemed dim and unfamiliar. "Gonna be a good day for ducks and rubber companies," Roy declared, as he pushed his mop into the room. "We're gonna have rain at last."

It was falling steadily by noon, when Debbie brought in her feeding. All at once a deafening noise, like the roar of an airplane engine, began somewhere close by. Hally caught her breath and looked up at Debbie in alarm. "Good Lord," she said. "What's that?"

"It's one of those gasoline generators they've got out on the porch," Debbie shouted. "They flew two of them in from Fort Dix last night." The noise stopped suddenly, leaving a dizzying silence. Hally looked out at the hall.

"Is it because of that hurricane they were predicting for south of here? Do they think it'll come this far?" Debbie filled the syringe from the paper cup on the bed table, but did not speak. "I guess they have to be prepared," Hally added and glanced toward the window. "In case of a power failure or something." The noise began again.

"With twenty-seven people in respirators," Debbie shouted, "they'd darn well better be."

It was still raining when the last visitors left that evening at nine. At midnight, Hally rolled on her back and squinted as someone snapped on the overhead light. Had she slept? She reached up over her ear for her tube and held the end out to an unfamiliar nurse. "I've been asleep almost three hours," Hally exclaimed, catching sight of the girl's wristwatch. Maybe it was the moist air spilling in from the window, she thought.

"That storm out there is terrible," the nurse said. "They say the subway isn't running and if they haven't got it going by four, when I get off, I don't know how the heck I'm going to get home." Hally stared. How could a little much-needed rain close down the Boston subway system?

The nurse glanced at Hally's window, and put down the syringe. "You've got water coming in there. Know that?" She moved around the bed to bang the window down. "This thing doesn't close right," she said and slammed it again. "It's leaking something awful. I'll tell them out at the desk." She picked up the empty syringe and switched off the light.

Hally lay curled on her side, looking out the window into the dark. Long ago at her grandmother's house, she and Ellie had lain tucked together like spoons in the sleeping porch bed, listening to the rush of rain in the drain pipe, thinking of the wet sand around the pine trees, the slippery grass, and the metal pail filling slowly by the kitchen steps. Maybe they would be able to play paper dolls in the kitchen in the morning and not have to go to day camp.

There was a sudden rumble of thunder and Hally lifted her head just in time to see a great zigzag of lightning tear through the clouds above, lighting the wet lawn for a moment and the iron fence, then it was dark again. Hally resettled her head on the pillow and dropped back into sleep.

When Hally woke the next morning, she crawled to the bottom of her bed to look out. The wind was blowing hard, whipping leaves and bits of branches past the window, and the rain was rushing down the window pane. That nurse had been right; it was a real storm.

No one had fixed the window, Hally noticed. The water was flooding steadily over the sill, down the wall, and opening into a small river on the floor. Hally stared at an outlet on the wall. The water parted on either side of it, as it ran down. That must be dangerous, Hally thought, especially when they were worried about the electricity. She crawled back to her pillow and pulled the bell rope. There was a tearing sound nearby and Hally saw a large branch crash down onto the lawn and lie with its green leaves streaming straight back. Hally shivered and pulled the bell rope again, but the buzzer echoed unanswered in the dim hall.

She eyed her wheelchair, parked close to the bed. Lou had lifted her into it each time she had used the chair. But maybe she could do it herself, she thought. She could slide out onto her good foot, then pivot, and drop onto the seat. Flushed with her plan, she pulled on her bathrobe. What if she fell? Miss Flaherty would have good reason to be annoyed with her then. Hally glanced out into the hall again. She could do it safely, she told herself. She slid down, sat, and looked around her room in triumph; now she wouldn't need Lou anymore. She was independent at last. But the window, she reminded herself, and pushed out into the hall. No one was in sight and the nurses' desk was empty. Hally pushed up to Dan's open door and looked in.

Dan lay on his side on the flattened bed, his head resting on his out-stretched arm. "Hi," he called out. "Come in. Isn't this storm something?" Hally pushed herself to his bed and stared out the window.

"It is," she said. "But my window's stuck and water's running in. It's going right over an outlet—or around it rather and . . . ."

"Nothing's plugged into it, is there?" Dan asked. Hally shook her head. "Then I wouldn't worry. You won't find anybody to fix it now, I don't think. I haven't seen a soul for the past twenty minutes." He smiled. "Your window's probably not the only thing that's leaking in this old place this morning." He twisted to look out again.

A small hemlock, whose side branches Hally could see from her window, was fully visible here, as the wind lashed it back and forth. The rain was rushing across the window pane in diagonal streams and several leaves were clinging to the glass. Hally glanced at the yellow glow of the lamp by Dan's bed and pushed herself closer. "At least it's nice and cozy in here," she said.

"We get storms like this in the mountains in Colorado," Dan started. "No fun when you're trying to herd."

"Herd?" Hally repeated. She glanced at Dan's sheet-covered legs. "Herd what?"

"Cattle mostly," Dan said. "My father has a ranch about forty miles north of Denver. Where we are in the foothills, a storm like this can go on for two or three days."

All at once the room was gray. Hally stared at the lamp; its yellow bulb had turned a cloudy white. She pushed her wheelchair back and peered out into the hall. "It's the whole place," she gasped. Dan pulled himself up on his elbow.

"Can you see any lights in that apartment building across the street?" Hally peered out.

"No and there're no street lights either. It must be the whole area." Dan nodded.

"Well, that's what those generators are for," he said. "They'll start them up in a second. Listen." They waited, not talking, as if the pressure of their silence could force the machinery outside in the rain to begin its roaring.

"The tanks," someone shouted. There were running footsteps in the hall. Hally turned her chair, then twisted to peer back at Dan's clock. The dial read 7:03; a minute had elapsed, almost two. There was an explosion of noise as the roar rushed in to envelop them; the lamp was yellow again.

"God. Less than two minutes," Dan shouted. "That's pretty darn good."

"Very good." Hally nodded, aware that she was inaudible now. Blue fumes blew out beyond the window, drifting for a moment, before they were dissolved by the pounding rain. Hally let her shoulders slump. Thank God for electricians and technicians, people who knew about these things, she thought, people who could plan ahead for crises. Dan smiled and let his arm down, so that his cheek rested on the pillow again. The lamp beside the armchair glowed, creating its warm circle.

The roar shook, then stopped. In the silence, the room was gray again. Hally pressed her knuckles to her mouth and turned to the window. "The generator," she breathed.

"Don't worry. There're two of them," Dan said. "They'll get the other going in a minute." He pulled in his arm and pushed himself up on his elbow once more. "Can you see them? The generators, I mean." Hally leaned forward at the window and peered. In the far corner, where the view included a piece of the porch, she could make out something metallic.

"I think I see the end of one," she said. "It looks wet."

"Damn," Dan muttered. "They should've thrown a couple of tarps over them last night."

"The nurses' home," a voice shouted in the hall. "Phone them. Quick." Footsteps sounded. Someone was dialing, talking fast. "It's general. No. It's the whole damn area. We can't hook-up." The voice was angry.

"That's the point. That's what the back-up's for. Hurry up, will you? What? No. Get them all up. Every minute counts."

Hally rolled herself to the doorway and peered out. Dr. Baldwin stood part way down the hall, his arms extended like a traffic policeman pointing to the critical ward at one end or the convalescent ward at the other, as he directed the interns and nurses, who were running past him, to one of the wards. Hally saw him point Miss Flaherty to the critical ward, and then Mrs. Ryan to the convalescent ward. Debbie rushed in, her bright yellow slicker, shiny with rain. She paused a moment to catch Dr. Baldwin's signal, then ran toward the convalescent ward without stopping to take her slicker off. A young kitchen worker appeared in a long, spotted apron. Hally saw the look of shock on his face, as he paused to take in Dr. Baldwin's direction, then ran on. The hall was empty again; Dr. Baldwin ran after the others, leaping down the tiled floor toward the critical ward.

"Everybody's rushing to the wards," Hally reported. "They must be going to pump the respirators by hand."

"They'll have to." Dan's voice was tense. "That's what they'll have to do now."

Hally stared down the hall at the critical ward. Orange heavy duty wires had been pushed across the top of one of the swinging doors, so that it was propped halfway open, revealing the long dim room within. She pulled herself forward hesitantly. Normally the swinging doors were shut; she had never glimpsed the ward before. Perhaps she could help, she thought, hold something, count. Maybe she could even stand and pump. After all she could balance herself on her good foot now. She rolled herself out into the hall. She could help, she told herself again, and felt her face grow warm with excitement, she could help; she would be part of this crisis too. She rolled hurriedly toward the ward, being careful not to push too close to the heavy clump of orange wires that stretched the length of the unlit hall, like a huge umbilical cord.

Hally pulled herself up to the half-open door and paused. She might be in the way, but . . . she wanted to see. She was here, after all. The huge respirators were pushed together in two ragged lines on either side of the room, with a narrow aisle down the middle, so that the protruding heads of the patients, pillowed on their narrow trays, lay side by side along the center aisle. Intravenous stands rose here and there and halfway down the room was a blank television screen.

[85]

Hally stared at the respirator immediately in front of her. A young man's head protruded from the end; his chin jutted upward, exposing his throat. A black rubber tube, running down from it, seemed to be making a wet gurgling noise. The man's face was pimply and he was gazing upward. But, as Hally stared, he rolled his eyes toward her, with a questioning look and she saw their pink-veined whites. Hally stared. She meant to smile, to speak, or make a joke even, but she only looked at him in silent terror. Voices sounded close by, Miss Flaherty's, she thought, Dr. Baldwin's, or was it Roy's? Someone was working the pump at the end of the man's tank, for there were loud whooshing noises.

It was a second's impression, confused, shifting, then came a shout. "Get out, Hally. Get out of here. Go back to your room." Dr. Mostello came into focus all at once, huge and angry in his long white coat. Then there were other faces; nurses, interns, Debbie's even. Everybody was looking at her, as Dr. Mostello's shout reverberated. "Get out, Hally. Get out." She backed up. She leaned forward clumsily, trying to turn, to avoid the orange wires, to get her wheels moving, to retreat, retreat, get back to her own room fast.

"Hally," Dan called out, as she passed his door. But Hally kept going. Tears had started down her face and her hands were shaking. "Hally," the voice came again, but she was in her room at last. Oh God, she thought, what a fool. What a fool I was and in this crisis. Did he think I was there to stare at him—that man in the tank? She bent her head into the darkness of her hands. Oh my God. And Dr. Mostello. "Get out." He knew she was only there out of curiosity. The man in the tank knew too and knew that he and all of them could die.

In the darkness of her hands, Hally heard another shout. She was under the big pine table in the living room that her father had been building. She had lifted the hammer to a long nail, and was about to pound it into one of the diagonal supports, just to help a little, just to show she counted. But her father's face peered under the table. "Get out, Hally," he yelled. "You'll ruin it. Get out."

"Hally. Could you come here?" Dan's voice had an urgent edge. Damn. She didn't want to go back in there now; she didn't want to leave this room.

All at once the edges of her fingers covering her eyes were pink; light was coming through. Hally jerked her hands away and turned to the hall.

It was yellow. The roaring was all around her. She looked back at her room. The light by her bed was on and beyond her window the blue smoke from the generator was blowing out once again. Thank God, she thought, as a cheering shout sounded somewhere down the hall.

"Hally. Could you just. . . ?" Dan's voice sounded muffled, Hally thought, as she rolled herself into his room.

"Could you . . . ?" Dan lay face down, one arm trapped under him. "It collapsed," he explained. "I was leaning forward to look and . . . ." Hally pushed close to the bed, and pulled herself up on her good foot.

"What do I do?" she said, leaning over him.

"Can you push my shoulder back?" Hally pushed. Dan's body tipped easily and he rolled onto his back. He lay looking up at her, as she straightened his arm.

"Thanks." He smiled. "That's great. I felt like an overturned turtle and with all that stuff going on. Thank God, they got that thing started." He peered at his clock. "Thirty-two minutes. God. What a drama. All those tanks they had to pump by hand. But they got that generator going at last." He sighed. "What did you see when you went down the hall?"

"I went down to the ward . . . I was a fool." Hally felt grateful for the fact that she could barely make herself understood above the generator's continued roaring. "I was dumb to go. It was . . . ."

"Well, you sure helped me," Dan said. "That arm was hurting like hell." The roaring modulated and the sound became softer, as though the generator had been moved further away. Hally settled into her wheelchair again. A phone rang in the hall and was answered. People were leaving the wards; the crisis was over at last.

Two nurses passed in the hall, talking. "I was sound asleep when they called and Brenda had those big pink curlers in her hair. There wasn't time to take them out. I barely found my bathrobe as it was." They laughed and continued up the hall.

"We'll tell our grandchildren about this one," Dan said. "But I'll leave out the bit about me falling over on my face."

"I'll leave out. . . . " Hally paused. The hot humiliation of that moment when Mostello had yelled at her seemed remote. That old vision of herself as the stupid one, the one in the wrong place, doing the wrong thing, had lifted. Hally gazed at Dan in grateful surprise.

The noise of Dr. Mostello's hard-soled shoes came from the hall. Hally turned. "Oh God," she whispered. "I'm going to leave. I don't want to see him." But Mostello was already in the doorway.

"Snap off that light, kids," he commanded. "Nothing nonessential until the city power comes on." As Hally turned to switch off the lamp, she thought of keeping her head averted until he left. But Dr. Mostello was talking, as though he had forgotten her appearance in the ward. "That thing took fifteen years off my life," he announced and sighed. Hally stared. It was a sigh of triumph, she recognized, not of exhaustion. It was the kind of sigh her father let out after a challenging case that he had won. "Worst kind of emergency for a respirator patient," Dr. Mostello continued. "But nobody lost a breath." He clapped his hands together with a hollow sound. "Magnificent staff. Magnificent." He nodded at them and turned back to the hall.

"It may well be a magnificent staff," Dan said in the sudden emptiness of the room. "But he had a lot of luck too."

"Luck?" Hally echoed. "What do you mean?"

"Well, if the power had failed at midnight or dawn say, he might not have had enough people to pump those respirators and. . . . " Hally stared. That was true, maybe, but she was still thinking of her father, of his intense black eyes, his energy, and love of crises. If she had known him better maybe, if he had not died. . . . "I mean just imagine what it would have been like trying to organize that job in the dark. That's what I mean by luck," Dan finished.

"I hadn't thought of that," Hally said slowly, pulling herself back from her own tangled associations. It was lucky too, she thought, that she was here with this young man in the cozy sanity of his room. "You know I never used to think about luck much," Hally said. "Now I think about it all the time."

13

Dr. Baldwin came into Hally's room, carrying a paper cup. "Time for your second swallowing lesson," he announced and put the cup on the bedtray. Hally looked up from her book, as though she had just remembered the appointment. But, in fact, her hair was freshly brushed; she was wearing her good pajamas, and the smell of cologne rose up around her. She smiled, as she spread a towel across her lap. Did Dr. Baldwin remember her stupid trip to the respirator ward the morning of the hurricane? Had he heard Dr. Mostello's shout? Maybe not, she thought. The huge drama of the storm and the power outage had probably blotted out any memory of her particular humiliation.

She raised the cup to her lips, took the liquid in her mouth, and positioned it carefully, as Dr. Baldwin had shown her how to do the day before. She let it drop down. Dr. Baldwin watched her and nodded. Hally went through the process once more. Dr. Baldwin had explained that for the time being she had no swallowing muscles and must learn to simply drop the liquid down her throat by gravity. The position and the timing were crucial, he had warned, otherwise she could get off balance and choke. It seemed simple enough to Hally. She would do this one or two more times, convince him she could graduate to a house diet, and then she would go home in another week or two. She looked up at him and he smiled. She liked the way his dark-rimmed glasses sat on his nose, still patched with adhesive tape on one side, and the way the crease between his eyebrows stretched up and smoothed out, when his slow, thoughtful smile began.

"You know this is such an amazing sensation," she said. "One swallow of apple juice after six weeks of no taste at all and the whole feeling of fall rushes over me." She put the cup down and leaned back on her hands. His smile had given her permission to expand a little, she thought. "I can see the pumpkins at the vegetable stand near my grandparents' country house, the gallon bottles of cider. I can even smell the new books at the beginning of the fall term." She twisted the short hair beside her ear, as she looked up at him.

"You could write a Proustian essay on taste," he said. Hally lifted her chin and laughed.

"Do you read Proust?" she asked. The doctor gave a self-deprecatory shrug and handed her the cup again. She must be careful, she thought. She mustn't intrude on his professionalism and yet.... Hally took another mouthful and dropped it down smoothly. But when she lifted her eyes to catch a look of praise, she saw Dr. Baldwin glance at his wristwatch; he was in a hurry then. She dropped the next mouthful quickly and the next more quickly still. Something caught; Hally's head jerked forward. Brown liquid rushed from her nostrils, splattering the towel, and a choking noise filled the room. She gulped, coughed, and reached blindly for the kleenex that Dr. Baldwin held out to her, as a rope of mucous swung down from her nose.

"I'm sorry," she said, mopping her mouth. "I . . . ." Hally wiped away the mucous and took another kleenex to dab her eyes.

"That always happens when you rush it," Dr. Baldwin told her.

"I guess," Hally said. The juice stung in her nostrils, but she straightened and sat back, meaning to regain her dignity. "How soon do you think it'll be until you take my tube out?" She paused. "I want to try my flute. I mean, you see I need to begin figuring out what I can do and. . . . "

"Of course," Dr. Baldwin broke in. "But there's no rush." Hally took the apple juice in her mouth and dropped it down again.

"I was working on the Mozart Flute Concerto No. 2 in D Major when I got sick," she began and wondered if it would sound self-congratulatory to add that she had played it with the Boston Pops the night before she came here.

"Ah, those flute concertos," Dr. Baldwin said. He turned and gazed out at the lawn. "My wife loves them, but I really think I like the choral stuff better myself." He looked back at her.

"Well, I ... I ...." Hally felt the paper cup shake in her hand. "I sort of agree. I mean I love the *Requiem,* but then I am an instrumentalist after all." She gave a little laugh and heard its high, self-conscious ring. Why hadn't it ever occurred to her that he might be married—that he would never be interested in her.

Dr. Baldwin took the cup from her and Hally watched him pour the left-over juice in the sink and drop the cup into the wastebasket. "See you tomorrow," he said and turned to the door.

Hally sat listening to his footsteps receding in the hall. He was married, married, of course. She looked out at the lawn and sighed. Perhaps there were children. Perhaps his wife sat nursing a baby, while she listened to the flute concertos, moving slowly back and forth in her rocking chair, beside a crowded bookcase, which contained French paperbacks, for it was she who read Proust.

A baby. Hally stared at the framed picture of her niece on the bedside table. Did polio mean that she would never know any of that? Perhaps she had already made that decision, she thought. There were all those evenings rehearsing, driving off on winter nights to performances in some high school auditorium, some Legionnaires' hall, always worrying about the acoustics, the tone, the interpretation, whether anyone would come. Maybe she should have been at a football game or a beer party, maybe she should have been smooching with somebody in a dark car. Ellie had done that—thoughtful, careful Ellie. She had picked Peter early and had made her plans; now there was little Hally and there would be other children, and houses to furnish and dogs to train, and piano lessons, and Christmas trees. And what about old Hally? What would she do? She had procrastinated, telling herself a man, a moment, would come soon enough, a musician perhaps, a director, a composer.

If she had married Carl, who had managed the New England Conservatory orchestra a year ago.... But she hadn't loved Carl. She had admired him, was grateful for his respect and for that world of European music she had glimpsed through him. But from the beginning there was something about his fleshy hands that had been wrong. And what if there were never anyone else? What if all the sensitive men, who listened to Mozart, were married? If her swallowing problems continued, if her voice was permanently disabled, her leg even, she would be a responsibility for anyone to assume.

Hally looked back at the lawn. She would continue with her music alone—if she could. Even if she couldn't play in concerts, there would be ensemble work certainly, and teaching. Or would there? Suppose she could never play her flute at all? What then? Hally saw herself with her profession broken into tangled pieces around her feet, her sexual longings floating out, like yellowed shreds of curtain too old to repair. She stared at a brown island in the grass. What would she do then, she wondered.

Dan lay waiting on his flattened bed, his sheet rumpled around his waist. He had had his enema at ten, but no bath yet, no shave, and his room still smelled of excrement. A wrinkle in the sheet was pressing into his back; he rolled on his side and saw a nurse pass in the hall. "Miss Lord," Dan called. "Miss Lord. . . . " But the nurse was gone.

Dan flopped onto his back again and sighed. Maybe he could get some news or some music even while he waited. His hand scrabbled on the sheet and he pulled himself over on his side, then realized that the bedside table with the radio had been pushed out of range of his arm. "Goddamnit." He yanked at his bell rope and lay listening to the harsh buzzing outside in the hall. Miss Lord appeared in the doorway and stood looking in, her face stern.

"What have you got your buzzer on for?" she demanded. "Don't you know we're busy out there this morning?" Dan lifted his head.

"I haven't had my shave or my bath or. . . . "

"Look here," Miss Lord said and put both hands on the large shelf of her hips. "We're busy. You ought to know that. We'll get to you when we can, not a minute sooner. Understand?" The gray metallic rims of her glasses matched her severe hair.

"You're always busy out there," Dan complained. "You in particular. You think more about your charts and your lists than. . . . " He paused, as he saw Miss Lord grip her hips more tightly. "I've been waiting for my shave for forty minutes now." Dan glanced back at his bedside clock. "Forty-five to be exact. I'll probably be lucky to get one by 11:30 and I'm not even talking about a bath or a bed change." He paused. Miss Lord moved her mouth as if to answer, but stared at Dan instead. "Would you crank me up at least? If you've got the time, that is."

The nurse moved to the bed and twisted the crank at the bottom, which made a ringing sound as it banged against the orthopedic frame on each revolution. But Miss Lord did not crank it far; she straightened and surveyed Dan again. "Now you just calm down, young man. All right?" She turned back to the hall. "We'll get to you when we can and not a minute sooner."

Dan let his breath out in a whistle as the nurse disappeared, then he spotted Hally, who was sitting in her high-backed wheelchair at one side of the door. "Calm down," Dan repeated angrily, almost shouting the words to Hally. "Calm down. Goddamnit. I wait here every morning, flat on my back, trying to be patient and there's always some lousy emergency out there." He let his head drop to the pillow, then lifted it with an effort once again. "I mean I'm a nice guy every day and what does it get me? Huh? An enema by ten, if I'm lucky, and a shave by noon. My chin itches, the bed's sweaty, and the room stinks. Just how much are you supposed to take? That's what I want to know." He dropped his head again and gazed around him. "This smelly pig pen, they call a hospital," he continued and looked down at Hally, who had rolled herself up beside his bed. "Unable to move, to. . . . "

"It's just one of those mornings," Hally started. "Besides you know Miss Lord. She's the worst."

"See that?" Dan pointed to the full urinal on the bedtray. "It's just lucky I don't have normal deltoids, because if I did, I'd reach over right now and smash that thing on the floor. I would, by God." Dan's voice was hoarse. He rolled his head and stared at the bedframe above him. "I'd shake this whole damn thing until it came crashing down too." He paused, breathing hard. "You don't believe me, but I would."

"I believe you," Hally said. She glanced at the sink in the corner, and rolled herself over, dampened a washcloth hanging on the side, and pushed herself back to the bed. Dan had covered his face with his elbow, but she leaned forward. "Here," she said and raised herself on her good foot, holding the cloth. Dan took his arm away and sighed as she laid the washcloth over his forehead.

"Thanks," he said.

"Miss Lord's awful," Hally said. "She's so mean." Dan let out a groan of agreement, but did not open his eyes. "She reminds me of a steam roller in a nurse's uniform with glasses on." Dan opened his eyes. "She told me I didn't deserve hot packs one night. That I really wasn't in pain."

"Oh, my God," Dan said. "Really?" He lifted the washcloth and rolled himself on his side. "Thanks again. I really didn't mean to carry on like that."

"I sort of admire you for being able to," Hally began. "I wish I could. I always seem to end up feeling guilty somehow. I mean I half believed Miss Lord that night." She paused and looked around the room. "Is your mother coming in today?"

"No. She flew home Monday. Dad had to go home last weekend," he added and sighed.

"Oh." Hally nodded. "I won't be seeing as much of my mother either now," she offered. "She's a teacher, you see, and she's got a lot of meetings in August before school begins."

"My mother'll be back in two weeks," Dan said. "Dad too, I hope, when he gets things arranged." His voice trailed and he eased himself onto his back again and sighed. "Family's funny though. You know? I mean my mother can make me so tense sometimes."

"It's a tense situation," Hally said. "You feel grateful and yet you're so dependent that you're sort of resentful too, or at least I am."

"That's true," Dan agreed and turned his head to look at her again. "Mother's great. But she can be so damn bossy. Awkward too. Her idea of making me comfortable is to tidy up the bureau, dump out all the flowers, and break the thermometer holder." Hally laughed.

"Do you have any brothers or sisters?" she asked.

"Two sisters," Dan said. "One's married and the other's just starting college this fall. I don't know them awfully well actually. I mean I've been away at Harvard almost six years now." Dan sighed. "My dad's my best friend really. When we're together, we talk and talk." Hally smiled.

"That's the way it is with Mom and me," she offered. "We live together, you see. Friends sometimes tell me that I ought to get a place of my own. But it's a cheap, cozy arrangement and we have fun. I have a married sister too," she went on. "She named her little girl after me. Oh, but I've already told you that." Hally covered her mouth with one hand and Dan smiled. There was a loud rattling as someone pushed a bedframe past.

"More beds, more admissions." Dan sighed. "No wonder they're tired and bitchy." He gazed around him. "You know it's funny about this room. Sometimes I really think I'd rather be on the ward. This place is so darn lonely at times. You know what I mean? I'd probably get more attention up there anyway."

"I know, but. . . . " Hally looked back at Dan. "I'd be on the ward myself except for this aunt of mine who's paying. Adding to what the March of Dimes puts out." She paused and gazed out the window. "Frankly I'd rather have a new flute or the extra lessons I'll probably need to retrain my lip. But it's her money and. . . . " She looked back at Dan. "Hey, did I tell you? Mrs. Harding's going to try me in a walker tomorrow. I just might come prancing in here on my own two feet one of these days."

"That would be great. Things are beginning to happen, you know, if you look at it all in geological time. Mostello says I'll be a 'clean case' in another week." He paused. "I bet you will be too. Then we can have some visitors outside the family. Won't that be something? I know my roommate'll come."

"My old music teacher wrote that he'd like to visit," Hally said, "and there're other friends."

"Hey, do you know what Roy calls you?" Dan asked. Hally shook her head. "Katharine Hepburn." Hally felt a flush rise and she lifted her hand to her lip.

"Well, he thinks you're Cary Grant."

"That makes us quite a glamorous couple," Dan said. "Cary Grant splayed out in bed, unable to move, and beautiful Katharine Hepburn with a tube in her nose."

Hally laughed. "I'm glad we got polio together," she said, "I mean if we had to get it at all."

14

*H*ally graduated from the walker to crutches in less than a week. But she was angry and disappointed to discover that her leg paralysis had left her with a clumsy limp. Mrs. Harding's unsubtle exhortations about straightening, pulling, looking directly ahead, irritated Hally. When the therapist was out of sight, she abandoned her crutches and hopped or limped; it was easier, even if she was starting bad habits. When Maureen was lifted into a wheelchair, Hally volunteered to push her. She could hold herself stable, by clutching the handles of the chair, she argued, and besides it was fun. "Where to this afternoon?" Hally asked, as she pushed Maureen out into the hall.

"Let's go visit your friend Dan," Maureen suggested. "He needs company, I bet."

"He's no more my friend than he is yours, Maureen," Hally objected. That wasn't really true, she thought, but she needed to fight off Maureen's implications of romance. "Okay," she said. "He'll be glad to have visitors."

Dan was sitting up in bed, wearing his horn-rimmed reading glasses. A book lay open before him, his place marked with a yellow pencil. "Study time's over," Maureen announced. "Some distinquished visitors have arrived." Dan smiled, shut the book, and pushed his glasses up into his hair.

"Not much studying going on here, I'm afraid," he said and sighed. "Just kind of going through the motions. I'm not getting anything done."

Hally rolled Maureen, who was wearing a lavender stole and a ruffled bed jacket, up beside the bed and settled herself in the armchair.

[96]

"You sound a little dour, Danny boy," Maureen observed. "Feeling a little down?" Dan nodded. "What we ought to have is a party like one of those you have at Harvard, where they cluster around the piano and sing, 'We are poor little lambs who have lost our way. Baa, baa, baa.' "

"That's a Yale song, Maureen," Dan said, laughing.

"No, it isn't," Maureen insisted. "It's Harvard and you're supposed to sing it at night."

"Not me," Dan said. "I have to study."

"Oh, you can study all day," Maureen protested. "At night you're supposed to sing and be a gentleman. That's what the song says. Right?" Hally laughed and curled her feet under her, as Maureen began to sing. " 'We are poor little lambs that have lost our way/ Baa, baa, baa./ Gentlemen songsters off on a spree, Damned from here to eternity. . . . ' " Maureen let the verse trail.

"Believe me, Maureen, that's a Yale song," Dan said again. "But I'll sing it. I'm a liberal. I'm not prejudiced about Harvard after all. 'God have mercy on such as we,' " he sang, laughing, and Hally joined in.

"Baa, baa, baa," Hally sang, but since she could not make the explosive "b" sound, she seemed to be singing, "ma, ma, ma." Dan and Maureen stopped to listen, letting Hally sing the last line of the chorus alone. Hally repeated it and they laughed. Dan smiled, flattered that Maureen should tease him about his academic life, and pleased that Hally was laughing about her voice.

"What's going on in here?" demanded Dr. Mostello, who had appeared in the doorway.

"It's Dan," Maureen explained. "He says that song we were singing, 'Poor Little Lambs,' is Yale. But it's Harvard, isn't it? I know I'm right." Dr. Mostello rolled his eyes at Dan and smiled.

"It's Yale, Maureen. But I don't expect to convince you of that or of much else either." He laughed and turned back to the hall.

"Dan's very fond of you, you know," Maureen said, as Hally pushed her wheelchair close to the bed. "He was laughing away when you sang."

"Oh, he just likes kidding around. That's all."

"Maybe." Maureen pulled off her stole and handed it to Hally. "Has he ever mentioned Jill?"

Hally had stooped to fit the stole into the bottom bureau drawer, but she straightened and looked back at Maureen. "Jill? Who's she?"

"She's an undergraduate at Radcliffe, Marian says he was going with last spring and. . . . "

"Good God," Hally interrupted. "Doesn't Marian have any respect for her son's private life?"

"Oh, she only mentioned it, Hally. Besides, I asked." Hally paused a moment, then smiled.

"I'm sure you did, Maureen. But she didn't have to answer you."

"Then I'll spare you the vulgar details, dear one," Maureen went on, and turned to pull herself up into bed. "Largely because I don't know them. But it didn't work out. They broke up last May."

"Hmm," Hally said and stood watching as Maureen lay back on her pillows with a sigh. "Dan's fun and I like being with him. But don't make it into a big romantic. . . . " She stopped and smiled. "You know what I mean. We're three good friends. Right?"

"Right," Maureen echoed.

Hally heard talk and male laughter as she approached Dan's door the next afternoon and, realizing that he must have a visitor, she tried to speed up as she limped past. But Dan called out, "Hey, Hally. Come in. There's someone here who thinks he knows you." Hally turned and moved to the door reluctantly; Harvard guys were usually snobby.

A tall young man in a blue button-down shirt, with the sleeves rolled up, rose from the armchair and smiled. "Mort Steinberg," he said with a laugh and held out his hand. Hally stopped on her crutches and stared.

"Mort," she said. "My gosh. What are you doing here?"

"I'm this guy's roommate," he said, smiling. "I'm responsible for all his troubles. I brought him here."

"You room with Dan?" Hally stared from one to the other, then laughed. She had known Mort in the high school orchestra, when he played the clarinet. They had dated even and. . . . Mort, old Mort, she thought, and felt relief spill through her, as she leaned against the bedframe. If Mort was Dan's Harvard friend, his roommate even, Dan's life beyond the hospital seemed closer and less awesome. She settled herself in the armchair, at Mort's insistence, and looked around. There was a package of photographs on the bureau and two library books sat on the bedtray.

"You've made me famous in the Square, you know," Mort said to Dan, as he settled himself at the bottom of the bed. "Everybody wants news about you and they all think I'm the source. Now I'll have to add news about Hally too." Dan laughed happily, but Hally only smiled. Who would ask Mort about her? She and Mort had moved in different worlds for at least six years. "Prof Robinson stopped me at the back door of the library yesterday afternoon," Mort went on. "He wanted a full rundown. Of course he couldn't hear anything I said, because he wasn't wearing his hearing aid and his eyes are so bad he probably thought he was talking to Eric anyway. But he nodded and shook his rosy jowls and told me he was delighted to hear of your progress. Absolutely delighted." Mort pronounced the phrase in the pompous English accent he used to do so well. Dan laughed and Hally joined in. In the old days she'd found Mort's imitations and his story-telling irritating, she remembered. But now it was clear that he was trying hard to entertain them both and disguise his own nervousness.

"Then there's your dear friend, Doris. Doris," Mort explained, turning to Hally "is universally agreed to be the most competitive graduate student Harvard has enrolled since 1902. She's so delighted to get your assistantship job in that American Intellectual History course, that she can't believe her luck. She keeps asking me, 'He isn't likely to just suddenly recover, is he?' " Hally laughed and felt Mort glance at her, taking in her tube and drooping mouth. There was a frantic edge to his story-telling, she thought. The poor guy was scared and longed to leave.

"Remember the time we played for graduation," she began, wanting to help him. "You had a bad reed and . . . ."

"Oh, my God," Mort said. "We met that crazy guy from the Conservatory at the dance after. Remember that?" Hally laughed. It had been an awkward night, not gay and funny, though it sounded that way now. She glanced at the floor, half wanting Dan to think there had been something between them and yet not enough to . . . what? She lifted her eyes to Mort again.

The two men were similar in ways—the laugh, a certain pulling down of the mouth, a kind of smoothness. But Dan was more sensitive than Mort, she thought; his thin face was almost poetic, and his long hands with their blue veins were beautiful. She could imagine him dressed like Mort—in khaki pants and a blue button-down shirt, open at the neck, with the sleeves rolled up—and yet they were very different. She twisted, trying to concentrate on what Mort was saying. Dan was a hospital friend, that was all. She was not going to spin off into some romantic fantasy over him, not after her silly infatuation with Dr. Baldwin. Besides they were both polio victims, for heaven's sake, both convalescent, both facing all kinds of uncertainties.

Dan sat smiling at Mort, aware that he had adapted most of those stories for the occasion. Dan wanted to hear about the historiography seminar he had had to drop when he got sick, and news of the first year crowd that would be arriving soon. But the pain in his abdomen had grown hot and his head ached with the effort to reach back into that world of school and Cambridge that seemed so remote now. Mort would rise and leave soon and then Dan could close his eyes. But for now he must show his appreciation. The guy had driven all the way out here after all. The thing Dan really wanted to know, he realized, was what Mort's relationship with Hally had been, high school orchestra, high school dates. What more? What did he know about Hally's involvements now, her life beyond her music? Dan watched, as Mort turned back to her. He liked Hally, yes, and admired her, of course. But he had not been in love with her, Dan thought, at least not recently.

15

Dan was sitting cranked up in bed, his arms suspended in their pillow ticking slings, when Hally limped into the room on her crutches, carrying some mail. When would he get up on those things, he wondered, and moved his shoulders against the pillow. When would he get up in a wheelchair for Christ's sake?

An unfamiliar intern, with thinning blonde hair and a rosy face, came to the door. "Good morning, folks," he said and glanced at Hally. "You're getting very expert with those." He nodded at her crutches. "Feel pretty natural now?" Dan stared. Who was this guy? One of the new group of interns apparently, but how did he know Hally? She made a little turn beside the bureau and smiled back at the doctor, as Dan studied them.

"Dan, this is Dr. Bullard," Hally said. "I guess you two haven't met." Dan nodded, but did not put out his hand. The intern had turned back to Hally anyway.

"How about coming down to the respirator ward with me this morning?" Dr. Bullard proposed. "I'll show you around now that you've got all this new mobility."

"The respirator ward?" Hally said and hesitated. She thought of the morning of the hurricane and that man with the gurgling tube in his throat. The sight was almost four weeks back, but the memory still made her stomach churn with shame. "The convalescent one?" she asked. Dr. Bullard nodded. "Now?"

"You really ought to see more of this great hospital we doctors work in." For a guy who'd only been here three days, this fellow had a pretty inflated sense of his identity, Dan thought. He saw Hally glance back at him for his approval, but Dan merely stared. Go ahead, he thought, if you want to spend time with that bald little turkey. Hally's questioning look changed to one of irritation and he watched her turn back to the doctor.

"Sure," she said. "I'd love to. It'd be an adventure."

Dr. Bullard stopped beside a laundry hamper near the nurses' desk and pulled out two surgical gowns. Hally pushed her arms through the loose sleeves and belted her gown around her thin waist. "If you didn't notice the slippers, you'd think I was just another visitor, wouldn't you?" She smiled, forgetting the crutches under her arms, the adhesive tape strip on her forehead, and the translucent tube protruding from her nostril.

"We transferred a respirator patient to a rocking bed yesterday," Dr. Bullard announced, as they started down the hall. Hally glanced across at him. The "we" had a pretentious ring; this intern had only just arrived and it had probably been Dr. Baldwin who had done the work. But she listened politely. "The bed's quite an invention really. When it rocks back, you see . . . ." He flapped his hand, keeping the palm flat. "It exerts pressure on the body, squeezing the air out of the lungs. When it tips up," Dr. Bullard held his hand vertically, "the organs are released and the air flows back in."

Hally nodded, but she was not concentrating. As they passed her room, she looked in with longing. There were her Impressionist postcards arranged around the mirror, the music scores on the table, and the picture of little Hally beside her bed. "You know actually, I think I'll just . . . ." Hally paused. She couldn't do this. She had always hated sickness, prone bodies in johnnies and pajamas, tubes, funny noises nearby. That morning of the hurricane had been horrible—those respirators, that man with that thing in his throat. She couldn't do this; she couldn't. But Dr. Bullard continued to talk.

"It's the same principle as a respirator really. But it works on gravity, you see, while the tank works on air pressure." Hally nodded uneasily. They paused at the door to the ward and Dr. Bullard reached into a small cardboard box tacked to the back of the door and pulled out two paper masks. Hally put hers on, then looked at Dr. Bullard resignedly, and followed him through the swinging doors.

Once again she felt herself stiffen with terror at the scene before her.

Huge tanks were lined close together on either side of the long room with a narrow aisle in the center, where the heads, protruding from the long machines, rested side by side on their trays. Intravenous stands rose here and there and some respirators supported vacuum cleaner-like oxygen tanks on top. Hally stared at the nearest head. The face was thin and pimply, the mouth drooling saliva; she glanced away. At least this time the room was full of light. Hally saw the face of a smiling druggist on the TV screen, midway down the line of respirators. He was holding up a tube-like package of Tums. "Tums for the tummy. Guaranteed to contain no soda." Hally fastened on his face as she began limping up the aisle behind Dr. Bullard. The protruding heads, which were at the level of her waist, felt uneasily close. One young man with rashy bumps poking up through the unshaven black hair on his chin, was smiling broadly. The smile was for her, Hally realized with a start. He had caught her reflection in the rectangular mirror above his head. She smiled back nervously. So that's what the mirrors were for, she thought, and limped on.

Two nurses were working at a respirator further up the aisle—their arms cut off by the black porthole openings on either side. Hally glimpsed two thin male legs, and a naked pelvis in the yellow light within the tank; she looked away. On her right side was a woman, whose black hair fell below the tray in a dark tangle and next to her was a short-haired girl or was it a boy? Hally couldn't tell. The uncertainty was scary. He, or maybe she, was making gurgling noises through a tube like the man she had seen the day of the hurricane. But that wasn't he, was it? Hally moved on. The word Tums appeared on the TV screen and Hally stared at it with an urgent concentration. Where was Dr. Bullard? A hot terror spread through her chest. Oh God, where was he? She saw a compartment at the far end of the aisle and spotted his white elbow jutting out. He was standing beside a wide, white bed, where a young man, with a bare chest that was still tan, was being raised slowly upward. Hally limped in beside the doctor and smiled at the half-naked man.

"Kevin," Dr. Bullard said. "I want you to meet our new head doctor." He nodded at Hally on her crutches. Hally smiled, embarrassed by Dr. Bullard's heavy humor. The man glanced at her, then looked down again at his moving chest, lifting, sagging, then lifting again, as though its effort required his concentration. His hair was sandy and the top curls were still orange from the sun. He'd done some kind of outdoor work, Hally thought. He had been a handsome man. But he was thin now and the tendons in his neck stood out as he breathed. Something was wrong with his arms, Hally noticed; they lay at his sides, tanned, but motionless.

"How's it going this morning?" Dr. Bullard asked. "Getting to feel a little more natural now?" Kevin nodded. He started to turn his head, but the bed moved him forward in its slow arc, leaving Hally and Dr. Bullard behind. "It's quite an invention, isn't it?" Dr. Bullard said. "He's doing well, considering. General paralysis. Arms particularly."

When the bed tipped back again, Kevin looked at Hally and asked, "How long have you been here?"

"Eight weeks," Hally said. She thought of her quiet room up the hall with its postcards and music scores and the African violet on the window sill and it seemed to her that, compared with this man, she had barely had the disease at all. She had never been in a respirator, even for a day or two.

"It's been six weeks and three days for me," Kevin said and sighed. "Seems like a year." The bed interrupted the talk once more, moving slowly backward to the end of its arc. When Kevin swung back to them, he looked at Hally with an apologetic smile. "I'd shake hands," he said and nodded at his shoulder. "But my arms . . . ." He nodded again.

"It's all right," Hally began nervously. "I mean I . . . ." She stopped and the man turned his gaze to Dr. Bullard.

"How soon they gonna take me off this thing anyway, Doc?"

"Well, it takes time, you know," Dr. Bullard replied.

"That's the theme song here, isn't it?" Hally said, clutching at something they had in common, something that might make him smile. "It takes time." She paused, delighted when the man laughed.

"You said it," he told her. "It takes time." His laugh made his naked rib cage heave, but Hally kept her eyes on his face.

"See? Here's the control," Dr. Bullard said. He pointed to an electric switch in the middle of the bedframe. "Try it," he challenged. "Turn it off." Hally leaned down uneasily and pressed the black switch to OFF. The bed stopped in its upward swing, arrested suddenly. Kevin looked over at Hally; his chest continued its heaving, the ropes in his neck stood out, and his brown eyes bore in on her. Hally felt a flush of horror at her sudden power over this helpless stranger and stooped to turn the switch to ON again.

Dr. Bullard looked down at his watch. "We've gotta go. It's nine thirty," he said. "I'll be missed on rounds." Kevin smiled at Hally, signaling a mutual awareness of the intern's self-importance.

"Good to meet you," Kevin said. "Come back again, why don't you?" Hally smiled. He meant it, she realized. He liked her, or at least he liked the distraction she provided.

"I will," Hally told him and glanced back at the lines of tanks with their protruding heads. "I will," she resolved. "I really will."

Hally did not stop to knock on Dan's half-open door, after she parted from Dr. Bullard; she simply limped in. She rested her crutches against the bedframe and sank into the armchair.

"I'm back," she said and sighed.

"What was it like?" Dan asked and rolled on his side to look at her. "What happened?"

"It's... it's overwhelming," she said. "Terrifying and yet...yet...." She paused and stared at him as she waited for the feelings and images to clear. "You see all these heads struggling to breathe, these people. I mean they smiled at me, one man did. They were watching television and Kevin, the one we visited, the one on this rocking bed, joked and ... and ... you see his arms are gone. I mean...." Hally stopped, then started again. "Sometimes I couldn't tell who was a man or a woman and ... I mean it's so...." She looked down at the floor. Dan nodded and started to speak. But Hally pulled in her breath. "Oh God, Dan," she said. "We're lucky. You know?"

Dan reached out his hand and touched her knee. Hally looked down. His fingers felt warm and she sat silent, wanting him to keep them there, wanting to hold the moment that was spreading out around them. She looked down at his hand again. "Hey," she said. "You couldn't reach that far last week, could you? I mean, that arm's gotten better, hasn't it?"

"You're right," Dan said and laughed. "My God, I didn't even notice it. My arm muscles are coming back." He raised his hand, pulled it in, then extended it again. "Look at that. I've got a whole lot more movement." He lifted the arm again. "Amazing. Mostello said he thought my arms would recover and damned if he wasn't right." Dan smiled broadly. "You know this just proves my point with my mother. She keeps talking about other hospitals—New York, Warm Springs, places where I might get more therapy and stuff. But Mostello's against it. He says that everything's changing now and there's no point in starting on a new therapy regime until we know what I really need."

"Sounds sensible," Hally said. "I mean this arm thing will change the picture a lot, won't it?"

Dan touched Hally's knee again. "You know, if it can happen to me, it could happen to that guy you met in the respirator ward." He paused. Hally nodded, but she was smiling. The terror of the ward was behind her now; she was with Dan. "I don't think a change makes sense now," he said. "Do you?"

"No. I don't think so either," Hally told him and smiled. "Besides you'd be missed here, you know."

*E*sther and Marian sat talking at a table near the door of the cafeteria. "I'm just so tired of all this waiting," Marian said and sighed. "I feel sure Dan would do better at Warm Springs or at that new Rusk Center in New York. I've made a number of inquiries. You see," Marian put one hand to the silk scarf at her neck. "My father has numerous connections in the medical world. He's retired now, of course. But he was at the Peter Bent Brigham Hospital for years and. . . . " She paused as Esther nodded.

"Father thinks Dan should be in a hospital that specializes in therapy. He's professionally cautious, you know. But I feel we've just got to make the transfer soon. Of course, Dr. Mostello wants to keep him here. He thinks the situation is changing daily, plus he's just so possessive." Marian sighed and looked around the noisy cafeteria, then took a sip from her water glass. "I confess if the setting were a little more civilized, a little more comfortable. . . . But the real point is Dan must have the absolute best in therapy and soon. I mean it's not a question of money." Esther looked down at her lap.

"It's so hard to know what to do at this stage," Esther began and glanced over at a March of Dimes poster on the opposite wall. It wasn't Marian's wealth that she found off-putting; it was her judgmental manner. "Hally keeps asking me to bring in her flute. But Dr. Mostello is firm; he says it's still too early."

"Dan can be so stubborn," Marian continued. "He always could. I mean, naturally none of us knows for sure which treatment is perfect. But that doesn't mean that. . . . " She lifted her elbows to the table, leaned on them a moment, and gave Esther a hard look. "I think you should know that I feel Dan is making these decisions about his hospitalization—or letting them be made for him rather—partly on the basis of his . . . his feelings for your daughter." She looked down, then up at Esther again. "I don't mean to imply that it's solely her fault or . . . I just want you to know."

Esther let an interval pass. "We all have our doubts, our frustrations," she said quietly. "But I don't think you can tell people, especially your own children, who not to love. At least I wouldn't want to."

Dan was reading from a pile of typewritten pages stacked on the bedtray in front of him when Jim Rickley came to the door. "Hey, look what came in the mail yesterday," Dan said and nodded at a notice on the bureau. Jim glanced at him uneasily, then moved to look down at the typewritten letter with the heading, Adams County Selective Service Board.

"My God. They've listed you 1A," he said and looked back at Dan.

"I'm going to tell 'em, if they want me, they'll have to come get me," Dan said and laughed. Jim smiled. "Funny, isn't it?" Dan continued. "You and I were just talking about the draft the other day, Korea and stuff." He laughed again. "Did you see the *Times* editorial this morning about Eisenhower's peace platform?" He paused. "Sit down. Take a load off."

"I can't." Jim shifted and moved to the end of the bed. "Actually I came to say good-bye." He moved a white towel hanging on the bed-frame several inches to the right, then back to the center again.

"Good-bye?" Dan stared. "What d'you mean?"

"I'm saying my good-byes," Jim went on. "I leave tomorrow."

"Tomorrow?" Dan repeated. Several of the interns had already gone, but Dan had assumed that Jim would stay on.

"Well, you know. It's the end of my contagious disease training," Jim explained. "Pediatrics is next. I'm going to Children's Hospital. Remember?" Dan stared. Jim had talked about that assignment a week ago, but Dan had not realized it was so close.

"But what about the epidemic?" Dan started. "I thought a lot of you guys were extending your time here." Jim couldn't just leave. Who the heck would he talk to now?

"I've been here eight weeks, instead of the usual five," Jim said. "A couple of people are staying—Artemis and Schmidt. But the new group's all moved in." Dan nodded, thinking of Dr. Bullard. "I'm planning to specialize in pediatrics, you know, so . . . ." Jim came around the side of the bed and put out his hand. "Just wanted to say good-bye. Wish you the best."

"Yes. You too." Dan shook his hand.

"I'll be back to check on your draft status." Jim's laugh was nervous. "I'll come visit as soon as I get settled." Dan nodded and glanced over at the armchair, thinking suddenly of those hot nights when Jim had sat there with his legs stretched out, talking, falling asleep. How could he just leave? Dan looked back at him in irritation. I just might not be here, he thought.

"I'll stop by again before I leave. Okay?"

"Fine," Dan said, but he felt anger pour through him as he watched the intern depart. So that's that, he thought. I'm just another contagious disease case; after weeks of talk and friendship, that's all.

"Look! Look!" Hally exclaimed, limping into the room. "My tube's out! Dr. Baldwin just did it." She turned to the bureau and leaned over to peer at herself in the mirror. "I look practically normal now." She leaned closer and fluffed up her bangs. "Just think. No more feedings! No more syringes. I go on liquids for a week or so, then soft food. And look," she pivoted partway holding her crutches out, like wings on either side, so that Dan could get the full effect of her appearance in day-time clothes for the first time. Her tan corduroy slacks were gathered in the back with a diaper pin, since the waist was too big, and her blue shirt hung down like a smock, giving her a waif-like look. She smiled triumphantly. "What do you think?"

Dan stared. Jim was leaving, now Hally had graduated from her tube and was wearing clothes and would be leaving too, probably in a week or so. He watched her turn to look at herself in the mirror again.

"So Dr. Baldwin took your tube out, did he?" Dan said. "That must have been a thrill." Hally peeled off an edge of gray adhesive, left on her forehead, and turned back to Dan.

"What do you mean?"

"Where's your wonderful friend, Dr. Bullard, this morning?" Dan demanded. "Isn't it just about time for your visit to the respirator ward?"

"Dr. Bullard?" Hally repeated. "I don't need Dr. Bullard. I can go to the

ward by myself now. I just delivered the mail down there and . . . ." She
stared at him, then moved to the foot of the bed and grasped the frame
with one hand. "Listen, Dan." She gave him a stern look. "We're hospital
friends and . . . I mean I'm sorry if my mobility and my new friends on the
ward depress you, but . . . ." She hesitated and clasped the frame with her
other hand. "I'm really sorry you're still in bed, but . . . ."

"But that's my problem, not yours," Dan finished. "Right?"

"No," Hally said. "That's not what I meant. I . . . ." She glanced around
the room and her gaze settled on the typed pages lying on the bedtray. "Is
that your thesis?" she asked.

"It was," Dan said and sighed. "The tentative beginnings. Seems pretty
damn remote right now."

"It's about the Oregon Trail, isn't it?" Hally said and perched on the
arm of the chair.

"Yes, it's kind of a history of it. Or it was. These are just preliminary
notes really. I haven't begun writing yet. I was planning to go down to the
National Archives in Washington this fall." Dan stacked the papers
together and stuffed them into a manila folder, holding the folder against
his chest, so that he could push the papers in with his strong hand. "Dad's
offered to pay for microfilm. But I don't even know what's in the
territorial papers or how they're organized."

"That's hard," Hally said.

"Yes," Dan said and let his breath out between his teeth. "But I'm going
to do it somehow. Not the whole thing maybe, but some version of it. I
mean. . . . Oh God, I don't know." He sighed and looked out into the hall.
"Did you know Jim's leaving tomorrow?"

"Jim Rickley?" Hally said. "He is?" Dan nodded and sighed again. "I
thought he'd stay like Artemis and Schmidt and . . . ."

"I did too," Dan said. "But he just came in to say good-bye."

"Oh God," Hally said and paused.

"Don't you leave too," Dan said.

"Oh, I'll be around a while longer, I guess." Hally leaned back. "It's
funny, isn't it? Your thesis, my flute. You know if someone would just say,
'Okay, Lewis. This is impossible' or 'This will be possible, but this won't'
or if they'd say to me, 'Hally, you'll never play concerts again, but you can
teach and. . . . ' But. . . . " Hally leaned forward. "That's the whole
problem, isn't it? The uncertainty."

"Yes," Dan agreed. "That's the real bitch of it all. If I knew I could just plain never do this thing, I could begin planning something else maybe, doing some reading or. . . . "

"I really want to try my flute, have it here near me," Hally began. "It's sort of my child, you see. I hate not to have it nearby. But Mostello says I've got to wait another week or two."

"You'll have it though," Dan said. "I mean if I gave up my Oregon Trail plan and if you thought you'd never do concerts again. . . I mean, if we thought all that stuff, we'd be awfully depressed, wouldn't we?" He let the question float a moment. "You know we had a hired hand once when I was little. He had a wooden leg and yet he was a good rider, a good herder and. . . ." Dan paused and looked at Hally. "I think I could ride again," he said. "I mean I really want to. That must count for something. Don't you think?" Hally gazed into his eyes, seeing that mixture of ambition and humor and hope that was familiar now.

"I'm going to play my flute again," she heard herself saying. "I'll go through any amount of retraining—whatever it takes to get my lip firm and make my breathing normal."

"You'll make it," he said, "and so will I, one way or another." Hally smiled, then looked out of the window and sighed.

"I don't know," she said. "You have more options, more ways to adjust things, than I do and . . . and . . . I don't know. I want to be optimistic." She looked back at Dan. "God knows, I'll work. But I don't know." Dan studied her a moment, as she sat gazing out at the lawn, then he reached out his hand.

"I'm awfully glad you're here."

Hally turned back at his touch. "You just like me now because I don't have a tube in my nose anymore."

Dan laughed and squeezed her fingers. "That's right," he said. "That's why I like you. My best hospital pal," he whispered and lifted her hand to his lips. He looked at her a moment over the back of her hand. "I don't want to be a problem to you," he whispered. "A nuisance or anything."

Hally smiled, lest he suspect the sudden sliding she felt in her abdomen. "You're not a problem," she said.

17

Hally glanced behind her to make sure the hall was empty, then opened the door to the roof passageway and stepped outside. The narrow walkway between the two buildings was open to the bright October sky and the blue space that suddenly enveloped Hally made her cling to the door handle a moment, startled by the rush of clean air and the brilliant colors around her. She stepped forward, and, as the heavy door swung shut behind her, she saw Artemis leaning her elbows on the metal railing, staring out. The young woman turned at the noise of the door and smiled at Hally. "This is beautiful," Hally breathed and moved to the railing beside her. "I've never been up here before. It's my first time outside. Nobody knows."

"Nothing like a little healthy rebellion to restore the spirits," Artemis said. "I won't tell."

"It's chilly," Hally said and rested her crutches against the railing to clutch her arms around her. "But then October's almost over."

Artemis pointed to two little girls, who were walking along the sidewalk beyond the hospital fence, one dressed as a witch in a tall, black hat, the other as a tiger with a striped tail hanging down behind her. "Is it Halloween already?" Hally demanded. Artemis nodded. "Oh Lord," Hally said and stared, as the little girls rounded the corner. "I used to love dressing up. I was a princess once. My mother made me a tinfoil crown and I wore one of her old evening dresses. Then for two or three years I went as a flutist." Hally leaned on her elbows beside Artemis.

"A flutist?" Artemis asked.

"Yes. I wore the top of my father's tuxedo and carried my flute case. I called myself Hally Flute until I was fourteen. Signed letters, Hally F. I was kind of pretentious."

"You were intense."

"I guess. My best friend was Barbara Oboe, but she switched to Economics later." Hally smiled and looked around her again. "You know it's hard to realize that life just keeps on going out there—Halloween, school, pumpkins. I mean I feel as though *everybody's* waiting to find out when they can begin on solid food, or get up in a wheelchair, or whether they'll wear leg braces."

"Or whether they'll survive," Artemis added. She gazed up at the glint of a plane high in the blueness. "Remember the time I sat in your room your first night here?"

"That seems a year ago, doesn't it?" Hally said slowly.

"A lot's happened," Artemis said.

"But so slowly," Hally added. "I mean it's almost four months now. Some people are getting discharged. Maureen's leaving Friday, you know. But not me. I'm still stuck." She sighed again and pointed to a lone fir in the driveway circle below. "I just hope I'm not here when they put Christmas lights on that tree down there," she said and they both laughed.

"When do you think they'll get Dan up?" Hally asked. "He's been in that room for weeks now." Hally thought of the half-pulled blinds at Dan's window, his pillow ticking slings hanging down, and the bedtray pushed back, blocking the door. She watched a crow settle on the roof nearby; its black wings gleamed in the sun. It seemed unbelievable that this vivid reality outdoors could be so close to that other claustrophobic one down below.

"I don't know," Artemis said. "Soon maybe." She turned to look at Hally. "Dan's come to mean a lot to you, hasn't he?"

"Yes, sort of," Hally admitted and paused. "Sometimes I think I'm kind of in love with him. But last summer I had a crush on Dr. Baldwin. So I'm not sure."

"You know," Artemis said. "Crushes, love, all that, can be a natural part of the recovery process."

"I guess," Hally answered. "I mean I am in love with Dan in a way. He's become very important to me. I feel happy with him. But I don't know. It's all so unreal. Sort of suspended, you know, as though we were becalmed in this ship of a hospital out on the ocean somewhere."

Artemis laughed. "So the Wahl's a ship?"

"Sort of," Hally said. "An ocean liner maybe. I mean it's so remote from the rest of the world, so. . . . " She smiled. "It's certainly not elegant though. No champagne cocktails or moonlight dancing on the deck." Hally laughed and tipped her head back to look up at the sky again.

"I'd probably hate an ocean cruise actually." She paused. "All my life—my adult life anyway—I've had goals, things I was trying to get to, musical techniques, interpretations. Now I don't know. I feel I'm drifting and. . . . "

"Don't torture yourself, Hal," Artemis broke in. She glanced at her watch. "Listen. We better get back."

Hally stood at Dan's window waving, as Dan watched her from his bed. "There she goes," Hally reported. "Ted's backing the station wagon and everybody's waving. Half the family's in that car. I can see Michael in the front, beside Maureen, and Connaught in the back with Kevin, I think. They're all waving. The car looks so funny with all of those arms sticking out." Hally waved again, then felt a sudden rush of irritation as she glanced back at Dan. "Damn," she said. "I wish you could see it." She felt all at once as if it was laziness or lack of interest that kept him stretched in bed, with his back to the window, not paralysis. She looked out at the car again. "They're starting down the driveway," she continued. "Did you hear that beep?" Hally looked at Dan again. Why did she always have to be the reporter, she thought, but she went on. "Now they're going through the gates and out into the street. Good-bye, Maureen. Good-bye."

Hally slumped into the armchair and sighed. "Oh God," she said. "I should be happy for her and . . . I mean I am. But it's so . . . ." Her voice shook. "Oh damn," she said.

"She and Ted really put the screws on Mostello to get her discharged, didn't they?" Dan said.

"In a way," Hally answered. "But she's realistic. She knows she'll never walk again and, as for her breathing, Ted's a respiratory specialist after all."

"I know." Dan nodded. "It still seems sort of dangerous though."

"Oh, I don't know," Hally said. "Why not get out of this dump if you possibly can? I mean God, I'd take the chance if I could." She leaned back in the chair and sighed. "Boy, I'm going to miss her. Remember the nutty things she'd do? That birthday party she gave herself and the Chanel No. 5 she used to spray around her room. Oh God. It's going to seem so dull around here without her."

Dan gazed at Hally a moment, then pulled himself up a little further on his elbow. "We'll follow," he said. "It's not that far off. A month for me maybe, less for you, probably."

"More," Hally said, "I'm still on fluids, remember?"

The elevator clanged, as it settled on the first floor. They heard the familiar bump of the meal cart being pulled off and smelled the odor of steamy food, as the cart was pushed down the hall. There was a loud rap on the door. "Room service for two?" Lou put two trays on the bedtray, lifted the round metal top from Dan's plate with a flourish, and bowed.

"Marvelous," Dan said, smiling. "Cordon bleu?"

"*Mais,* of course, monsieur," Lou said and twisted the ends of an imaginary moustache. Hally settled her smaller tray on the table beside the armchair, and sat down again, unsmiling. She stared at her tray while Lou continued to kid and talk. He bowed again and left the room finally. Hally sighed.

"Do we have to go through that routine every night?" she sulked. "It loses a little of its witty flavor the sixtieth time." Dan glanced at her without answering and unfolded his napkin. "Look at this," Hally said and pointed to her tray. "Greasy chicken soup again and apple juice. I've been on a liquid diet for six weeks and this is all they can think of to give me every single night." She rose and plunked her tray on the bed table. "Hey," she said, staring down at Dan's plate. "You've got french fries." She picked one up and held it in front of her. "I bet I could swallow that." She bit off the end, chewed it, and dropped it down. She reached for another and put it into her mouth.

"Don't, Hal," Dan said and spread his hand across the plate. "Don't. You'll only get into trouble." But Hally snatched up the oval dish of potatoes and sat down in the armchair.

"I'm fine," she said, dropping two more. "I thought I could do this. I'm going to tell Baldwin tomorrow. I'm going to show him that . . . ." Her words stuck and a gagging noise began. Dan yanked at his bell cord. The sound of Hally's loud raking cough blanketed the room, interspersed with deep shuddering gasps. Dr. Baldwin rushed in, followed by Miss Lord.

"Get the suction machine," Dr. Baldwin ordered and stooped down beside Hally, who was bent over one arm of the chair. He grasped her chin with one hand and punched her diaphragm sharply with his clenched fist. Hally stared at him wildly a moment, then flopped over the chair arm and vomited, spattering the floor with bloody saliva and gooey bits of potato. She hung there, gasping, making loud honking noises, as she struggled for breath. Miss Lord returned, pushing a collection of bottles and black tubes on a wheeled table.

"Okay," Dr. Baldwin said. "We've got some of it, Hally. But not all. I've got to put this tube down." Hally nodded weakly as Dr. Baldwin tipped her head back and pushed a black tube down her throat. A motor started up with a low whirring noise and the large bottle began to fill with pinkish water and brown potato flecks. Dr. Baldwin turned off the motor after a moment and extracted the tube. "What were you eating anyway?" Hally pointed at the remaining pile of french fries in the dish beside her, then leaned over to spit again. Dr. Baldwin stared. "Maybe this'll teach you a lesson," he said. "We're not just being mean, you know." He sighed. "The fact is Hally, you're still in a dangerous condition. Just because you're up on crutches and don't have pain. I mean that's why you're here. Don't you see that? You can manage the liquid diet now and later when you get some more muscle return, you'll graduate to soft food. For now you've just got to . . . ." He studied her wearily. "But you understand all that." Hally nodded and closed her eyes.

Dr. Baldwin pulled the suction machine out into the hall and Dan turned to Hally. "Don't you ever do that again," he whispered angrily. "That was so stupid. That was. . . . " Hally lifted her head and stared at him in surprise. His face looked white and his chin was shaking.

"I'm sorry," Hally began. "I just wanted to see if. . . . " Miss Lord appeared with a mop and they watched silently as she cleaned the floor.

"I only wanted to see if I could swallow a little," Hally continued, as Miss Lord carried the mop out into the hall.

"I don't care. It was so dangerous, so stupid . . . so. . . . " Hally stared at Dan again. Everything was changeable and fragile, she thought. Swallowing was dangerous and so was friendship or love.

Dr. Baldwin returned to the room and stood at the bottom of the bed, leaning against the metal frame. "Going to take a little break this week-end." He took his glasses off and rubbed them on the lapel of his medical coat. "Going up to the White Mountains." He resettled the glasses. "First time away since last June."

"Going to ski?" Dan asked. It was a relief to think about the head resident. He let his eyes travel down the doctor's pants legs, half-covered by the medical coat, and took in his athletic-looking rubber soled shoes. He had some shoes like that at home in the closet, Dan thought, though his were a darker brown. He was a pretty good skier himself, cross-country anyway.

Dr. Baldwin shifted, as if to shrug off Dan's gaze. "We hope to. They've had some snow. Beautiful clear days." He smiled. "Well, I better get a move on." He turned to the door, then looked back at them. "Get to bed soon, Hally. You'll feel okay by morning." He waved. "See you Monday."

Dan and Hally sat listening a moment to the sound of the doctor's footsteps receding down the hall. They heard him stop and imagined him standing at the nurses' desk a moment. Then the sound came again, far off, but distinct, ending as the elevator clanged.

"It's weird to think he can just leave this place," Dan said. "That he goes out into the parking lot and just drives home." Hally nodded.

"And off to the White Mountains," she said, "while we stay here, trapped." She closed her eyes. There is no ski slope, no lodge full of skiers, no snowy landscape to distract us, she thought. The feelings building between us in this crowded, over-familiar space can't be covered; we will have to confront them soon.

18

Hally held the elevator door open with her hip and pulled Dan's wheelchair backward out into the hall. Dan peered around him eagerly, but a wide band, strapped across his chest and tied behind, held him upright in the chair and prevented him from twisting to look behind. "Don't go too fast," he said, as Hally started pushing him. "This is historic. I want to see everything."

"I know, I know." Hally's voice was high with excitement. "But we need to get there before your glutes start hurting. I told Kevin we'd be up around three."

Glutes, for gluteus medius, Hally thought. Four months ago she'd never even heard the term, but now they used it twice a day or more, referring to those crucial muscles at the back of the thighs. She backed the chair through a swinging door, and pushed Dan down the center aisle.

The men's ward consisted of a group of beds arranged in a rough semi-circle at the sunny end of the long room. A smiling young man, who looked like Gene Autry in a cowboy hat and jeans, slid from his horse to light up, as two men in wheelchairs gazed at the TV image, which was queerly striated and unaccompanied by any sound. Dan peered around him. The room seemed partially deserted, but this was the ward at last.

Hally pushed Dan over to Kevin Christy, who sat in the wheelchair nearest the television. He was the man Hally had met on a rocking bed during her first visit to the respirator ward, Dan remembered, and he had bad arms. An aluminum frame, attached to the back of the wheelchair, curved above the man's head and his forearms were supported by two pillow ticking slings, which hung down from it. "So you finally brought your friend upstairs," the man said to Hally and enclosed Dan in his smile. "Name's Kevin," he said. "How are you?" he nodded at his suspended hands to explain the lack of a handshake and Dan smiled back. The man looked surprisingly vigorous, with his curly reddish hair, his arms and neck still tan, despite weeks in the hospital. Dan thought of Harley back at the ranch and glanced down at the man's knees. Kevin used to be a telephone pole climber for Bell, Hally had said. He won't be doing that again, Dan thought, and saw his own desk, the row of sloping books at the back, the shoebox file, and the typewriter; he was lucky. He shook his head to jostle the image. "It's great to be here," he said. "I've heard a lot about you."

"We've heard about you too," Kevin said. "You've got to meet the gang." He turned. "That's Henry," he began and pointed to a man behind him, who was hunched over a thick book that looked like a Bible. "Henry's the reader." The man raised his head. His staring eyes were magnified by the thick lenses of his glasses and his forehead was marked with a wide piece of adhesive tape, just as Hally's had been, holding a dangling tube. He did not comment, but looked down at his book again, as the other man beside the TV turned his wheelchair toward Dan. His face was pocked, yet handsome and there something defiant in his manner as he rolled himself up close to Dan.

"So the bourgeoisie from the private rooms downstairs has come up to visit the ward proletariat," he said and thrust out his chin. "How do you rate that room down there anyway?" he demanded. "The March of Dimes sure isn't paying for it."

"Ah, Jack, knock it off. Will ya?" Kevin broke in. "The guy just came up to visit."

"If we're the bourgeoisie," Dan started. "God help the ruling class." He smiled nervously, but the man beside him did not respond. Dan heard Hally give an uneasy laugh, as a loud, nasal voice behind them announced, "The Lord giveth many mysteries that man can neither know nor see." Dan turned his head. The words came from the man with the Bible. His bulbar voice was solemn, despite its nasality. "Many mysteries," he repeated. "It is not for man to question."

"We call him Isaiah," Kevin whispered to Dan. "We get a lot of this." The belligerent man beside Dan rolled his eyes upward and shook his head. Dan shook his head in imitation, grateful to the Bible reader for his distraction. "That's Jack beside you," Kevin said. "Always good for laughs." Dan turned; he had heard about Jack. Hally had mentioned him in her reports of her ward visits. He was the real leader, she said, bright, but moody and critical.

"You'll meet the others soon. Billy's up the hall flirting with the nurses and Ted. . . ." Kevin nodded at a body curled on a bed in the corner. "He's sleeping as usual."

"So how're you doing with the muscles?" Jack demanded. "You got any abdominals left?"

"Not a lot," Dan told him, relieved at the shift in subject matter. "Still on enemas every day. But I'm up in this vehicle at last." Jack nodded.

"What kind of therapy are you getting? Leg stretching? Anything else?"

"That's pretty much it right now," Dan said. Jack nodded again and pulled himself closer.

"What do you think of this place?" he asked. "Of Mostello? You think he's the brilliant diagnostician people say he is?"

"Well, I guess he saved my life," Dan started and paused. "I mean he's obviously very good in the field. I'm willing to stick with him a while longer. But I don't know. I get kind of sick of his God Almighty act!" Jack's face moved into a smile. He looked at Kevin, then back at Dan.

"I know what you mean," Jack agreed. "Here in his blue heaven." He glanced at the wall beyond him. "Puke green rather. God, if this is heaven, I wonder what the other place is like." The others laughed and Dan watched Jack as the sound settled. Funny that Hally hadn't said more about him. Was he the kind she really liked, he wondered, tough, experienced, unsentimental—not a rich man's son studying an impractical subject like history. He tried to twist to look back at her, but Jack leaned toward him again.

"So you're a graduate student at Harvard. Right?" he paused. "What are you planning to do? Teach? Write books?"

"A little of both, I hope," Dan began. He gazed at the door, exhausted by the man's hostility. The long-anticipated adventure of coming up to this place had gone sour; his glutes and back were aching.

"I'm a gaffer myself, or I was," Jack offered. "You know what that is?"

"Part of a production crew," Dan ventured. "The guy who holds the mike?"

"There you go. Harvard's good for something." Jack smiled. "I never got to finish college. But I've done some script work. City beat mostly. I work for radio—WEEI. I won't be doing the gaffer stuff now. We've got a strong union though. They'll take care of me. Besides I was pretty good at the script biz." Dan gazed at Jack again. Where was he from, he wondered. What other kinds of writing had he done?

"So what's the deal with you two anyway?" Jack demanded. He gave a snort and looked up at Hally. "You engaged or something? You've got rooms next door to each other. Right?" Dan saw Hally give Jack a teasing smile.

"We're thinking about tearing down the wall in between," Dan said. "It'd be a lot more convenient." Jack laughed and Kevin joined in.

There was a sound of rapid footsteps approaching. Hally turned. "Oh Lord, it's Mrs. Harding," she said. "She told me she'd come up after us, if I didn't have you back in your room by three."

"Ah, the hell with Harding," Jack said, as the therapist strode toward them, her black ponytail bouncing on her shoulders.

"It's after time," she began. "Dan, you're going to have some serious pain tonight, if we don't get you back in bed."

"Come again," Kevin urged.

"Yeah, pal," Jack joined in, "Come back tomorrow, why don't you? We'll be here." Dan smiled and promised, but his thighs were throbbing and the shapes and colors of beds, bathrobes, and magazines slid together in a dizzy blur, as Mrs. Harding pushed him up the aisle and down the hall to the elevator.

19

*H*ally came out of the supply closet, carrying a pair of scissors and a towel. She paused by the door to the front passageway a moment and looked out, then hung on her crutch rests and stared. The single fir tree in the driveway circle stood glittering in the cold dark—its branches decked with red and orange lights. Hally sighed, then glanced down at the scissors she was holding, and limped down the hall.

"The time has come," Hally announced as she put the towel and scissors on the bed. Dan, who was sitting in his wheelchair, held up a Christmas card from the collection in his lap and Hally stooped to peer at it. "Great," she said. "I'll add it to the exhibit." She knelt on the bed and pinned the card to one of the two long strips of red cloth she had taped to the wall. A knitted stocking hung from the end of the bedframe and a red poinsettia dominated the bureau. Hally draped the towel around Dan's shoulders and opened and shut the long scissors. "I really am quite good at this," she said, "I've even done my brother-in-law."

"I trust you," Dan said smiling. "I am as putty in your hands." Hally laughed and began to snip.

"You know I feel a little nervous about Mom's Christmas dinner plan," she said. "I mean our apartment is small and well . . . it's sort of shabby. I mean I'm not sure your mother will really. . . ."

"Don't worry," Dan broke in. "It'll be fine. Esther's great to invite us all. A hotel Christmas could be kind of grim."

"I guess our real problem is whether Mostello'll give me permission to go," Hally interrupted. "I mean I told him we'd take the suction machine.

But you know him. He'll wait to the last minute to hand down his verdict." She snipped some hair over one ear and stepped back to look. "All I say is if you get to go to my house for Christmas dinner and I have to stay here . . . ."

"Oh, he'll let you go," Dan said. "He can't not. We just have to be careful. That's all." Hally nodded and snipped again.

"It's funny, isn't it?" she said, moving around to the front. "I mean here you are struggling to get the strength to sit upright for two hours and waiting and waiting for that damn leg brace to come and meantime I'm up and dressed and whipping around and even going without my crutches a lot of the time and yet it's me that's complicating things. I'm the one in real danger, or so Mostello says."

"It is funny. But it's going to work," Dan said. He waited for Hally to finish cutting the hair above his ear, then added, "I'm so damn excited. Do you realize in just five more days we're actually going to see the outside world again after six months—six whole months in this place. It's going to be incredible." He smiled at Hally and lifted one hand in a cheering gesture. "Just plain incredible."

"It will be," Hally said. She glanced out the window, moving a little so that she could see beyond the reflection of the lamp to the lights at the end of the driveway and the lighted windows of the brick apartment house across the street. There were two windows she could see clearly from this room and her own—a piece of a picture on the wall in one, a lamp in the other. She had been thinking about the lives in those room for months, she realized, and bent over Dan to snip again.

"It's funny," she said. "I was determined to try my flute by the end of November, no matter what, and I still haven't even got it. But right now with you and Christmas . . . I mean I don't know, it just doesn't seem so urgent anymore." She finished her trimming and surveyed Dan from the front. He smiled and she leaned down. "The barber's privilege," she said and kissed him on the cheek.

"I'm fond of the barber." Dan caught her hand in his. "You know I was thinking this morning how much better life is now. Better, bigger. All our friends on the ward, the respirator ward too, the different feel to the days, the trip out at Christmas, and . . . and most of all you." Hally smiled and pulled her hand back, as the shuffling sound of slippers came from the hall. They turned to see Billy, an adolescent bulbar case from the men's ward, standing in the doorway. He was wearing a spotted maroon bathrobe, and he looked excited as he pressed his forefinger to the tracheotomy tube in his throat before he spoke. "Hey, you two," he called into the room in his thick voice. "Guess what? There's big doings on the convalescent ward. A whole pack of good-looking girls are in there singing carols."

"Carols?" Dan said. "Already?"

"Hell, man. It's only five days to Christmas. You expect them to come out to some hospital and sing on Christmas Eve?" Dan laughed and pushed himself forward.

"And it's going on right now?"

"You betcha." Billy nodded. "You guys get down there quick. I'm going up to tell the ward."

The center aisle of the convalescent ward was crowded with young girls, who stood bunched together singing. They held paperback carol books between them and looked up with nervous smiles, then down at their music again. The sounds filled the long room, muffling the watery noises of the tracheotomy tubes close by and the intermittent roars of the oxygen pumps. Hally gazed down the rows of rocking beds, as she stood leaning against the wall, one arm resting on the back of Dan's chair. Red tinsel letters spelling "Merry Christmas" were pasted to the window at the end. She looked along the walls, surveying the effect of the Christmas cards she had scotch taped to the tiles on either side, watching them flutter as the rocking beds moved slowly up and down. Over half the convalescent ward had graduated to rocking beds, she realized, and counted the seven respirators still left. They were in the aftermath of the epidemic now.

Hally peered at a gray-haired woman who sat playing *O Little Town of Bethlehem* on a small electric organ by the door, while the girls harmonized. Jack sat in his new walker on her other side and Kevin was in his wheelchair, while Billy leaned against the bed near the door. He caught Dan's eye and lifted one hand to draw a sexy silhouette in the air, making Dan chuckle. Hally stroked Dan's neck and giggled when Jack shook his head in mock disapproval.

The gray-haired woman looked back at them and tipped her head, indicating that the audience along the wall should join the singing. Dan's bass voice rung out. "The first Noël, the angels did say. . . . " Hally raised her hand to hold her lip in place and joined in. What did it matter if her voice sounded thick and wavery; she sang out with the rest. *The Holly and the Ivy* followed and then *Good King Wenceslas*. When the girls embarked on *O Holy Night*, Jack leaned toward Hally and whispered, "This one always gets loused up."

"They've pitched it too high," Hally whispered back. "Where are they from anyway?"

"Some convent school nearby," Jack said. "Saint Mary's, Saint something. I don't know." The girls were folding their music. They smiled at the patients on the rocking beds and then at those in the row of wheelchairs along the wall. They were glad to be leaving, Hally realized. How terrifying it would be to stand in this crowded room for the first time, with respirators and rocking beds, and half-paralyzed men in wheelchairs, and a woman on crutches with a crooked smile. It would be frightening, especially if you were only sixteen. "Good-bye." "Merry Christmas," the voices called back and forth. The girls pushed through the swinging doors and all at once the room seemed spacious and familiar again.

"Well, what did you think of those little do-gooders?" Jack said, turning his walker to Dan.

"They weren't bad." Dan smiled. "Not bad."

"Damn good, I'd say," Jack told him, "especially when you consider they were scared shitless." He smiled broadly and glanced around the group, as the others laughed. Dan patted his knee and Hally sat down on his lap, draping her legs in her red corduroy pants over the arm of the wheelchair. Dan tickled her; she twisted and struggled to her feet, as the group laughed again.

"You shoulda done that while them girls were here, Dan," Billy called. "Given them something to think about."

"Hey, Hal. They left that organ," Dan said. "Why don't you give it a try?"

Hally hesitated, then limped to the organ and sat down. She played some chords, and paused. How strange it felt to make musical sounds after so long, even the tinny electronic noises of this instrument. She played another chord combination and shivered, then clutched her arms around her. Part of her wanted to rise and rush up the hall to her room. The flute was her love, her instrument, not this vulgar electric thing. But Dan had pulled himself up behind her and Jack was leaning from his walker flipping the pages of the carol book on the music stand.

"Here. Start with this one," he ordered. Hally glanced back at the others and tried the first bars of *God Rest Ye Merry Gentlemen.* Dan sang out strongly and Miss Flaherty leaned on the back of Kevin's chair, singing too. Hally moved into *Silent Night* and on to *We Three Kings.* The familiar music, weighted with its memories, rose around them.

"Okay. One more, Hally," Miss Flaherty announced. "Then you people have got to get to bed." Hally played *O Come All Ye Faithful* and they all sang. As the carol ended, the group looked around at each other smiling, laughing a little to disguise a sudden sense of closeness.

"If you've gotta get a disease," Jack declared, "this is the best or the worst," he added, laughing. "Getting stuck with a bunch of clowns like you guys for six months. Jeez."

"Come on, kids," Miss Flaherty urged. "You've got to get to bed. It's almost nine."

Dan lay flat in his dim room, which was lit only by the gooseneck lamp, while Hally stretched to push the canvas slings up on the overhead bar above him. She poured some water into a paper cup, inserted the bent straw, and put the cup within his reach on the bedtray. "What an evening," she said and sighed as she sank into the armchair. "I'll remember this a long time." She glanced out into the hall. "Funny how quiet it is now after all that singing and laughing." She hooked one slippered foot under the bar that ran parallel to Dan's mattress and he reached out and clasped her ankle. They sat in silence a moment.

"You've got to get to bed," Miss Lord announced, glaring at them from the doorway. Her eyes moved from the neck of Hally's bathrobe, where the lace frill on her nightgown poked up, to Dan's hand, holding her bare ankle. Hally met the nurse's stare.

"Two more minutes," she said. "I always take my chloral in here anyway, then I go back to my room."

"Hmph," Miss Lord sniffed and turned. "You'd better."

"God in heaven," Dan said, as her footsteps retreated. "What's wrong with her? You've taken your sleeping stuff in here for weeks now."

"Oh, she's just cross because she's on by herself tonight. Marge went home early."

"So that's why it's so quiet out there," Dan said. "We're alone almost."

"As alone as we'll ever be here," Hally said and smiled.

"I have a question for you." Dan withdrew his hand and scrabbled on the sheet a moment to push himself up on his elbow. He got himself balanced and paused. "Will you marry me, Hal?" he asked.

"Dan," Hally breathed. She brought her foot to the floor and stared at him. "Dan."

"Not tonight or soon, but sometime," Dan hurried on. "I mean there'd be problems. Sure. But think of it—being together, sharing stuff, my work, your music, friends." He stopped and paused again. "I love you, Hal. I want to go on together—like now." He paused. "Only better, because we'd both be well—or almost."

"Dan," Hally breathed again. She rose from the chair and sat close beside him on the bed. "I want to go on together too," she whispered and leaned down to kiss him. But Dan's elbow slipped and he tipped forward so that her kiss landed on his ear. Dan eased onto his back and smiled as Hally bent over him again. They kissed, pressing their lips together hesitantly at first, then exploring them with their tongues, sucking, pulling finally, as their hands fumbled. Dan clutched Hally's bathrobe; his fingers stroked her neck and moved down to her breast, as she caressed his ears. There was a sound in the hall and Hally pulled back.

"We don't want old Lord to see us," she whispered.

"Damn," Dan muttered, but he was smiling. "Confirm all her suspicions. Sex rears its ugly head again." He laughed softly.

"Oh Dan." Hally gazed down at him. "I'm so in love with you."

"And me with you," Dan said. "I want to share everything. You know? Show you all the stuff I love. I can't wait until you see Valley, the mountains, the view, and my horse, Star. Oh God, she's such a beauty. We'll have such fun."

Hally pushed back her hair and glanced beyond Dan to the dark window. For a moment Marian seemed more vivid to her than the mountains or Dan's beloved horse, Marian with her blue-gray hair, moving among the flowered cretonne-covered couches, that Hally imagined in her living room. "What about your family?" she said. "Your mother? I'm not sure she's going to be too pleased. I can't blame her really. After all, I'm hardly the perfect bride. I've been very sick too."

"I know, I know," Dan said. "They'll worry, of course. But give them time. They'll love you when they know you. Dad already does."

"I don't know," Hally said, but she was smiling down at him. Time was the important thing. His parents, Valley, Star—all of that was a long way off. Meanwhile she and Dan would recuperate happily here, planning their lives together. They would live in Cambridge, somewhere small and cozy when they married, she thought, letting her imagination dart ahead, and if Dan could never ride again, if he had to use a cane. . . . Well, they would face that later. He would still write and teach and . . . .

"You know I think I could modify my Oregon Trail stuff somehow," Dan began. "I mean it doesn't have to involve all that hiking and backpacking. I could still . . . ." He smiled as Hally stroked a frown line in his forehead. "We'll work all that stuff out. The important thing is . . . ." He tipped his head back, as she bent to kiss him again. Hally straightened and sat gazing down at Dan. He would definitely figure out a way of doing that thesis and she and Marian would definitely become friends, since they both loved Dan. But what of her flute? The thought slapped against her and she drew in her breath.

"There's an awful lot to work out," Hally said and put one hand to her lip.

"Yes," he answered, "but there's an awful lot to look forward to, too."

20

Dan sat waiting in the passenger seat of a rented Cadillac, as Roy helped his father fold the borrowed wheelchair and fit it into the trunk. Hally, who was in back with Marian, felt enveloped in the dizzying richness of Marian's perfume. Her elegant fur jacket and silk scarf had made Hally feel frumpy, when she climbed into the car minutes earlier. But she forgot her self-consciousness in her excitement when the car started and turned to wave to Roy, left behind in the driveway. Hally pulled in her breath as they passed between the brick gate posts with their round lamps; the street was almost deserted on this bright Christmas morning. Hally peered at the apartment building opposite the gate, remembering the nights she had gazed out at it, longing to be there or anywhere but the hospital. The scuffed front door surprised her and the trash can, lying on its side nearby. A group of pigeons was clustered by the curb. Hally could see the intricate designs on their wings, but their flat, red-ringed eyes looked strange. A diamond of light gleamed from the chrome side of a parked car, and beyond it was a hexagonal stop sign in brilliant yellow. The car turned, following the shiny trolley tracks. "Look at that little girl," Hally exclaimed, as two children came down a driveway, one pushing a baby carriage. "I bet the doll inside is a brand new Christmas present, maybe the carriage too."

"What about the brother though," Dan said, pointing to a little boy, trailing behind. "He only got a cap." They laughed as Mr. Lewis drove on.

Sights replaced each other in kaleidoscopic fashion; a man in a red and black lumberman's jacket was peering under the raised hood of his car, while a huge bottle of Schenley's whiskey rocked up and down in a slow pouring movement on a billboard above him. A gas station window, displaying a pyramid of Pennzoil cans, was decorated with cotton balls and sparkles. They passed houses, where cold bushes in front glittered with red and orange Christmas lights, and front doors were decorated with plastic wreaths, poinsettia leaves, and paper Santa Clauses. When Mr. Lewis turned onto Storrow Drive, the river spread before them, its crinkled water, shining in the sun. "Look at that," Dan exclaimed. "It's so blue and bright. Isn't it amazing?" He turned back to Hally.

"We've been living in a dull green world so long, we don't even know what real colors are," she told him. "Just dirty browns and cracked green walls and . . . ." She let the sentence hang and peered out again. Her mouth was dry and her jaws were trembling. But this was only the beginning, she reminded herself. There was home and Mom, and the reunion with Rosie, and then . . . then after the dinner, the pie and the mints, Dan would tell them. They had agreed that he would begin. There was so much and yet she must not appear feverish and excited. Marian would be bound to have her doubts about Dan's engagement to another polio patient—Tom too, probably. She must show them how strong she was, how steady and sane.

The Blessings' dining room felt crowded with the table opened out so that one side almost touched the keyboard of the piano and the lace tablecloth was cluttered with dessert dishes and wine glasses. Mr. Lewis sat at the end of the table, finishing a sliver of apple pie while Marian, who was sitting under the portrait on the wall, dabbed her lips with her napkin and tucked it back in her lap.

"More pie anybody?" Esther asked. She looked a little flushed in her black wool dress, and a lock of white hair had slipped down over one ear.

"Couldn't possibly, Esther," Tom Lewis said. "But thank you anyway."

"What about wine?" Esther smiled at Tom.

"I think we need a refill, Esther," Dan said, lifting his glass. "Hal and I have an announcement to make." Hally smiled and covered her lip with one hand, as she stared down at the tablecloth. She had only been allowed a glass of apple juice and she felt a sudden ache of hunger for her mushy portion of chicken back at the hospital and her mound of orange squash.

"We've decided we want to get married," Dan began and looked from his father to Esther and then across the table at his mother. "Nothing soon, of course, nothing sudden. Obviously we both have a whole lot of stuff to figure out first. But we want you three to know that that's definitely in our long range plans."

There was a pause and the sound of a breath being drawn in as Marian pressed one hand to her throat. She turned to her husband with an urgent look. Tom nodded at her slightly, clasped his glass, and raised it. "I think this is . . . is wonderful," he started, "but. . . ."

Esther rose. She slipped around behind Dan's wheelchair and bent to kiss him. "It's wonderful," she said; she put one arm around Dan and the other around Hally. "It makes a wonderful Christmas more wonderful still." She hugged Dan to her and looked across the table at Marian. "We've all had to learn to take things one at a time and whenever this happens, this year, next, or five years from now, it will be wonderful." She patted Dan's shoulder. "You know I was afraid I might lose you as my old friend, just because you're getting well, Dan. But now you're going to be my son-in-law." She hugged him again.

There was a scratching of toenails on the bare floor as Rosie scrabbled to her feet and poked her graying muzzle out from under the tablecloth. She looked up at Hally with her brown eyes, which were partly obscured with a bluish film, then plunked her head down on Dan's knee. "That's a sign," Hally said. "She's welcoming you." But she felt the tension spread out around them, as Tom's toast hung interrupted. This news had clearly surprised the Lewises, who had not been able to visit weekly like Mom, and lacked her more immediate sense of what was going on. They seemed enveloped in shock. Their only son had announced that he would marry a crippled girl with a nasal voice, who could not swallow, and who had been even sicker than he.

"This is indeed wonderful," Tom began, as they raised their glasses. "But we just hope—Marian and I—I mean we're very glad that you aren't going to rush into this. As Dan says, there's a lot to work out and time is so important." Hally stared down at the empty champagne glass again. Time, she thought. The Lewises probably believed that she and Dan would realize the impossibility of this romantic plan in time. They would get discouraged and frustrated, as the weeks went by and gradually they would abandon the affair. Time—it was a wise, old tactic. Were they right? Would it work?

"We just hope you won't rush," Marian said and her glass trembled as she held it up. "We want you both to be healthy again first." Hally looked down at the gray hairs in Rosie's muzzle. A dizzy fatigue had enclosed her all at once, pressing her in. She thought of her hospital room with the bed, her blue nightgown. Maybe the Lewises were right. Maybe it was too much, too soon.

She looked over at Dan and saw the dark indentations below his eyes and the gray look of his thin face. His glutes must be aching, she thought, his back too. Oh God, you're right; she glanced across the table at Marian. We're too tired; we're still too sick. We need the hospital now.

21

*D*r. Baldwin stopped in Dan's room one gray morning after New Year's. "You said you had something you wanted to talk to me about," he said and leaned against the bedframe.

"Yes, I. . . ." Dan glanced out into the hall, then back at the doctor. "Now that we've. . . ." Dan began and looked out into the hall again. "Now that I've survived the Christmas outing, how about letting me go out another time? I mean I. . . ."

"Sure, sure." Dr. Baldwin's voice had an impatient edge. He straightened and poked his glasses up into place. "I told you when the weather gets better, when the ice melts and. . . ."

"I know," Dan said. "That's not what I wanted to ask." He looked down at his knees, covered with a white bath blanket. "I wanted to ask you if. . . ." He paused. "Can you sit down? I mean can you take a minute?" Dr. Baldwin nodded and sat down on the bed. "I've been seeing a lot of Hally lately." The doctor nodded again and covered his knees with his hands.

"And?" Dr. Baldwin asked. Dan drew in his breath and raised his head.

"Is there something the matter with me?" he demanded. "I mean has this damn disease taken that too?" Dr. Baldwin sighed and took a metal mallet for testing reflexes from the pocket of his white coat.

"No, probably not," he said. "But you won't feel the old way for a while."

"How long?" Dan demanded.

"No way of knowing really." Dr. Baldwin met Dan's eyes. "A year.

Maybe more. It could be less. Your body's undergone a terrific trauma. It's different in every case. It might be just a matter of a month or two."

"Oh God." Dan let his breath out slowly and stared down at the floor. "A few months ago it didn't matter much, but now . . . ." He paused and glanced out into the hall. "You see, Hally and I are planning to get married. Later, I mean, of course."

"That's great." Dr. Baldwin smiled. "Good for you." The smile faded and his face became serious again. "You know your very eagerness could be a factor right now. You could talk to Mostello, if you want, or your own doctor. But my guess is there's really not much you can do, but wait and try not to worry."

"Try not to worry," Dan repeated. "Hell, I just told you I want to get married. I'm in love. How can you sit there and say, 'Try not to worry'?" His voice sounded loud and shaky with emotion and he paused. "I'm sorry," he added. "I . . . I . . . ."

"I know." Dr. Baldwin looked down at the mallet and sighed. "I hear that phrase in my sleep. All of medical technology and modern science and we end up repeating it two, three times a day sometimes, 'Try not to worry. Wait.' " He put the mallet back in his pocket and looked at Dan again. "Listen. That's great news about you and Hally." He reached out to Dan and shook his hand. Then he rose and turned to the door, "Don't brood about this sex thing," he added, turning back again. "Chances are you'll be fine. A little time, a little patience, like all the rest of it. Okay?"

Dan nodded his thanks and turned to the window. It was gray outside, but at Valley it would be bright and sharp. He saw the horse pasture, the wooden gate and the side door into the barn. That had become a familiar mental journey here—imagining the grained wood, pushing the door open, smelling the hay inside, the manure, seeing the pegs on the wall with the bridles hanging down, the row of hats, the jumble of dusty ropes in the corner, starting down the aisle between the stalls. But this afternoon he stopped in the outer office room instead, stared at the stove with its red coals and the desk cluttered with charts and files. He was unable to walk down to Star's stall; he would probably never ride her again. He would never take Hally there; he was an invalid, crippled, impotent, and that whole dream of love and marriage was impossible.

Dan turned his chair to the hall, then back to the window again. Oh God. What should he do? Hally had taken to coming back into his room at night after the hall lights were dimmed. Marge Flaherty had never objected; no one had tried to stop them, in fact, save old Battleax Lord and she wasn't on nights anymore. Hally would sit on his bed in her bathrobe and they would talk. She would lean over him and kiss his ear, nestle herself close. Her fresh smell, the feel of her hair against his cheek, the soft bathrobe were cozy, precious things he had come to expect; but that was all. Two nights after their Christmas outing, an image of Jill's bedroom had dropped before him, as Hally leaned over him. He saw Jill's striped sheets pushed down in a tangle, the pink quilt tossed back, and their clothes dropped in clumps on either side of the bed. He thought all at once of that rolling and clutching, their moans and perspiration, and he realized he had felt none of that for Hally. None. Was it over for a little while, a few months maybe, as Baldwin suggested? A year? Or forever?

Dan watched a car move down the driveway and pause at the gate. He thought of Hally tonight, tomorrow, of her expectations. The fact was he felt only a happy warmth with her; the old rushing urgency was gone. Even if he could have turned and pressed her to him, climbed on top of her . . . even if. . . . But he couldn't. And he probably never would. Dan sighed. His love-making with Jill seemed to float behind him now like some island far apart, another man, running up the library steps with a green bookbag on his shoulder, riding a naked woman among crumpled sheets, and a horse with a white star on her forehead.

Hally stood balanced on a straight chair beside the bed in Dan's room, unpinning Christmas cards from one of the long red strips of cloth she had taped to the wall. The morning outside was dark; a cold rain had turned to sleet and the room had a harsh look, lit by the overhead light on the ceiling. Dan pushed himself in, scraping the door frame with one wheel. Hally turned at the sound and looked down at him.

"What're you doing up there?" he demanded, staring up at Hally. "That's dangerous. You could fall."

"I'm all right," Hally told him. "I'm being careful." She turned back to the wall and dropped a Christmas card, which fluttered down to the pile on the bed, then leaned forward to unpin another. "I just want to get your room cleaned up. That's all. Christmas stuff looks depressing after New Year's, don't you think?" Dan did not answer. "Do you want to save any of these?" she asked, pointing to the cards still pinned to the cloth. Dan shook his head. "None of them? What about these snapshots of the ranch?"

"Throw them out," Dan said. "I'm sick of them." He backed the chair noisily.

"What's the matter?" Hally asked, and turned to stare at him. "Is your back hurting?"

"No," Dan said. "I'm fine. I've got something to tell you— something we've got to discuss. That's all." Hally eyed him suspiciously and stepped down from the chair.

"What?" she said.

"It won't work. I've been thinking about it a lot and we can't get married."

"What do you mean 'it won't work'?" Hally demanded and put one hand on her hip. "We love each other. We've told our families and we. . . ."

"It won't work," Dan broke in. "You'd be marrying an invalid. Don't you realize that? I may never get out of a wheelchair."

"Who says?" Hally stared at him. "What's the matter with you, Dan? What do you mean 'invalid' anyway? What kind of a word is that?" Dan let out a sigh and pulled his wheelchair closer, as Hally stood studying him. "What's this mood anyway? Some kind of self-pity?"

"It's not self-pity. I'm trying to look at the facts. I'm not just talking about the obvious stuff—the paralysis. I may never be any good in bed. Don't you realize that?" Hally glanced toward the hall, closed the door, then looked back at Dan.

"Oh, come on," she said. "Cut it out. Is this supposed to be news? I've thought about this stuff too, you know. Half the men in the ward upstairs are brooding about impotency." Hally stared at Dan a moment, then stooped down in front of the wheelchair and pressed his knees. "That's not the point, Dan. We love each other. We want to spend our lives together. Remember? We can figure out the rest."

"Don't talk that way, Hal." Dan jerked the wheelchair back, leaving Hally's outspread hands pressing the air. She wobbled and caught herself. "Don't," Dan said again. The word reverberated like a shout, as Hally rose. "You don't understand. I'm talking about no sex, no children maybe. Christ, Hal, I can't ask that of you."

"You're not asking it, Dan," Hally said and gripped the metal bed-frame. "Even if sex is really a problem, and we don't know that for sure, it's what I want to do. Marry you, that is." She let her breath out, then rushed on. "You act as if I'm some fluffy little Radcliffe girl—your friend, Jill, maybe—who'd come here for a visit." Hally felt heat pour into her face; in all these weeks, Dan had mentioned his old girlfriend only once. Hally hurried on. "We met in this place. Remember? I have polio too. I've known you since last July and I've seen you every day practically." She paused and gripped the bedframe. "Damnit, Dan. This stuff isn't exactly new and besides the decision isn't just yours, you know."

"But you don't know how these problems'll feel when we're beyond this place, Hal—when you're living inside them. The sex is major, but there's all the work too. I mean the fact is you're convalescent yourself, but you'd have all kinds of heavy stuff to do taking care of me—washing urinals, making beds, lifting, carrying. What about collapsing one of these things and lifting it into a car?" He slapped the guide wheels on either side of his chair. "Have you thought about that? I wouldn't be able to help, you know." He pushed the wheelchair back an inch, then forward again. "I know it's not just my decision, but I've thought about it a lot. I can't think about anything else actually, at least I haven't for the last two days. I talked with Baldwin Monday, you see, and he. . . ."

"What did he say?" Hally demanded.

"Well, he doesn't know. None of them do. Time. The same old stuff. But what I see now is that getting married is impossible. It really is. The work would structure our lives, your life. You wouldn't have any energy left over for your music, your. . . . " Dan hesitated.

"My flute?" Hally supplied. She narrowed her eyes and glared at him. "You seem to assume I'm unable to think about my own life at all." She looked out the window at the sleet-covered lawn. "Oh God, Dan," she said after a moment and her voice was dull, as though exhausted by her anger. "It was all going to take courage. There were going to be plenty of hard times, dangerous ones too. But we thought we could do it; we wanted to." She moved to the window and stood, looking out, then she turned back to Dan again. "It was your idea, remember? That night after the carols on the ward? You've always been the optimist, Dan, the believer. You got me believing too. I mean we've lost so much else." She paused and stared down at him. "Now you're saying that we've lost each other too?"

"Oh Christ, Hal. I don't know. I'm just trying to think it through, to really look at the problems. It doesn't look happy and adventurous anymore, the way it did at first." He stared down at the floor, then raised his eyes to her again. "It looks irresponsible to me—insane, in fact. I just can't do it. That's all." Hally waited. What about love, she started to ask, but drew in her breath.

"You see some problems. I see others." Hally turned to the window and continued with her back to him. "We're certainly not some nice normal couple," she said. "That's true." She watched a trash truck rumble down the driveway, as the feel of Christmas dinner rose around her again—the hot anticipation, the lace tablecloth, the dessert dishes, Dan's announcement, Marian's tension, and Tom's awkward toast. "Maybe there are no normal couples," she said slowly. "I would have had a lot of work to do to win over your parents, your mother, even if I'd never gotten polio. But damnit, Dan." She looked back at him again. "We were going to help each other, support each other, try. That's what I thought, but . . . but. . . . " Hally's voice shook. She glanced back at the lawn, then at Dan again. "I'll tell you one thing; I'm not going to plead with you to hang onto me." She mopped one cheek with the back of her hand. "I think you're being stupid and melodramatic. You're exaggerating things you can't possibly . . . ." She stopped and pulled in her breath. "Dan, if I lose you and my flute too. . . . " Her voice shook again and she put both hands to her mouth. "Oh Dan, Dan." Hally squeezed past the wheelchair and left the room.

"Hal, wait," Dan shouted and pulled himself to the doorway. "Wait." But Hally had retreated into her room and shut her door.

22

*D*an and Jack sat at the ward window, peering down at an elderly Buick in the snow-filled parking lot. Its spinning wheels made a high whining noise and its headlights cut into the gray morning light, while its exhaust fumes blackened the snow behind. Roy stood in front of the car, signaling with a red, ungloved hand, as Mrs. Ryan rotated the steering wheel. But despite his directions, the tires continued their futile rotation, scattering snow, as the scream continued.

"That dumb bastard," Jack muttered. "He ought to tell her to back it— roll it back." Dan nodded in agreement, but the problem seemed remote. The emptiness of the past two days without Hally had a scary quality. He had felt self-conscious eating his supper with a book open beside him, hoping against hope that she would come limping through the doorway and make her shadowy enveloping presence actual once again. But she was avoiding him, he realized, and it was better to come on up here to the ward.

The car pulled forward suddenly, freed of the icy gullies behind it, and pushed cautiously through the rutted snow to the black ribbon of plowed driveway ahead. Dan and Jack watched it pause between the gate posts, where the globed lights wore peaked white caps, then it turned out into the street.

"This weather is so Goddamned depressing," Jack said. "Makes you feel ten times more trapped than you were before." Dan nodded. Some soap opera was playing unwatched on the televison beyond. Was it "The Secret Storm"? "Elsa came in last night," Jack went on. "Three weeks I don't see her at all and then she chooses a snowstorm." He sighed and looked around the room. "I said just about everything that I told you I was going to." Dan studied Jack's pocked chin and his plaid bathrobe. "I told her I couldn't take her messing around anymore," Jack went on. "I said it was bad enough before polio. But now . . . Christ. I told her she'd have to decide."

"How'd she take it?" Dan looked down, remembering an earlier talk with Jack. The man he had been four days ago, counseling Jack with cheerful confidence, seemed a ghost, someone he barely knew.

"Didn't seem to surprise her really. Said she'd file for a divorce, if that's what I want." Jack sighed again.

"It might be a relief," Dan suggested. "The decisive thing." The phrase seemed to drop with a thump. Decisive? God, he had been plenty decisive when he'd wrecked his relationship with Hally.

"In a way. Sure," Jack agreed. "But I gotta think about after this." He glanced down at his pajamaed legs sticking out below his bathrobe, his thin ankles mottled with brown, and his feet in their terry cloth slippers. "I have my job, you know." He looked up at Dan again. "The union's guaranteed that. But setting up in an apartment somewhere with all these problems." He glanced down again. "Alone? Jesus." He paused. "I mean Elsa drives me crazy sometimes with her flirting and her restlessness, and her sloppy ways around the place. But what am I going to do, that's what I ask you? How am I supposed to manage now, get breakfast, get my clothes on, go to the bathroom, for Christ's sake? You know what an operation that is." Dan drew his breath in to speak, then nodded instead.

"Oh, well. You can be sympathetic," Jack said. "You can probably afford a French valet or whatever they're called. I'll be lucky to be making three thou, when I go back." Dan pressed his lips together and glanced out of the window again. Jack looked at him, then out at the snow. "I'm sorry," he said. "That was a lousy shot." He paused, but Dan said nothing. "Listen, pal, what's the deal with Hally? She seems so depressed, you know? I guess maybe it's her flute and stuff. But she says you guys have decided not to see so much of each other for a while." He waited, then pulled his walker closer. "Jeez, Dan, why now? It's the middle of winter. We're all locked in. Why fight now?"

"Did she say we'd had a fight?" Dan asked. "What did she tell you?"

"No. Hell. I'm only guessing. You know Hally. She didn't say much of anything. And God knows, I'm in no position to give advice."

Henry shuffled toward them in his maroon bathrobe, his Bible in one hand. "You should pray," he said in his heavy nasal voice and looked sternly from one to the other. "Both of you. I could have been in a wheelchair too, but I prayed to the Lord and He gave me the power. He put me on my feet and . . . ."

"Ah, Jeez, bag it, will ya, Henry?" Jack muttered. "The only reason you can move better than the rest of us is you didn't have any leg paralysis to begin with. You had bulbar, damnit. Can't you get that through your head?"

"Prayer," Henry repeated. He turned and shuffled slowly up the aisle.

"That guy makes me sick," Jack said. "Prayer, my ass. This damn disease is different in every case. The only real thing to do is wait."

"Oh, it makes Henry feel better to think he has some control," Dan said and studied Jack, sitting beside him on the folding seat at the back of his walker. "What about Hally?"

"Nothing more than what I told you. She just seems damn depressed to me. Listen, I gotta go," Jack groaned and rose in his walker. "Milk-a-mag last night again."

As Dan watched him start down the aisle, Margaret, a thin young woman who liked Hally, stepped back to make way for Jack, then came up to Dan on her crutches.

"I can't cut your hair this morning," she told him in her heavy East Boston accent. "Miss Lord says it's against the rules for patients to use scissors." She laughed briefly. "I'll do it this afternoon, when she goes off. Okay?"

"Don't worry about it," Dan said. Margaret had three little boys under ten and during her long months in a respirator, she used to talk to Hally about toilet training and Cub Scout meetings and her relations with her mother-in-law, who had moved in for the duration. Had Hally told her about their fight, Dan wondered? Had she told Margaret to cut his hair? Dan heard the theme music of "The Secret Storm" as he turned his chair. The sound filled him with weariness. Those voices—a widowed father, a girl named Susan—had drifted into his room from a television set somewhere down the hall during the hot summer days, when there was nothing else to listen to or no energy for anything more. "I'm going down to my room to do a little work," he told Margaret, raising his voice over the music. He pushed himself up the aisle and out into the hall to escape that glimpse of a sicker self. But who was he kidding? What work?

Hally sat hunched beside the upright piano at the far end of the empty cafeteria, playing a Bach Two-Part Invention. The tentative notes sounded incongruous, rising near the bare table tops, where catsup bottles, sugar jars, and paper napkin holders were clumped together. Dan listened in his wheelchair in the doorway, unseen by Hally. From the kitchen came the clatter of dishes and the crackle of frying oil. "Hey, Eddie," a voice yelled. "Don't pile 'em there. I gotta have that counter to work."

Hally finished the piece and sat staring at the music on the battered stand, as Dan rolled toward her down the aisle between the tables. "That was good," he said, smiling. "You have to have real talent to get music out of that old thing." He drew his chair up to the scarred piano. "Was it Bach?"

"Damnit, Dan." Hally turned back to him. "What are you doing down here anyway? We're trying not to see each other."

"I know," Dan started. "I just heard you playing and I . . . ."

"But don't you see? Meeting, talking, all that stuff, only makes it harder."

"I know. But Hal, I just wanted to tell you that it's great you're doing this, playing here, practicing, developing this skill."

"What skill? This?" Hally glanced down at the keyboard, then back at Dan. "You don't understand. I don't want to play the piano. I want my flute." Hally twisted on the low piano stool and looked straight at Dan. "This isn't practice; I'm just filling up time. This isn't therapy and God knows it's not an alternative. I want my flute."

Hally twisted her hands and looked down at the linoleum tiles on the floor. She didn't want to talk to Dan, but she wasn't really talking to him, she thought, she was talking to herself, turning a private sorrow in her hands. "My flute was my baby," she said softly, "my child. I never went anywhere without it. I used to take it with me to market, tuck it into the wire basket, pile it on the library table beside me with my books. I never ever checked it on trips: I kept it in my lap or in the seat beside me on planes and trains." Hally turned from Dan and clutched her arms around her. "I say all that, but I haven't even seen it. I want Mom to bring it in, but I don't." Her voice shook and she clawed her sleeves with her fingernails, as she went on talking. "I keep putting it off week after week. She was going to bring it at the end of November, but it's January now. The fact is I'm terrified about whether or not I can ever play again; I don't want to know." She spun herself back to Dan on the piano stool and stared at him. "It's so different for you. You've got a plan and you've got the courage and the . . . ." Her voice broke. "I mean you'll do it. Get your thesis written one way or another. You'll make your life work. . . . But I . . . I don't know. I feel so trapped. Mom talks of other instruments and Ben, you know, my old flute teacher. I told you. He's been urging the piano since last fall. But somehow I can't seem to move—to make up my mind."

Dan reached out to pat her knee, but stopped and stared at the curving ribs of brown corduroy. The linear pattern seemed to hold a new perception that might blur, if he raised his eyes. Her problem was absolute; it confronted her like a wall. His thesis, how he would walk and when, whether he would ever ride—all those were changeable, shifting questions, demanding compromise and adjustment. But her flute? In all probability, that life was gone.

"All I do is twist things back and forth, piddle around down here, and feel sorry for myself," Hally continued. "And my God, there are people still in tanks upstairs. Kevin's arms are paralyzed and you . . . I mean I'm so ashamed of myself." Hally covered her face with her hands. "No wonder you didn't want to marry me." Her voice was muffled by her fingers and her shoulders shook. "Sometimes I wish I could just get out of it all . . . just bring the whole stupid business to an end."

"Don't, Hal. Don't." Dan kneaded her corduroy knee. "It's going to be all right." But what was "it," he thought, as Hally's sobbing broke the heavy quiet of the deserted cafeteria. How could "it" become "all right"?

"Whatdya mean twenty-seven house diets on One?" a voice yelled. "Shit. Yesterday they told me twenty-three."

Hally pulled a kleenex from her pocket and dried her cheeks. "I'm sorry," she said and rose. "I shouldn't have gone on like that. This can't help," she added and looked down at him. "Being together this way." Dan stared up at her. Her face looked gray with shadows beneath her eyes. What were they doing, he thought. Why couldn't they comfort each other at least?

"Look, Hal," he began. "If we just talked like friends."

"But we're not friends, Dan. We're . . . ." She hesitated. "We decided to separate." She drew her breath in sharply. "This won't work. It only hurts more." Dan felt conciliatory phrases twitch at his lips. *But, Hal . . . We can still help each other. We can. . . .* And yet she was right. They had planned to marry and had decided not to. They couldn't help each other now. Should he call Esther, he, the crippled boyfriend who had backed out of becoming her son-in-law? Could Jack help? Oh God. Was it really completely beyond him now? Her face had closed, the anguish was covered and she looked efficient and calm.

"We've got to avoid each other, Dan. Okay?" Dan sighed.

"Okay," he said. "But that's not going to be exactly easy here, you know."

23

"*L*ove and marriage, love and marriage," sang the radio voice, as Dan pushed himself down the ward aisle. "Go together like a horse and carriage." Dan winced to block out the sound. They'd been playing that inane song for months. Couldn't they think of anything else? He rolled over to Kevin's chair.

"Five days of this stuff," Kevin said, nodding at the snow outside. "Jeez. Seems like there's nothing to look forward to now that Christmas is over. I mean at least then we had carolers and visitors. Now it's nothing but the waiting again."

The ward doors opened and Jack came through, walking carefully on a pair of new Lofstrand crutches—metal canes with cuffs that held his lower arms. He looked surprisingly tall, almost commanding, risen from his cage-like walker. He was a good-looking man, Dan thought, with his sharp, mobile face, and his cocky smile. "When did he get those?" Dan whispered to Kevin.

"Yesterday morning. He's been showing them off ever since." Dan watched Jack move toward them down the aisle to the wheelchairs by the window.

"Whatdya think?" Jack demanded and stopped in front of Dan.

"Looks great," Dan said. "How's it feel?"

"Good, good," Jack told him. "Little tricky at first. But I'm getting the hang." He rested the crutches against the nearest bed and pulled himself up. "Takes it out of you, though." He wiped his forehead with a limp handkerchief. "But it's exciting. Suddenly you feel as if you can do so much more." Dan felt his jaw tighten as a hot envy rose. Why the hell couldn't he . . . ? Jack eyed him and added, "You'll be getting them yourself in another coupla weeks. In another year or three anyway." He laughed. "Who knows?" Billy had followed Jack in and was leaning on the bedframe beside him. Dan was noticing that Billy's teen-age acne had spread out around the adhesive tape strip holding his tube to his forehead, when he saw Hally from the corner of his eye, slip in after the other two and stand beside the TV.

"Speaking of being able to do stuff," Jack continued. "Billy and Hally and me have come up with a great idea." Dan looked down at his pajama-covered knees. So that was the way it was. If Dan was through with her, Jack would move in. Great. He moved his gaze to Jack's slippers, dangling from the side of the bed. Damn him. Damn his confident, busy-body ways. "What we thought of is a show, see?" Jack went on. "A hospital show."

"Whatdya mean a show?" Kevin said. "Who'd do it?"

"Us," Jack told him. "All of us. It'd be a kind of variety show with a skit. See?" He looked around the group, then hurried on. "There'd be a take-off on the doctors, Mostello, Baldwin, Miss Lord too. Complaints, bitching about the food, the therapy, Mrs. Harding. You know. Funny stuff." Dan listened sullenly. It didn't sound funny to him.

"But we've only got four people that can walk," Kevin objected. "Hally, you, sort of, Billy and Henry. Oh and Margaret," he added. "Five. That's it."

"We'll do it in wheelchairs," Jack said. "What the hell? Be fun. Hally's got this idea for a wheelchair chorus." He turned to her. "Tell 'em about it, Hal. Go ahead. Sing it." Dan saw Hally flush, then smile. She was wearing her usual brown corduroys and her blue sweater, but her face looked brighter, he thought, more animated. What did Jack mean to her? What were they doing anyway? The Goddamned two-timer, he brooded. A married man and he'd been warning Dan about her depression. Jesus Christ.

"Remember that song, *Waitin' for the Train to Come In*?" Hally asked. Kevin nodded. "Well, I thought we'd use the tune, but sing different words. Like this. See?" She smiled and began in her wavering nasal voice. " 'Waitin' for the nerves to come back,/ Hoping that they're not out of

[146]

whack . . . .' " She paused and glanced around the group, avoiding Dan. The others laughed and nodded.

"Cute, huh?" Jack said. "She'd write more. Three or four maybe." Cute, Dan thought. God, man. She played the flute with the Boston Symphony. Don't you know that?

" 'S good," Kevin told Hally. "But I don't know about a musical. I can't keep a tune."

"I can't either," said Henry, who stood behind Billy. "I can't sing."

"I'll be the audience." Kevin laughed.

"Aw, come on, you guys." Jack looked around the group in annoyance. Dan glanced down, as he felt the beam of Jack's gaze. Goddamn, he told himself. Stop it. Will you? Jack's not stealing Hally and even if he were, she's not yours anyway. Jack's a friend, stupid—your best friend here right now. "You gotta be the MC, Dan. Okay?" Jack demanded. "You've got the voice." Dan met Jack's eyes and smiled. What's the matter with me, thinking such garbage about this guy, he wondered.

"Okay," he said. "But what about the skit? We oughta have a script, a cast. Hey, Jack." He laughed. "You be Mostello. You're bossy enough." Dan laughed again and the others joined in.

"Swell," Jack agreed, "and Billy can be Baldwin." Billy looked up from a magazine he was eyeing.

"Me? Baldwin?" He put his finger to his tracheotomy tube and looked around the group. "Listen. Let's get the nurses to do a number. How about it? I wanta see Marge Flaherty dance."

"Look, fella," Jack said and punched the air beside Billy's ear. "You keep your sweaty little hands off Marge. She's engaged to a naval officer. See? Besides the staff's too busy to get involved. Now look. Dan's right," he said and slapped his knees. "We've got to have a script." He looked at Dan again. "What about you writing it? You write on that thesis all the time."

"Sure." Dan said. He hesitated and looked around the group. Who knows, he thought. He and Hally might work together on this thing. "Sure," he said again and smiled. "I'll give it a try."

"What about Dr. Mostello?" Henry demanded in his nasal voice. "You need his permission, you know." Jack glanced over at him, then back at the group.

"Oh, the hell with Mostello," he said. "He should be pleased. Besides I'm Mostello now anyway." He laughed and the others joined in.

Dan was sitting up in bed, writing on a yellow pad of foolscap, when Hally came into his room, carrying some mail. "It's nothing much," she said. "A circular or something. I'll leave it on your bureau. All right?"

Dan watched her nervously, meaning not to talk. But, as she turned to the door, he said, "By the way, I've been thinking up some commercials for the show. Have you got time to hear one?"

"Sure." Hally limped back to the bed and leaned against the frame. Dan lifted the pad. "This is the first one. 'Are you bored, sitting around in a wheelchair all day? Wanta get up and dance? You'll be embraceable in Dr. Popovsky's shiny new leg braces. Delivery guaranteed in ten to twelve months. Adjustments, bendings, whackings into place not covered under the warranty.' "

Hally laughed. "That's great. Any more?" Dan gazed at her a moment. She tipped her head back a moment as she laughed, which made Dan think of Star, tossing her long blonde mane.

"Any more?" Hally asked again.

"Well, yes," Dan said. "I mean I was just starting on this one." He raised the pad again. " 'Tired of steak and roast duck night after night? Artichokes and French burgundy? Drop by the Wahl and enjoy a delicious homemade dinner of hamburger pinwheels and old potatoes boiled in grit, served attractively on battered metal trays with cartons of soured milk, at the fashionable dining hour of four. You only have to contract polio to qualify for this rare gourmet experience. Even a mild paralytic case will do.' "

"That's wonderful, Dan." Hally perched on the end of the bed. "Listen. Jack's getting a microphone. Did he tell you?" Dan shook his head. His smile felt stiff and new. "It's mainly for you," Hally continued, "A mike'll make those commercials really audible. Oh and guess what?" Dan shook his head again. "Henry's going to play the patient in the skit."

"Henry?" Dan said.

"Well, he's the only one of the four of us, who can walk, that can get up on that gurney. We'd need an orderly to get Billy on it and. . . . "

"But will Henry do it?"

[148]

"He will," Hally announced. "I didn't even have to persuade him. He asked me."

"Amazing," Dan said. "What about the Roy part? Did you ask Margaret if she'd play him?"

"She's delighted and you know Margaret. She borrowed one of Roy's uniforms and she's already hemmed up the pants. Oh and listen. I called Mort and he's going to play the piano."

"He is? Mort?" Dan smiled.

"Well, he offered last week when he was here and we were chattering about it. Remember? It'll be much better than trying to do the choruses *a cappella.*" Hally smiled at the word. "Oh and I've thought up some more words to another song. Remember that old one, *There's No Place Like Home for the Holidays?*" Dan nodded. Maybe the long gray time was over, he thought. Maybe they were all emerging at last. Hally's voice was thick and wavery, but the words were distinguishable. " 'There's no place like the Wahl for the holidays,' " she sang, " 'No matter who your doctor is.' " Dan smiled.

"That's great, Hal. Great." He paused, embarrassed suddenly. She had been stern last week in the cafeteria about their separation. He didn't want her to think he was exploiting the show just to get close to her again or. . . . Should he tell her that or let it pass?

"Don't worry," Hally said, as if she felt his uncertainty. "This is different." She rose and gathered the envelope of mail. "I mean we're not talking about ourselves. We're just doing a job together. Okay?"

Dan nodded. "Okay," he said.

Hally was pinning a large round sign that read "AMERICAN TORTURERS ASSOCIATION" to the sleeve of a therapist's white uniform, when Dan knocked on her door and pushed himself in. "Look at this," Hally said. "Do you think it's big enough? Will they be able to read it?" She straightened and glanced back at him. "Hey, it's time for you to get dressed."

"I've got some bad news," Dan said and rolled himself over to the bed.

"What?" she demanded, taking in his grave face. His father, she thought in a rush. His heart. "Is it from home? Is it . . . ?"

"No. It's not that. Maureen's back. She's got pneumonia. She's in the critical ward."

"Maureen?" Hally stared at him. "Oh my God."

"They've got her in an oxygen tent," Dan explained.

"An oxygen tent!" Hally repeated and pressed her hands to her mouth.

"It's not as bad as it sounds." Dan pulled his chair closer and touched her arm. "I mean it's serious, but she's going to be okay. Baldwin thinks they've caught it in time." Hally clutched his hand in both of hers.

"It's scary," Dan continued. "But Baldwin said they'd probably let us go in and see her tomorrow." Hally let out her breath and sat down on the side of the bed. Maureen had been doing so well or so she had reported to Hally by phone. In another week, she would celebrate her third month out of the hospital. Hally imagined her terrified and humiliated, her head and shoulders encased in long folds of clear plastic, while an oxygen tank roared beside her at the end of the critical ward. Hally glanced down at the therapist costume.

"God, all this seems so stupid," she said. "How can we put on a show tonight when Maureen's . . . ?" She squeezed her hands together.

"She'd want us to go on with it, Hal," Dan said. "You know Maureen." He looked over at the sign. "It'll make a good story to tell her tomorrow when we go visit." Hally gazed at Dan and nodded slowly.

"You're right," she said. "It will."

The rows of chairs in the cafeteria were already occupied by families and friends of patients, who sat talking in loud whispers, waving to each other, and laughing, as cigarette smoke rose. Esther signaled to the Christys, who made their way down the aisle to two seats she had saved in front. The ceiling lights went off and the crowd grew quiet, as Mort began to play. Behind a tan curtain, separating the dining area from the kitchen, the wheelchairs were jammed together, the men on one side, the women on the other. The women were heavily made up, with gleaming red lips, false eyelashes, and ropes of pearls around their necks. The men looked ridiculously unfamiliar with their lipsticked mouths and rouged cheeks, as they sat waiting in their wheelchairs, their mop wigs in their laps. A row of aluminum pots glowed in the dim light above a stainless counter, which was cluttered with incongruous objects—an eyebrow pencil, a cluster of hairpins, a yellow comb, and a creased copy of the script.

Hally moved past a gurney on her way to Dan. "How do I look?" Henry demanded in a low urgent voice. Hally glanced down at the heavy, dark-haired man, stretched full length on the narrow table. He was dressed in a pair of blue pajamas and his black eyes shone with excitement.

"Wonderful, Henry," Hally whispered. "Nice and sick." She slipped around the other wheelchairs to Dan, who sat close to the curtain with the microphone on his lap. There was a shushing noise as Jack began to address the cast in a tense whisper. "Listen. This is the deal," he said. "See?"

"Oh Lord," Hally murmured to Dan. "I just hope he doesn't get too bossy."

"We've got it all worked out about moving the wheelchairs," Jack continued. "Hal and Margaret and one of the kitchen guys. But no back talk. See? Just let them do it. One person bitching about his place could louse up the whole works." Jack glanced around the group sternly. "Now they're going to have to jam these chairs in tight, because they've got to pull Henry's gurney through for the skit. Okay?" The group nodded seriously, as Mort's rippling chords continued to rise from the other side of the curtain.

Margaret pushed past the others to check the pillow she had pinned inside Jack's medical coat. She unpinned it, raised it an inch, pinned it again, and buttoned the white coat on top. She surveyed Jack a moment, then gave his stolid-looking front a sharp tap. Jack rocked backward but caught himself on the counter, as his metal canes clattered to the floor. "Holy shit, Margaret. Watch it, willya?" he whispered. "I'm not too steady, you know." Hally bent to retrieve the crutches and Jack settled his forearms into the metal cuffs. He breathed in a moment, then turned to the boy at the curtain, and nodded. "Okay, Eddie," he said. "Let's go."

Hally pushed Dan onto the side of the stage and all at once his loud, amplified voice was moving out over the rows of people in the dim room. "Tonight poliomyelitis has brought together a collection of talent unique in the whole country," he began. Hally limped backstage to help Margaret and Eddie pull the wheelchairs into a double line across the curtained stage.

"Can you see okay?" Hally whispered to Kevin. He nodded, straightened his wig, and sang out loudly before the curtains were fully open. "Oh, there's no place like the Wahl for the holidays, no matter who your doctor is . . . ." It was all moving so fast, Hally thought, as she began dragging the chairs offstage again.

Margaret entered stage left, dressed in Roy's gray uniform, a pillow pinned at her waist. She pulled the dolly with its bucket halfway across the stage, took out her mop, and moved to the gurney, where Henry lay stretched out. "Another terrible day," she said. "Sludge falling and eight more people dying up there in the ward. God rest their souls." She shook her head gloomily and leaned on her mop. Hally rushed onstage in her therapist's uniform, brandishing the long muscle charts she had made from shelf paper.

"Good morning, good morning, Mr. Hotpack," she began, plunging into her lines. "How are we this fine morning? Ready for our little stretch?" she asked in an imitation of Mrs. Harding. Hally's face was burning, and, aware that her excitement had made her voice thicker than usual, she began to pantomime. She put down her charts and whipped the sheet off Henry, who lay groaning on the gurney. Between Henry's legs was an extra leg that Hally had constructed by dressing one of the pink leg casts Dan had used last summer in another blue pajama pant. Even to Hally it looked eerily real, matching Henry's pajama-covered legs. She bent over it, feigning astonishment at the sight. "Right leg, left leg," she began and hesitated. "Middle leg?" she asked and raised it partway. The audience laughed. "A gluteus medius?" She paused again, then lifted the false leg higher, supporting the heel in one hand, the calf in the other. "Oh well," Hally continued and gave an exaggerated shrug. "Let's just start with it." She lifted the leg, stretching it higher and higher, shouting out degree numbers. "Eighty, eighty-five, ninety. Amazing, Mr. Hotpack. Amazing. One hundred degrees," Hally exclaimed. "This is extraordinary, Mr. Hotpack. Truly extraordinary."

Hally stretched the leg a little further and it came off precisely at the moment that Dan made a loud ripping sound in his throat directly into the microphone. Hally held the amputated leg above her head, turning from right to left, then bunched it together and flung it across the stage, where it hit Margaret's bucket with a ringing slap. Jack and Billy took the cue and entered stage left.

"What's this leg doing here?" Jack demanded. He stood still, staring down. Hally thought he looked remarkably like Dr. Mostello in the padded medical coat, with Dan's striped tie and button-down shirt underneath. Standing composed and stern, he waited until the laughter had subsided. "You know I don't want legs left around in the halls," he said to Billy. "Messy. Depress the patients." He continued to berate his head resident, who looked sweaty and excited in another borrowed medical coat. When they left the stage, there was loud applause.

It was almost over, Hally realized, as she pushed the wheelchairs back onstage for the final chorus. Then they were all together, smiling and waving in the curtain call, while the crowd pushed forward to congratulate their own, pulling back chairs, stepping over them, encircling the performers, who sat smiling in their wheelchairs, their make-up smeared with perspiration.

One end of the curtain rod rolled off its nail and fell to the floor with a crash. Hally felt a hand clap her shoulder, as she bent to pick it up. "It was terrific," Dr. Mostello said. "Terrific. There were people laughing here tonight that haven't laughed since last July." He lifted his hand and stood smiling at her. Hally felt a flush run through her. Was this the prize that she had wanted, she wondered, the climax of it all? She started to point to Dan and Mort, who were watching Roy do a dance step beside the piano—Roy, who was almost unrecognizable in a black three piece suit. But when Hally raised her arm to point, she realized that she was holding a full urinal.

"It's not real," she said, glancing back at Dr. Mostello. "It's apple juice. But I can't remember now whether I ever took it onstage or not."

Hally and Dan waited beside the elevator together, as scraping noises came from the cafeteria behind them, where chairs and tables were being pushed back into place. Hally's face was flushed, her eyebrows were still dark with make-up, and Dan had a smear of lipstick on his chin. "Tired?" Hally asked, as she pushed the UP button. She gazed down at Dan, who nodded and let his shoulders sag. Hally waited, then pressed the button again. "It was incredible, wasn't it?" she said.

"Incredible," he repeated and let his eyes close. Hally looked down at him, waited a moment more, then raised her fist and pounded the elevator door. Dan opened his eyes. "That thing's going to fall off its hinges someday," he said and smiled. There was a groan, then a familiar clanging as the elevator bumped itself down into place. Hally held the outside door open with her hip, pushed back the collapsible door inside, and shoved the wheelchair in. She slammed the inner door, punched the button for one, then squeezed around Dan and slumped against the back wall.

"You're tired too, aren't you?" Dan said, looking up at her. Hally nodded. "You should be. It wouldn't have been much without all your work."

"Or yours," Hally said and smiled. Dan gazed at her a moment.

"Would you bend down here a minute?" he asked. Hally bent over and Dan put his arms around her. He pulled her close and kissed her cautiously. Hally bent to him and pressed her mouth to his. She put her arms around him, as he pulled her closer. The elevator groaned and bumped into place, but Dan and Hally continued to kiss. Someone pushed the button on the floor below and the buzzer sounded.

"Oh Dan," Hally whispered and drew back. "What are we going to do?"

"Something," he said. "We'll figure something out."

"But . . . ?" The buzzer sounded again.

"Send that elevator down, willya?" A voice yelled.

"But what?"

"I don't know, Hal. You and I have something we've got to hold onto somehow and. . . . "

"Slam that door, willya?" the voice yelled. "We're waitin' down here."

"Just hold your horses," Hally muttered. She pushed the heavy outer door open, then pulled the wheelchair off. "Okay, it's on its way," she yelled down the shaft. The elevator clanged and departed, as Hally leaned back against the battered door and looked down at Dan in the quiet hall. "I don't know what we're going to do. I mean . . . ."

"We just need a little more time, Hal, a little more strength." Dan caught her hand and kissed it, then holding it still, he let his shoulders slump.

"Strength." Hally sighed. "It's funny, isn't it?" She pulled back her hand and caressed his head. "The show gave us a glimpse of something we can be, maybe. Something we could be together." She gazed down the hall at a hot pack machine in the corner, its cord hanging down. "But . . . but there's so much other stuff. We're not there yet, are we?" Dan shook his head and looked down.

Hally grasped the handles at the back of the chair; she felt small and vulnerable, as she pushed Dan down the dim hall and into his room again.

24

Hally watched Maureen stretch out her freckled hand and inspect the fingernails she was filing. Her new room was larger than the old one, but it was already just as crowded. "What really happened?" Hally asked. "Did you catch a cold from one of the children or what?"

"I was tired and nauseous." Maureen peered at Hally over the top of her glasses. "I'm pregnant, you see."

"Pregnant?" Hally echoed. "My God, Maureen."

"Well, I told you I don't like odd numbers."

"But you've been awfully sick."

"So? Things have to go on, you know." Maureen surveyed her fingernails at arm's length, then started on the other hand. She glanced at Hally again. "How are you and Dan doing?"

"Oh, I don't know, Maureen. It's so complicated. I mean we love each other or we think we do. But there's all the other stuff: his walking, my swallowing, his thesis, his feelings about . . . well, about sex. I mean, you know, and then, of course, there's my flute." Hally sighed and looked out at a leafless bush beside the wall. "We had such fun working on the show and everything. But now all the other stuff's crowded back in again. We've sort of decided not to see so much of each other for a while. It's just too hard being together somehow."

"Look, Hally." Maureen pulled off her glasses and leaned her pale forearms on the bedtray so that she sat imperiously among her satin pillows, staring down at Hally. "You can fuss around and make things complicated if you want to," she said, "or you can assume they'll go all

[155]

right and just keep on." Hally looked out at the bush again and sighed. A pale leaf was caught within the intricacy of its dark branches. Was she caught too? Hally turned back to Maureen.

"What do you mean?" she said.

"That I think you two love each other. That I think you should respect those feelings instead of anguishing over all the unknowns."

"But, Maureen. We've both had this disease, damnit." Hally's voice rose in a whine. "We're not some sweety-pie little couple that can just pick a date and a china pattern and . . . ." Maureen gave Hally a long look, put on her glasses again, and picked up her emery board.

"I just told you what I think," she said. "That's all."

Dan stood near his bed, balanced on a pair of new wooden crutches and gazed around him dizzily, as Mrs. Harding hovered on one side and Lou on the other. A long steel brace was strapped on his left leg on top of his blue pajama pants, its calipers fitted into a laced brown shoe below. Dan glanced down; that brace shoe and the one beside it looked incongruous below his loose bathrobe and faded pajamas and the surface of the black and white tiled floor looked hard and far away.

"Want to try again?" Mrs. Harding asked. Dan swallowed and nodded. He moved his right foot forward slightly in a slow shuffle, then dragged the left leg after it. He paused and breathed out. "That's better," Mrs. Harding encouraged. "How do you feel?" Dan turned his head and looked at her cautiously, as if even that slight movement was vaguely dangerous. He had been anticipating this event for weeks, imagining the sensations. And this was it, he thought, the great moment of getting the brace at last, standing up on crutches, trying to walk. When he had imagined this moment, he had thought of the first time he had mounted Star again after his appendectomy, the summer of his sophomore year. He had felt a moment of astonishment at his height in the saddle, a sudden flush of fear in the familiar stable yard. Then the old confidence had flooded back and he was riding easily once again. But now . . . he felt so tall, so brittle and uncertain. The crutches cut painfully into the flesh under his arms and that pull it took to bring the braced leg up beside the other one was heavy, awkward work. How did he feel, Mrs. Harding wanted to know. Scared, he thought, and disappointed—damn disappointed.

"I thought it'd be a lot easier," he started. "I mean I thought I'd just. . . ."

"It'll get easier soon," Mrs. Harding told him. "You'll see. Just a little time and you'll get very good at this."

"I hope so," Dan eased his head up and rolled his eyes, taking in the room. "Right now the whole concept of evolution—this rising up and walking around on my hind legs seems highly unlikely to me, highly dangerous too." Mrs. Harding laughed and Lou joined in. That's the ticket, Dan thought. Keep it light, keep it slanted and funny. God knows, if you look at this thing straight on, you might well crack.

"Mind if I come in?" Artemis asked. She closed the door behind her and stood looking at Hally, who was hunched in her armchair by the window. "You seem sort of upset. I thought it might be those barium swallowing tests you had at the Lane General Hospital last week." Artemis glanced around her and sat down on the side of the bed. "Did Mostello give you the results or what?"

"Just now," Hally said. She straightened and looked across at Artemis. "They say I'm still dropping the stuff by gravity—that there's almost no muscle activity yet." She paused and sighed. "Seven months in this place and I'm still dropping the food. I could be here another month or two or three." She paused. "Honestly, Artemis. I could."

"Still no muscle activity at all?" Artemis repeated. "Boy, that is hard. What else did those tests show?"

"Actually," Hally began. "Dr. Atkins, who did them, says he feels it's on the verge of happening. He says it sometimes goes that way—a long period of virtually nothing and then the muscles finally begin to work. He wants to test me again at the end of February and see. He thinks the picture could be very different in two or three weeks. I mean I'll probably never swallow normally, but the muscles could return enough so that I wouldn't be in danger."

"Well, then," Artemis said. "It's not all that bleak."

"No," Hally said. "It isn't really. It's just . . . well, you know Mostello. He's so damn possessive. His patients, his cases . . . sometimes he acts as though he never wants me to leave." She glanced out of the window, then back at Artemis again. "I don't know," she said. "That's not the whole thing. Something's happened to me. A kind of fear or. . . ." She sighed.

"You still haven't tried your flute, have you?"

"No." Hally turned back to the window. "I haven't even talked to Mom about bringing it in. I. . . . It's funny." She looked back at Artemis. "When Dan and I were talking marriage—back at Christmastime, you know—when we were wrapped in that romantic haze, that . . . oh, I don't know. I think I sort of thought somewhere inside—well, that'll be it. My life. Our life, his degree, his teaching and books, kids maybe. I thought I can stand not having the flute, because I'll have him." Hally clutched one knee against her chest and went on. "I mean, I never said that to him or even to myself, but it was part of it somehow and now. . . ." She turned to the window again and let out a long sigh.

"Hally, I think you have to try that flute," Artemis said. "You have to face up to that whatever you and Dan decide, whatever the swallowing tests indicate, or Mostello decrees about your discharge. You have to get that flute and try it." Artemis paused and studied Hally. "I mean, don't you think so?"

"Yes," Hally said slowly and dropped her hands to her lap. "I guess you're right."

25

Dan walked with a new confidence, as he moved slowly up the hall toward the nurses' station. The learned stages of his walk—the deliberate placing of his crutches, the angle at which he leaned, the timed pull of his left foot, then the shuffle, were becoming familiar and he no longer needed Lou beside him, although Mrs. Harding stood watching him from the nurses' desk. As he approached the desk, Dan remembered the glass door just beyond it, in which he had sometimes seen his reflection. He was wearing daytime clothes—a shirt, khaki pants, and a green cable knit sweater, and all at once he wanted urgently to assess this new effect. Mrs. Harding was looking down at a chart; Dan moved closer to the door and stopped. There he was, tall and familiar, thin certainly, but surprisingly energetic looking—almost normal. He smiled. He wasn't a bad looking guy, by God, despite the crutch rests hiking up his shoulders, and the long stiff look of his leg with the shape of his brace, visible beneath his pants. He was okay. Dan breathed out. Not Cary Grant maybe, but he wasn't grotesque—not someone you'd turn from or. . . . Damnit, he was okay.

"That was good," Mrs. Harding said, coming up behind him with the wheelchair. Dan twisted to look back, hoping Mrs Harding hadn't noticed him, staring at his reflection. "You've done enough for this morning. Don't want to overdo." Dan positioned himself in front of his wheelchair, Mrs. Harding took his crutches, and he plunked down on the seat. "I'll be back for these in a sec." Mrs. Harding leaned the crutches against the wall. "I just have to whip down to the convalescent ward."

Jack approached on his Lofstrand canes and stood smiling down at Dan. "You're getting pretty good," he said.

"Did you see me just then?" Dan asked. "I got all the way up here with just two stops." He breathed out triumphantly. "I couldn't sleep last night, thinking about trying it again. I just wish they'd let me practice alone."

"Go ahead and practice," Jack said and glanced up the hall. "To hell with the rules. They're meant to be broken anyway."

"You know, it's funny," Dan said. "Suddenly all kinds of things seem possible. I mean once you get up on your feet, you feel you can do stuff, you know?" Jack nodded and Dan leaned toward him confidentially. "I've been thinking a lot about Hally lately. I mean all this politeness crap—this caution and talk about the future—all this worry about what if this, what if that—this endless indecision. I mean hell. We've got to take some chances—get on with our lives—get married. Why not?" Jack smiled.

"Don't ask me, pal," he said. "Go ask her." Dan nodded and started to turn his wheelchair toward Hally's closed door, then glanced back at the crutches resting against the wall. He leaned forward, hoisted himself up out of the chair and locked his brace.

"Don't tell on me. Okay?" He took the crutches from the wall, fitted the rests carefully under his arms, and stood upright. "I believe in dramatic presentations." He winked at Jack, who smiled and watched as Dan started across the hall.

Hally stood beside her bed, clutching her abdomen as she stared down at her flute case on the striped bedspread. She straightened at the sound of Dan's knock, then dropped a sweater over the black case. "Who is it?" she called and stared, as Dan moved into the room.

"How do you like this?" He stopped beside the bureau, lifted one crutch slightly, and wiggled it to show his control.

"Fine," Hally told him. "You're getting very good." Dan moved to the end of the bed and clasped the frame.

"I came in because I want to talk to you about something, Hal." He paused and smiled. "You see I've been feeling so good since I started walking. I feel it's opened up so many possibilities somehow." He hesitated, watching her, then glanced around the room. A row of Impressionist post cards was lined in the mirror frame and a pot of white violets stood on the window sill, beside a stack of music scores. The room was gray without the ceiling light and yet he could detect a rectangular box on the bed underneath her sweater. My God; it was her flute at last. He stared at the shape, noting one edge of the black case on the side. "Have you tried it?" She nodded and Dan took in the white shocked look of her face for the first time. She must have just tried it, he thought, and it hadn't worked. Oh God, what would she do now? He watched her turn and look out at the frozen lawn. "It didn't go too well then?" he asked.

"It doesn't go at all," Hally said. "I can't do anything. I can't even make a sound." She pulled the flute case forward and opened it, revealing the silver parts of the instrument fitted snugly into their blue plush beds. Dan stared down.

"Gee. It's beautiful, isn't it?" he said and was disgusted by the sound of his own well-meaning comment. Dan shivered. He felt he had come from the warm room of his own life, colorful with new possibilities, into this dim space, where Hally was trapped, and he must bring her into his own world somehow. He lowered himself onto the bed, rested the crutches beside him, and peered down at the instrument. So this was her baby; he watched Hally fit the parts together and move to the bureau.

"Look at this." She focused on her reflection in the mirror, then raised the flute, holding it shoulder high, pursed her lips, and brought her mouth to the embouchure. A wet blowing noise sounded in the room. Hally glanced back at Dan, then turned and blew a second time. The wet noise came again. "See what I mean?" Hally demanded and lowered the flute. "See? It's not just the lip paralysis. It's my breathing capacity too. You have to have good lungs." She laid the instrument on the bedspread beside the open case and sank down into the armchair with a sigh. "Oh God, Dan," she breathed. "This is it. No wonder I delayed all these weeks and months. No wonder. Now there's no hoping anymore." She stared down at the floor as a long minute passed.

"But, Hal," Dan started and heard his words drop into the silence of her gloom. He must cheer her, divert her, help get her past this crisis. "There are other instruments." He paused and glanced at the bureau. "You play the piano. You compose. Look at all you wrote for the show." Dan knew, as he said it, that the remark was dumb, but somehow he must pull her out of the awful emptiness of this room.

"The show," Hally repeated. Her voice was harsh. "My God, Dan. The show."

"But the piano," Dan persisted. He had begun and now he had to keep on. "If you can play that battered old thing down in the cafeteria, just think what you could do at the Conservatory."

"Don't, Dan," Hally broke in. "Please."

"But you will, Hal," Dan went on. "You'll get going again. I'll begin a new thesis and you'll start a new instrument." Hally covered her face with her hands and shook her head. "You've got to think of other things, Hal." Dan reached out and touched her knee. But Hally made no sign that she had heard his words or felt the pressure of his hand. Dan gazed at the window, then down at his new crutches, resting beside him at the edge of the bed. He thought suddenly of his reflection minutes earlier—of that man, who was not grotesque after all, but familiar, almost handsome. Plenty of disabled people married and went on with lives. He remembered Jack, waiting outside in the hall to hear what he had said to Hally and what her answer had been. Dan leaned forward. In a way this wasn't the time and yet maybe it was.

"You've just got to think of other things," he told Hally again. "Like me, for instance." He gave a little laugh and felt a pain begin in his chest as he waited for her to lift her head and smile. "Hal, I want to marry you," he said in a rush. He sucked in his breath, watching for the moment when she would remove her hands from her face and raise her head. But she did not. Maybe she hadn't really heard. "Hal," he repeated. "I asked you to marry me."

Hally took her hands down at last and looked at him with a sigh. "Oh, Dan, stop pestering me. Will you?" She covered her face again. Dan stared.

"Pestering you," he repeated. "Pestering you, for God's sake." He glared at the postcards that framed the mirror, then down at the flute again. "Look. I have some idea of what this instrument means to you, Hally. How important it is." He waited again, but Hally did not look up at him. "Honest to God, I think I really do understand some of what you're going through. But I'm talking about love, commitment, marriage, damnit— going on with what we've got left." He stared at her and she stared back, but did not speak. "You've got serious problems, Hal. But so do I. I made a mistake after Christmas, tearing us apart. I mean I see that now." Hally said nothing.

"I want to share things with you, Hal. The good stuff as well as all the bad. I've been stuck in bed for seven months, waiting for this brace, for the muscles to use it, and now. . . ." He waited again, but Hally was looking at the floor. "I mean, God, when it finally happens and I start walking, you . . . you . . . ." Hally gazed at him with an expressionless face. Dan waited, then drew in his breath. "Christ, Hal. Say something. Will you?" But Hally only stared. "Okay then. Never mind." Dan made his voice sound ordinary. He locked his brace, pushed himself up from the bed, fixed his crutches under his arms, felt his knee to make sure the brace was locked, then looked down at her again. "Mourn your flute," he told her, "if that's what you want. I've had enough of your sick gloom. I've tried. Now I'm leaving."

Dan's eyes were glazed with anger as he moved across the room. He stopped in the doorway a moment and stood looking out, unaware of the hall, the nurses' desk beyond him, the elevator clanging, and Roy's bucket, parked just outside the door. He would go back to his room, he thought. No, he would find Jack. No, the room. He moved his crutches forward, not stopping to assess the stretch of wet tiles gleaming ahead of him. The right crutch skidded out; he toppled forward, and crashed down, hitting the handle of the wringer. There was a thud, then a loud clatter as the crutches rayed out on either side. Dan lay crumpled on the floor; the dolly was flipped on its side, its black wheels spinning slowly, and a pool of gray water from the overturned bucket, was spreading toward Dan's head. In the doorway behind him, Hally pressed her hands to her mouth and screamed.

Dr. Baldwin leapt down the hall and knelt beside Dan's head. Mrs. Harding bent over him, helping, as Lou and Dr. Baldwin rolled him onto his back. Dan's face was expressionless. Blood oozed from his forehead, past his eye. "Get that foot. It's twisted under him," Dr. Baldwin shouted. Hally stooped and clutched Dan's shoe. "No, Hally," Dr. Baldwin ordered. "I mean Lou."

Hally froze, then stepped back, but she stayed in her doorway, watching. They weren't going to scare her off the way they had in the hurricane. Dr. Baldwin moved one finger in front of Dan's eyes, then lifted his lids one after the other; Dan was clearly unconscious. Had he broken his foot? His leg? Oh God, did he have a concussion? Lou left and returned, pushing a gurney. Hally watched as he and Dr. Baldwin lifted Dan's limp body onto it and rolled it down the hall to the elevator.

"I'm so ashamed, Maureen," Hally said and clutched her arms around her as she sat beside Maureen's bed. "It's all my fault. My fault. Don't you see?" Her teeth were chattering loudly and she blotted some tears with the heel of her hand, then clutched herself again. Maureen reached for a sweater at the bottom of the bed and handed it to Hally.

"Put this on," she directed.

"I was so melodramatic, so false, Maureen, just so . . . oh God. What if he's really hurt? I mean what if . . . ." Hally put her hands over her face and Maureen reached out and stroked her arm. "The fact is, I've suspected for weeks, months even that I'd never play again," Hally began. "I mean I knew my lip was paralyzed. I knew—part of me really did know—that it was impossible. In a way it wasn't a shock. I always thought I could go back to the piano, just as Ben, my flute teacher kept suggesting. But after Dan and I broke up or decided not to decide, you know, I got mad." Hally leaned back. "I wouldn't think about the piano and I wouldn't try the flute. I couldn't seem to do anything or I wouldn't."

"You had a major disappointment," Maureen said. "It was natural to feel. . . . "

"But Maureen, it's as though I was punishing Dan because I can't play my flute. It's so stupid." She covered her face again.

"Dan's not the only one who's been punished," Maureen said. They heard footsteps in the hall and looked up as Dr. Mostello appeared in the doorway.

"He's going to be okay. No breaks. Sprained his ankle, but it's not bad. He's conscious now, dazed of course. But that's to be expected. Got a bad cut on his forehead. But Dr. Strout's on his way over. Fine plastic surgeon. One of the best. The scar'll probably be minimal." He started to turn, then looked back at them. "If he'd just obeyed orders. He wasn't supposed to be walking unsupervised."

"It wasn't that." Hally sat forward. "He was upset. We'd had an argument. It was my fault. I . . . ."

"Thank you for reporting to us," Maureen interrupted. "We really appreciate this. Both of us. And we have a lot to be grateful for." Dr. Mostello nodded and turned back to the hall.

"Hey, Hally," Debbie announced, coming into the room. "You've got a long distance call from Denver. A woman. Where's Denver anyway? Wyoming?" She stood with one hand on her hip peering at them.

"It's Marian." Hally looked at Maureen in alarm. "I can't talk to her. I can't."

"Yes you can." Maureen told her.

"You can take it out at the desk," Debbie said. "It's quiet right now. We've had enough excitement for one morning."

"Hally?" Marian's voice sounded startlingly close, as Hally stood holding the receiver. "We've just talked with Dr. Mostello," Marian announced. "He says the X-rays show Dan hasn't broken anything."

"Oh," Hally breathed. "I mean I know. It's so lucky."

"Have you seen him?" Marian demanded.

"No," Hally said and thought with panic that perhaps Dan had never told his mother of their break-up. You don't understand, Hally imagined saying. The whole reason it happened is because Dan was furious with me, because I was selfish and. . . . "I've been terribly scared," Hally began instead. "I . . . ."

"Of course you have. Now I called my father about the plastic surgeon and it turns out he's excellent. One of the best." Marian's voice shook slightly. "Hally," she started again. "If you and Dan do decide to marry. I mean if you . . . ." She paused. Then she did know about their indecision, Hally thought with relief. "Tom and I only want what will make Dan happy—you and Dan happy, that is." Marian's voice shook again. "Things like this make you realize . . . ."

"Yes," Hally broke in. "But, Marian, we're not certain at all. I mean it's complicated and . . . ." Her voice trembled. "I don't know what will happen when Dan gets better and . . . ."

"Well, none of us knows. Now Hally, you try to relax and we'll talk soon. All right?" Hally finished the call and limped back to Maureen in relief.

It was late afternoon and Hally was sitting alone by her window, waiting, an unread music score open on her lap. Dr. Baldwin appeared in the doorway. "Want to see him?" he asked. "He wants to see you." Hally rose quickly and followed the head resident into Dan's room. Dan lay flat, his forehead marked with a large, white bandage, but he smiled as their eyes met.

"Hi," he said. "I knocked myself out."

"I know." Hally smiled back.

"What did I hit?"

"Roy's bucket," Hally told him.

"That figures." Dan let out a little laugh.

"Does it hurt?" Hally asked.

"Not much." Dan reached for her hand. "Boy," he said and breathed out slowly, "I'm sure glad you're here."

26

*L*ou cranked Dan's bed to a sitting position and lifted a round metal cover from his supper tray with the familiar flourish. Hally sat watching the ritual shyly. Dan's forehead was still bandaged, but he had been up in his wheelchair for an hour in the morning and again in the afternoon, enjoying the attention he had been receiving from patients and staff. This dinner was the first time they had been alone together since the accident and Hally was so full of the speech she wanted to begin that she could barely wait for Lou to leave and close the door behind him.

"Dan, I'm still sick about the way I behaved Monday," she started. "The day you fell. . . . The. . . ."

"Don't agonize over it, Hal. We were on different tracks. That's all. It was stupid of me. I was excited about the walking, and . . . ." Dan paused. "It's funny. I'd seen my reflection in the door earlier and . . . ." He stopped again. "Don't worry about it," he said.

"But I do," Hally protested. "I mean I was so awful and . . . ." She paused. The point was not to apologize really, but to bring them back to that moment in Dan's feelings, to. . . . But she couldn't begin this way. "You're doing wonderfully," she started. "Mrs. Harding told me the sprain's so mild she's going to get you up on your sticks in another day or so."

"Yes. Old Harding won't let me sit around." Dan opened his paper napkin and spread it on his chest. "What about you? Any news about that second round of tests you took?" Hally looked down at her lap. She wanted to talk about that morning, her shock about her flute, and . . . and his proposal. But this was not the moment maybe. Such talk would take time, like everything else.

"I'm still waiting to hear the results," she said as she watched him peel open a packet of pepper and shake it over his hamburger. "It's been almost two weeks now. All Mostello has to do is phone, but he keeps delaying or forgetting or.... I don't know. I'm almost sure I did better this time—significantly better. I mean I feel I'm ready to graduate to the house diet now." Hally stared at the mounds of baby food on her plate. Why was she talking about this? It was him she wanted to discuss—him, her, their feelings about each other.

"What's delaying Mostello anyway?" Dan asked.

"Oh, you know. Crises. There's a meningitis case upstairs or they think it might be." She sighed. "Dr. Atkins, the guy who did those tests, said I might have to drop my food for years, but that gradually I would learn tricks so that I could handle almost anything. If Mostello would only get the results." Hally looked down. Beside the mound of ground chicken on her plate was an orange mound of squash. Rivulets from the two hillocks ran together in a brownish stream at the side.

"There's something so enervating about waiting," she began. "I have this flabby feeling, this sense of powerlessness." She stirred the squash, but did not lift the fork to her mouth. "Everything seems to blur together, all the decisions. Do you know what I mean?" Hally leaned forward. "I've got to make something definite, something clear." Did she mean Dan, she wondered, and looked down at the squash again.

"We all feel that way," Dan said. "My God, look at Jack. Up on those sticks for six weeks now and they're still talking about his balance and stalling on his discharge." He opened a small carton of milk and poured a white stream into his glass. "If the test results are good," he said, "and I bet they are, you'll go on a house diet this week or next. You'll be out in two weeks probably, end of March at least, and I'll follow. Harding says I should be walking normally in three weeks maybe." He paused and smiled. "Who knows? You might get a call in mid-April, asking for a date." Hally stared. *A date? They had agreed to marry at Christmastime. Now he was talking of a date.* Phrases crowded into her mouth. You can't just ... I mean, Dan.... My God, we were in love. Remember? Hally swallowed, then looked over at him.

"Where'll we go? Out to dinner?"

"Well, dinner would kind of depend on the step situation. But we could roll straight into the movie theatre."

"That's right," Hally said. "The Unie in Harvard Square doesn't have any steps, does it?" Dan shook his head. He was keeping himself safe. She had hurt him and for the moment direct methods of healing were impossible.

"Do you like Ingrid Bergman?" she asked. Dan shook his head.

"I like Katharine Hepburn best," he said, "especially when she's playing with Cary Grant."

Hally stood in the hall, listening to the unfamiliar sound of a typewriter in the room next door. The clacking noise came in a series of little bangs, then a pause, then it started up again. She listened a moment longer and opened Dan's door. He sat in his wheelchair by the window, typing on a portable typewriter, which kept slipping toward him on the tilted bedtray. His foot was propped on a stool and he still wore a large square of white gauze on the side of his forehead. Dan shoved the typewriter back once again and studied the foolscap pad beside him.

"Is it working okay?" Hally asked. "Can you manage that way?" She nodded at the typewriter, then at the pages beside him. "You look busy."

"I am," Dan said. He smiled and pushed his glasses up into his hair. "I told you I wrote Professor Henning and guess what? He answered." Dan waved a typewritten letter. "He says he'll be glad to look over my thesis proposal, if I want, and he has this neat idea. He suggests that I concentrate on the history of ranching in the 1870s, instead of trying to follow the Oregon Trail. It makes a lot of sense, because it's really the subject I was dealing with anyway and. . . ."

There was a clatter in the hall as Mrs. Harding pushed a walker past the door. Dan smiled at Hally.

"She's coming for me next. I just want to finish these notes before she gets here." Hally opened her mouth to say something, but Dan looked down at his foolscap pad again.

She returned to her room and stood by the window, her arms clutched around her, as she stared out at the melting mounds of snow. Next door the typewriter clicked, stopped, then clicked again. Hally moved to the bureau and gazed down at her flute case. She opened it and stared at the silver sections, nestled in their blue plush beds. Hally drew in her breath;

she closed the case, snapped down the locks on either side, and bent down to put it in her bottom drawer. Standing in front of the mirror, she stared at her reflection, her uneven mouth, her dark deep-set eyes. If she could . . . if she could just. . . . She took some change from her top draw and left the room.

"Ben." Hally stood at the pay phone in the basement hallway, startled to have reached her old music teacher so easily. "It's Hally." She stretched her mouth so that her ennunciated words would be heard over the noise of tables being shoved back and stacked in the cafeteria behind her. "Hally Blessing." She waited. "No. I'm still in the hospital," she explained and gave a little laugh. "I'm still here." She paused and began again. "Ben, I've been thinking about piano lessons. What you suggested and. . . . Your friend, Andreas. . . . Do you think he'd take me on? Do you think I could study with him? You see, I don't want to just diddle around. If I'm going to start, I want to work hard." She waited a moment and nodded. "You do? You think he would? About the payments," she went on. "I thought maybe I could copy music for him. It's my old skill. Remember? It really pulled me through those last two years at the Conservatory. I mean, I could copy out parts for him. He still runs that chamber music group, doesn't he?" Hally paused to listen. "No," she said, "Actually I'm not even on the house diet yet. But it can't be much longer. It really can't. I mean, I'll certainly be out by April, and when I get home I want to start studying seriously. That's what I've decided. I mean, I know now that's what I want to do." She listened a moment. "You will, Ben? You'll ask? Oh, wonderful. Now don't oversell me. I might not be that good, you know. But if he'd give me a chance. Mid-April maybe. If we could start and see how it goes. . . ."

Hally hunched forward in her armchair by the window, a three-point pen in one hand, a pad of music writing paper on her lap. She dipped the pen into an open bottle of india ink on the sill beside her, lifted it cautiously, and drew a wavery G-clef on the empty pad of bars. She stared at it, then drew another, and a third more quickly. She made an F-clef, a sharp sign, a flat, and another sharp, then paused to look at the page. "Making accidentals," she murmured to herself and smiled. She tried a quarter rest. What a lovely squiggle, she thought, and made an eighth rest and a whole.

She drew another G-clef, turning her pen to extend the loops, so that the curl at the bottom had a professional grace.

"Got the results of your second tests this morning," Dr. Mostello announced. He stood in the doorway, his hands in the pockets of his medical coat. "I'm going to put you on a house diet today."

"You are?" Hally rose, clutching the music pad with its wet symbols in one hand, the wet pen upright in the other. "A house diet?" She glanced down, worried that she had dropped ink on the bedspread; one lone black bead lay on the floor beside the bed. She put the pen on the sill, capped the ink, and turned back to Mostello.

"Two weeks," he said. "Then, if all goes well, I'll consider discharge."

"Discharge," Hally whispered. She stared at the doctor, smiling and familiar; several strands of black hair were rumpled together as usual over the bald place.

"You look shocked." He laughed. "Would you rather stay?"

"No, no," Hally said. "I mean, I'll miss you and everybody, and Dan, of course, but I. . . ." She smiled, then swallowed, glanced down at the pad, then up at the doctor again. "Dr. Mostello, I just called about piano lessons. . . . I think I can study with this really good teacher at the Conservatory in return for some music copying jobs and . . . I mean, I. . . ."

"Good for you," the doctor broke in. "That's the stuff." He swung out one white-coated arm and peered at his watch. Hally gazed at him. Goodbye, old friend, doctor, father, she thought. Soon I will be leaving you. I have loved you in my way, been awed by you, frightened by you, irritated, grateful.

"Now you've gotta take this slow." Dr. Mostello put his hands on his hips. "I don't want any trouble. Hear? We haven't got extra suction machines just sitting around." He smiled at her and left the room. Hally stared at the bed, the window sill with the pen lying beside the ink bottle, her bureau. Half an hour ago she had put away her flute and had made a new plan for her music at last. Soon she would put away this hospital life. And Dan? She sighed. If they were to go on, they would have to transcend this world anyway.

27

Hally stood on the roof passageway, looking out. The March morning was strangely warm and a green haze hung over the damp lawn, promising grass and spring. Hally tipped her head back to the wide blue arc above; there were buds on the maple branches, tight still, but beginning, and the smell of new growth rose from a muddy flower bed below. She leaned her elbows on the metal railing and watched a withered leaf spiral down. Next week she would be leaving at last. Dan had teased that she would miss the reek of Lysol in Roy's mop water and the clanging of the elevator in the hall, but it was Dan she would miss, and below her excited talk, she felt a knot of panic. She wanted to clutch at him, to cry. She would visit him during the next weeks and he would be out by mid-April probably. But . . . but. . . . They had become constrained and polite with each other of late, as if they were both evading something dangerous that neither could articulate.

Why? Hally wondered. She thought of Dan, handsome and vigorous looking in his green cable knit sweater walking on his crutches again. She saw his familiar smile and the long blue veins on the backs of his hands. For weeks now, they had permitted themselves only little pecks on the cheek, pats on the arm, the shoulder. And yet Hally ached to kiss him passionately, to push her tongue between his teeth, to stroke his neck and suck him into her warmth. She wrapped her arms around herself, as a familiar sliding sensation began in her abdomen and she entered an old fantasy. She would push off her corduroy jeans, her underpants, and tunnel down beside him under the sheet, press herself close, kiss him, caress him, show him that it was all right, that it could be good between them, wonderful, in fact. But, but ... she couldn't do that. And yet he wanted it too, she felt. But he was terrified of humiliation, of not being the man he had always imagined he was maybe: the Western rider, the herder, the historian in a cowboy hat. But Dan was so much more, Hally thought. There was his love of music, his way with people, his courage. If this dizzying sweetness, for which her whole body yearned, slipped past her...? Hally gripped the railing. If she and Dan moved into conventionalities and awkwardnesses out there in that impersonal world beyond, if they lost each other and....

Hally shuddered as she watched a long, dark car turn into the driveway. Oh God, a hearse. But it was the administrator's black station wagon, pulling into its parking place. Death, she thought. She could have died last summer. She watched the balding administrator pull his briefcase from the back of the car. Charts and budgets, Hally thought. Soon she would have her work too. She would begin piano lessons at the Conservatory and her old music copying job. It would be all right, she told herself. Dan loved her; she knew that. And with time, he might feel confident about marriage. She could wait for love and passion, as she had waited for health. And if she didn't have all she wanted, well she had learned about compromise.

"Hey, Hal. Whatcha dreaming about up there?" It was Jack's voice. Hally turned and looked down into the ambulance entrance on the other side. Jack and Dan were leaning on their crutches below, Jack in his baseball jacket, Dan in his tweed sportscoat.

"Come down," Dan yelled. "It's beautiful."

Hally smiled. "I'll be there in a sec," she shouted.

"Isn't it an amazing day?" Hally said smiling, lest some trace of her naked thoughts on the roof passageway above were still visible in her face. "Look," she said as she stood with the two men, beside the dry weeds at the edge of the driveway. She flung out one arm and pointed to a nest of light above them in a hemlock tree. "Can you believe it's already the tenth of March?"

"Enjoy it, kid," Jack told her. "Probably begin snowing again tomorrow." Dan laughed and looked up at the brick building beyond them.

"God, it's hard to believe we're all going to be leaving this place soon," Dan said. He stared up at the rows of windows, the venetian blinds pulled down at some or pulled up at others, where clumps of slats hung crookedly. "Is that my room?" He shifted one crutch so that he could reach out his arm to point at the row of almost indistinguishable rectangles that formed the line of windows on the first floor.

"No. That's mine," Hally said. "See the violets on the sill. Yours has the typewriter. The fourth one. There." Dan peered and nodded.

"A lot's happened in that old garage," Jack said. "Remember the summer? The heat? Those admissions pouring in? I used to read the obits every morning. Jesus."

The door to the emergency entrance opened noisily. "Hey, you guys. Don't be so exclusive," Margaret called from the doorway, as she pushed Kevin down the ramp. Billy followed, and Henry brought up the rear. "This is beautiful," Margaret said. "We ought to bring our lunch trays out and have a picnic."

"The heck with a picnic," Kevin said. "Let's make a break for it. Go stop the trolley, Jack. Tell 'em to wait."

"We'll hire a limo," Jack said. "Or a hearse. We could all squeeze into one of those." The others laughed.

"Say, Hally," Margaret said. "Where's Maureen? Wasn't she supposed to be back last night?"

"Oh, she's still on her trial weekend," Hally reported. "I predicted she wouldn't make it back last night. Ted'll come toodling in with her about noon, I bet." They laughed again and Dan glanced at his watch.

"It's just about time for physio," he said. "Does Mrs. Harding know where we are?"

"The heck with her," Jack said. "Let her look."

"Fresh air's better for us than stretching anyway," Kevin said and nodded at a cat that had darted out from behind some trash cans near the wall. Hally stooped to brush the tarred surface with a dry weed. The cat stood a moment watching, then hunched to pounce. But the door behind them crashed open again and the cat ran off. Roy wheeled a trashcan down the ramp on its battered rim and brought it parallel with Dan.

"Didya hear the news?" he asked.

"No," Dan said. "What?"

"Mrs. Hogan," Roy answered. "Maureen." He paused a moment and

ANN L. McLaughlin

looked around the group. "I hate to be the one to tell ya, but she's dead. God rest her soul. Died this morning right at her own dining room table."

"What?" Dan said. "What do you mean?" He leaned forward and scowled at Roy. "Maureen?" The group pulled close together, listening.

Roy put both hands on his heavy waist, aware of his solemn power as news bearer. "It's God's truth," he said. "So help me. She died right after breakfast a coupla hours ago—right there with her family. Started one of them terrible coughing fits of hers and. . . . Warn't nothing they could do. Even her husband, the doc, you know. He called Mostello, just twenty minutes ago. Terrible broke up, of course."

Hally pressed both hands to her mouth as she stared at Roy. "Oh no," she said and let out a cry. "It can't be. No." Dan moved one crutch in front of him, so that he could put his arm around her, but Hally twisted out of his reach. "I'm going in," she said and limped hurriedly up the ramp to the door.

"You're absolutely sure about this?" Dan said to Roy. "When did you hear it anyway?"

"I told you. Dr. Hogan just called. Not more than twenty, thirty minutes ago. If you don't believe me, talk to Dr. Baldwin or Marge Flaherty," he said. "They'll tell you . . . maybe. Or their faces will." He turned and bent over the trashcan again. "Be cleaning out that room soon," he said. "That's going to be a job." He let the can rest on its bottom and straightened once more. "It's a terrible thing," he said. "Terrible. She was a great lady, that Mrs. Hogan. Always had a good word, a joke. I tell you." He paused, waiting for some corroboration, but the group was silent. Roy shook his head and rolled the can toward the others, lined against the wall.

"Ah, shit," Kevin said and glanced around him angrily. "Shit." He twisted to look up at Margaret. "Get me out of here, will ya? The hell with the beautiful day. I wanta go inside too."

Jack held the door open as Margaret pushed Kevin in. Billy shuffled through next, then Dan. Henry held the door for Jack. "It's not fair," Jack muttered to Dan, as they stood waiting for the elevator. "It's just not fair, Goddamnit."

Hally was not in her room, so Dan made his way down the hall to Maureen's doorway. Hally was at the bureau staring at the picture of

Maureen, surrounded by her nine children, but she looked back at Dan. "I can't believe it," she said. Dan gripped the frame at the bottom of the bed and nodded. "She was so alive . . . so . . . ." Hally pointed to the picture. "How can she be dead? I mean it doesn't make sense, it . . . ." She brought both hands to her mouth. "Oh God, why Maureen?" Her eyes filled with tears and she turned and pressed her head against Dan's chest. He put one arm around her cautiously, holding the bedframe with the other, and felt her shoulders shake. Hally pulled back all at once, snatched his free hand, and kissed it hard. "Dan," she said. Her teeth were chattering and her eyes were big, as she stared up at him. "Dan . . . ." There was the sound of footsteps outside in the hall. Hally pulled back.

"You two'll have to get out of here now," Miss Flaherty said, coming into the room. "Roy's got to clean." She put a brown suitcase on the bed and turned back to Hally. "I'll come get you later, if I need some help. Okay?" She paused and studied Hally. "You go on back to your room now. Stay together, why don't you? Lunch'll be up in a little while."

Hally led the way up the hall to her room and Dan followed, moving his crutches deliberately, tense with a longing to go faster, to comfort her. It was like a mother's death, he thought, for Maureen had been a mother to Hally. After Dan had gotten himself into the room, Hally shut the door behind him. She moved close and clutched the lapels of his jacket. "Dan," she said. "I want to marry you. I love you. I really love you," she whispered. "Marry me, will you? Right away. Please."

"But, Hal . . . ." He looked down at her in surprise, but Hally covered his mouth with hers, pulling him into a deep kiss. He felt her hands clutching his shoulders, her fingers on his neck, his ear. Dan pulled her closer, smoothing her hair with his free hand. Did she mean it? Now? Yes. Yes, she did. He moved his hand to her breast. At last, he thought. Oh my God, at last.

"You're not afraid?" he asked. "All the stuff ahead? The decisions, all the limitations."

"No. No. I love you. Maybe there're not so many limitations anyway," she whispered, as they began to kiss again.

"Oh God, Hal. I'd almost given up. I thought. . . . Oh, baby, I thought. . . . " He wobbled suddenly and reached out to grab the bedframe. Hally drew her breath in with a jerk and stepped back.

"Don't you wreck everything by crashing on your head again." Dan smiled and plopped down on the bed. Hally watched him unlock his brace and pull his leg back, then she squeezed up close beside him and they kissed. "We need each other," she whispered. "There's a whole lot of frustration ahead and. . . . "

"I know. I know," Dan answered. "I've thought about that a long time." He held her face between his hands a moment, studying her. "I love you," he said again. "I'm crazy about you. I want you with me all the time." He covered her mouth and moved his hands to her sweater, stroking her breasts. One crutch rolled off the end of the bed and dropped to the floor with a clatter, but they continued to kiss. Dan pulled back finally and smoothed her hair, as he began to talk.

"If you get out of here by the end of the week and if I'm out by early April. . . . I mean my ankle's practically healed now and. . . . There's going to be a lot of stuff, Hal," he said, interrupting himself. "School, my thesis, your music. Learning to manage. There's a lot we've got to figure out." He paused. "But we'll be together. I mean we'll wait a few months and all. Then in July or August anyway. . . . "

"Why wait?" Hally interrupted and clasped her hands. "Why not now? We could even do it here. Mostello's probably a justice of the peace along with everything else. Who knows? He might be." She rose and turned to the door. "I'll go ask Marge." Hally wheeled back to Dan; her face had a look of horror. "Maureen. My God. I forgot. I completely forgot. Oh Dan." Hally sat down on the bed again. "I forgot all about her."

"No, you didn't," Dan said and put his arm around her. "Neither did I. This is our way of celebrating her, don't you see?"

"Celebrating?" Hally repeated.

"Her life, her spirit, her love of you, of us both. She'd want this far more than she'd want us crying." Hally stared at Dan a moment, then dropped her head and pressed it against his chest.

"You're right," she whispered, looking up at him again. "It's what she always wanted for us. Maybe that's what I was thinking when I suggested it. But I got carried away and . . . ." The chattering of Hally's teeth made a low shaking sound in the quiet room. "Oh Dan, I'm so excited." She rose again. "I want to call Mom and Marian and Tom and . . . ." She looked at the door, then back at Dan. "You know they could use some good news up there in the ward," she said. "Let's go up and tell them now. Invite them to the wedding." She tugged at his hand. "I know we can't have it here or all that soon maybe. We want our families after all. But we can tell them, Dan. Can't we?" Dan glanced at the door, then back at Hally.

"Yes, sure. But let's wait an hour or two," he said. "They're still in shock, you know. We'll go after lunch. Okay?" Hally nodded.

"We'll have a Wahl wedding," she said. "Dr. Mostello and Baldwin and Artemis."

"And Jack," Dan added. "And Billy and Henry." He smiled and pulled her to him. "We'll ask them all."

Down in the men's ward, Kevin sat in his wheelchair by the window, biting his lip as he stared out at the leafless trees. Behind him Jack leaned forward on his crutches, switching the channels on the TV. "Goddamned set," he muttered. "What the hell's the matter with it anyway?" Kevin did not look back at him, but Henry, who was turning the pages of his Bible, glanced over at Jack and sighed.

"You just don't like none of the stuff that's on," Henry said. "That's all that's wrong with that thing." Billy seemed unaware of them both, as he sat on the bed beyond them, fingering his rosary.

Miss Flaherty's voice on the phone was calm, but she gripped the edge of the nurses' desk, as she talked. "No. It's no trouble," she said. "Of course not. We'll have everything packed." She paused and listened a moment. "Yes, certainly, Dr. Hogan. Good-bye." She hurried down the hall to Maureen's room, and stood a moment in the doorway, looking in. The suitcase was open on the stripped bed, which had been pulled away from the wall. Roy was mopping, moving slowly backward toward the door. But he stopped and leaned on his mop, when Miss Flaherty appeared. Margaret stood at the bureau, stacking cards in one pile, photographs in another. "I appreciate this, Margaret," Miss Flaherty began. "I really do."

Margaret shook her head, and turned to tuck the photographs into the suitcase. Miss Flaherty moved over to it, gazed down at the soft mound of a lavendar nightgown, then turned to the bureau. "You've got everything in the drawers?" she asked. Margaret nodded.

"I'll be back in a minute, sweetheart," Roy said to Margaret. "Gotta get another rag for them baseboards. Now don't you go lifting that suitcase, you hear?"

Dan glanced at the window. "It's still an amazing day out there, isn't it?" he said. "Let's go look at it again." He pushed out his braced leg, slid the lock down into place and rose slowly, using the bedframe for support. Hally handed him one crutch, then the other. He settled them under his arms and walked to the window. They stood there close together, looking out.